The Eyrie

Also by Stevie Davies

FICTION

Boy Blue
Primavera
Arms and the Girl
Closing the Book
Four Dreamers and Emily
The Web of Belonging
Impassioned Clay
Kith and Kin

NON-FICTION

Emily Brontë: Heretic
Unbridled Spirits: Women of the English Revolution 1640–1660

The Eyrie

STEVIE DAVIES

Weidenfeld & Nicolson
LONDON

First published in Great Britain in 2007
by Weidenfeld & Nicolson

T. E. Nicholas translation on page vii by Joseph Clancy, from the
Bloodaxe Book of Modern Welsh Poetry, edited by Menna Elfyn
and John Rowlands, Bloodaxe, Highgreen 2003

A CIP catalogue record for this book is available
from the British Library

ISBN 978 0 297 85141 7

Typeset by Input Data Services Ltd, Frome

Printed in Great Britain by Clays Ltd, St Ives plc

Weidenfeld & Nicolson
An imprint of the Orion Publishing Group
Orion House, 5 Upper St Martin's Lane, London WC2H 9EA

www.orionbooks.co.uk

To the dear memory of my mother
Mona Davies
who did so well by me

I Aderyn y To

T. E. Nicholas (Nicholas o Glais)

Wele friwsionyn arall am dy ganu,
A darn o afal i felysu'r bwyd.
Daw sŵn dy bigo cyson i'm diddanu
A da yw gweld ar dro dy fantell lwyd.
Daethost, fe ddichon, o dueddau Penfro
O'r grug a'r eithin tros y Frenni Fawr,
A buost, dro, ar ardain lwyd yn cwafro
Uwch Ceredigion deg ar doriad gwawr.
Cymer y bara: pe cawn ddafn o winoedd
Gwasgfa'r grawnsypiau pêr o'r gwledydd pell,
Mynnem ein dau, ynghanol helynt trinoedd,
Gymun, heb groes nac allor yn y gell.
Mae'r bara'n ddigon santaidd am y tro,
Offrwn o galon nad oes arni glo.

(*Llygad y Drws, Sonedau'r Carchar*, Wasg Gee, Dinbych, 1940)

To a Sparrow
by T. E. Nicholas (Nicholas of Glais)
(*Swansea Prison, 1940*)

Look, here's another bread-crumb for your piping,
And a piece of apple as a sweetener.
It gladdens me to hear your steady pecking;
It's good to see your cloak of grey once more.
You've travelled here, perhaps, from Pembroke's reaches,
From the gorse and heather on Y Frenni's height,
And maybe on grey wing you've filled your measures
Above fair Ceredigion at dawn's first light.
Accept the bread: had I a drop of wine
Pressed from a distant country's sweet grape-cluster,
We two could take, amid war's turbulence,
Communion, though the cell lacks cross and altar.
The bread's as holy as it needs to be,
Offering of a heart not under lock and key.

(translated by Joseph Clancy in *The Bloodaxe Book of Modern Welsh Poetry*, ed. Menna Elfyn & John Rowlands, Bloodaxe, 2003)

Prelude

Venturing inland from the silver oval of Swansea Bay, the oystercatcher's eye hovers above the ruins of a Norman castle on the hill's green breast before flying across a valley to a lushly wooded limestone scarp. Go back 180 years and the creature's ancestor would have circled above a quarry and a lime kiln raising choking clouds of smoke and dust and a furore of industrial noise, where ant-like workers, glad of a pittance, toiled and died for their masters.

But, veering east along the ridge, it would have come upon leafy woodlands, a choice spot for a copper master to build a sanctuary, round the coast from the poisonous fumes of his arsenic and copper works at Llangyfelach and Clyne. The black disc of his top hat might have been visible as he surveyed his workmen erecting this retreat, *Nyth Eryr*, a limestone homage to himself. Constructed according to the most fashionable Gothic design, it is a whimsy with crenellations and pilasters, bays and balconies featuring rails of intricate wrought iron and copper, a brand-new coat of arms, a magnificent curving staircase and three gables topped with gleaming weather vanes.

The great age of copper gives way to tinplate. The copper master dies and is carried over the scarp to the elite cemetery, where he rests under a seven-foot angel carved from high-quality veined Oystermouth limestone, indistinguishable from marble. The copper magnate's idle heirs, offended by the fumes and din of the quarry which has expanded eastwards, leave for London and New York. Boarded up, the abandoned folly decays. After two world wars it is gutted by fire. Quarrying comes to an end and the ridge ripens into a forest in which strewn copper artefacts lie half-buried. Larking girls cycle down from Hafod, break in and picnic in *Eryr*'s corrupted splendour.

As the twentieth century nears its end, the place is recognised as a gold mine: *Nyth Eryr* – reconceived, renovated, renamed, advertised and sold out within a year – is divided into the largest feasible number of superior flats. Singletons and other nomads, often women, often elderly, find refuge under its roof.

The seabird soars above the frosted slate roofs of The Eyrie, perches on a gleaming copper vane atop a gable, then descends to a balcony rail. In the dim interior, a woman with a fine ancient face pulls down a leather-bound book from a shelf. Sighting the black-faced predator, with its long red bill and particoloured livery, perched so insolently on the margin of her world, she stands still in fascination, listening to its bold, look-at-me *kleep-kleep.*

A small, birdlike woman in a red woollen hat and a green coat down there in the frosted garden offers crumbs to sparrows, but when the oystercatcher takes off with a thunderclap, she looks up, crying, *Sea pie! There goes sea pie!* and marvels at its arrogant wingspan. A plump person in middle age labours over the fore-court carrying bags filled with more goodies than one woman could possibly eat. She turns as a cab draws up: out climbs a dark-haired girl, who glances up as the white-haired, hawk-eyed woman cranes down from her balcony.

1

She had fallen, with the Wall, into obsolescence. For her first eighty years or so she had not acknowledged mortality at all, not a fig, not a bean. The night those Berlin youngsters had leapt and derided and crowbarred the Wall, not only had Red Dora's spirit sunk but her joints had twinged dismally. Yet thirteen years had passed since then, without significant loss of vigour or wits, or the wilting of anything vital except political hope. Nobody would *dare* to call me an old lady! she fiercely told the mirror.

Ach! she thought, facing the crinkly mountain-map reflected there: put me away, please, I have seen enough.

Turning her back on her reflection, Dora retreated to the window, to be soothed by the gentleness of Oystermouth. A ribbon of fishermen's cottages, painted pink, lemon, cream and blue, unfurled below the forecourt, drifting west in an arc that led down the sheer slope through the village to the sea – though little of the village and none of the sea could be seen from The Eyrie, for the intervening hill shouldered them out. Yet Dora intuited the presence of the sea and guessed its moods from the look of the light above the hillside. The invisible waters qualified her world by their subtle alterations in a constant drama of reflected light, blushing rose-pink into the sky or bleeding it scarlet, or, as now, turning it a piercing thrush-egg blue. Her temperament had always been fiercely active: now Dora paused, breathed in deeply, tasted beauty and allowed herself the pleasure of reverie. The sea at this moment would be lying as still and cold as turquoise glass, an oval pool in the sweep of the bay that ended in Mumbles Point. Later she'd walk down to check. But by then it would have changed.

When Dora had been shown the flat seven years ago, the estate agent lassie had explained that this view in itself would add value to her property in what was already an *executive area*. She had nattered on about how the high-class flats had originally been a mansion.

'Aye, I know. A copper baron's palace,' Dora had said.

The copper millionaires had fled the chemical smoke of industrial Hafod and Treforys, to the clean air and romantic scenery of the coast, ploughing back their stolen profits into stately abodes that had mocked them by decaying and, a couple of centuries later, had been reclaimed and renovated as executive flats, forsooth.

'Yes, yes, copper!' the lassie had exclaimed. 'Unique Welsh fittings! Original copper balustrades! Well, I think they're original. Antique wrought-iron rails to individual balconies!'

Turning to the window, with scathing anti-capitalist words on the tip of her tongue, Dora had fallen in love. Just like that. Nor was I wrong, she thought now. Moss and grass had mocked the architecture both of copper mansion and Norman castle, and winter winds had sabotaged the works both of the invader and the capitalist. The winds were temperate, of course, in this soft and courteous haven that welcomed Scots Commies and retired English blimps alike into its liberal muddle of palm trees and mountain pines.

Autumn here, Dora thought, fades straight into spring. She stepped out on to the balcony to get what her neighbour Eirlys called a 'fix' of morning air. Crisp and sharp-but cold? No! She had been brought up in Glasgow, and directed her school in Morayshire, where, aye, you knew what real cold was. Thank God she had been brought up hardy and spartan, without such luxuries as central heating. Yet, to tell the truth, she was glad of the clemency of this place. It embraced without confining her. The trees encircling the castle still carried a vestige of crimson and ochre into December, despite the icy purity of the day.

Perched up here among sycamore and beech woods that lined the limestone ridge, The Eyrie commanded one of the village's highest points, nestling on three sides into the sheer wooded slope. In the allotments at the base of the opposite hill, older folk could be seen tending their patches of onions and carrots, and building autumn bonfires that blessed her with strange scents through her always open window: wood smoke and sea salt, like the Diggers and the Levellers with their wee communities of brotherly equals, she thought. Here, unexpectedly, after a lifetime of makeshift pads, Dora had secured a perch for her talons where she could look down on the world, surrounded by her few belongings.

Was it a betrayal? How could a Scots ex-Communist, ex-Trotskyite, still live any version of the faiths of her socialist comrades, when those comrades were chiefly underground, discredited or apostacised? How could she abide in this gentle and genteel backwater of Wales among the little people and satisfy herself (and here was Eirlys with a bag of shopping) with queening it, as she undoubtedly did, here at The Eyrie? Nobody at The Eyrie was quite like Red Dora! That was for certain.

The knock on her door was Eirlys bearing gifts. Eirlys had just seen these in the window of Bevan the Bread and they had looked so fresh and delicious that it had been impossible not to think of one's elevenses.

'Indeed,' Eirlys said, 'they spoke to me from the counter. They were eloquent. They told me to buy them.'

Dora accepted the paper bag and peered inside. 'Eirlys, my dear lassie, you've brought me doughnuts! Good gracious. Are you wanting to plump me up?'

Dora opened the paper bag and counted four.

'All for me?'

'I think you can manage them, can't you?'

Dora cast Eirlys a wry glance. The lass was incorrigibly sanguine, uncontrollably kind. If her neighbour weren't so commonsensical, Dora would worry for her sanity. Do anything for anyone. Salt of the earth. Etcetera. But she worried for Eirlys. A part of her brain was missing, the part programmed for flight or fight. Eirlys didn't do either. She just smiled warmly and patted the wolf on the head.

And she must be doing something right, for she had survived about five decades tempting the wolf to the feast. Something, however, had clearly unsettled her as she had entered her middle years. For Eirlys had taken early retirement from social work. Stress, she'd once said, vaguely. Dora had not pried.

'Sinful they are,' said Eirlys. 'So I thought you'd like them, Dora.'

Dora laughed. And really they did look tempting.

But how could she live, she wondered, after her neighbour had bustled out, in a world of doughnuts? Fare of Uncle Sam, patron of capitalist imperialism? But these were Welsh doughnuts and would go down nicely with a pinch of humour, which, thank heaven, Dora had never entirely lacked. Cosy doughnuts, like their dragon. *Y ddraig goch.* Eirlys, who was madly patriotic, had as her door knocker a brass dragon making hideous grimaces. A gargoyle, Eirlys, upon the temple of your niceness. She wouldn't be without dear Eirlys, the nourisher, who, despite her Plaid Cymru footlingness, had a highly developed internationalist consciousness in the field of feeding, and kept a goat for a family in Rwanda. Sharp brain on her, though: a blade to cut the cake, if only she'd use it.

She put Eirlys's gift down on the breadboard and returned to the window. If she craned her neck, she could see part of the tower of the small grey church at the centre of the village, fronting the sea. Dora snatched a glance. Withdrew. Blinked. The sight stuck like a dark fleck at the corner of her eye. Always beneath the peace of this place lay boundless unease. A deep qualm passed through her. She had retired to Wales to be near to her daughter at last. For no other reason. Yet in seven years she had not quite brought herself to visit the graveyard. She was self-condemned to live here, waiting near to a grave she still evaded, though Rosa's unseen resting place drew Dora daily, like a magnet against the contradictory current of her fear.

Rosa, aye, stayed in the earth, and had stayed there for four decades. She had died in prison in England. Her common law husband, Dewi Lloyd, an ex-miner, had taken possession of her ashes (*fine by me*, Dora had said, *do what you like, she is gone*) and borne them home to Glamorgan, where he had had them committed to the earth according to the rites of the Anglican communion. Since both he and Rosa had been atheists, she presumed that his highly respectable parents had taken over this decision. And poor Dewi had died young, of silicosis. How come it had taken Dora over thirty years to recognise the reality of Rosa's death?

For she had – to her shame – attended neither the funeral nor the interment.

Almost impossible now to conjure up the state of mind that had absented her from her own daughter's funeral. She had visited the body in hospital and registered the death herself, in an almost business-like way. But then, in broad daylight, towering waves of grief had built above Dora's head, high as houses, bitterly dark. To have let them crash down on her would have meant the end of Red Dora. So back to work, no time to lose. Callous, no doubt, she had been thought, or crazy. And perhaps she *had* gone mad when Rosa died, refusing to know that she would never in this world (and there exists no other) see her daughter's face again.

She had broken some taboo, hadn't she? Dora had brought Rosa into the world and failed to see her out. In doing so, she seemed to have cut herself off from any tender or beautiful memories. Quarrels, rancour, harsh words: these were all she remembered. Rosa at twenty-nine had still not stopped rebelling against her mother because Dora had never relinquished possession of her daughter.

She pressed her thumbs on her eyelids. At heart Dora had always known herself to be a coward. The coward ran away to pursue crucial political work, which, look, would not wait! The struggle had dwarfed the death of a daughter. But Dora's Communist faith had long ago wavered: after Spain, she'd been denounced as a traitor to the Party. Her whole emotional and ideological life had been bound up in comradeship. She'd tried to keep on believing, moved from the Party to Trotsky, but ultimately the knowledge of Trotsky's mass butcheries had sickened her. Her daughter's anarchism she could not embrace. Red Dora had gravitated after the Sixties towards the peace movement and feminism, whilst never abdicating her socialist allegiance.

Where could you go, when all faiths failed you? She had become in the modern world a community of one, holding her borders against all-comers, most especially against those who had shared these hopes and losses with her.

Now she was the pit pony released out in the friendly light. But still Dora had so far stopped short of entering Rosa's garden. Visiting the library at Oystermouth or walking the foreshore, she'd catch sight of the flag flapping at her from the tower of All Saints, reminding Dora that she had come here for the sole purpose of ending her days, near a certain rebellious, dishonest and occasionally vindictive person with whom painful conversation had painfully ceased in 1968; and can there be a developing relationship beyond the death of one? She thought, aye, there can and there must be, yet always she had bent her head under a thunderbolt of pain and looked away from the flag.

She'd been told there was no headstone. No names at all. It was a wee garden, Rosa's son Keir had said, with a pretty show of snapdragons and wallflowers, very tasteful. Dora's heart had spasmed uncontrollably. She scorned her bourgeois grandson. Yet at the same time she was glad to know about the flowers in the homely garden, and remembered Rosa's careful fingers as a girl, as she bent with delighted curiosity to pinch open the delicate yellow mouth of a snapdragon.

Will I go today? Aye, go. Do, Dora, go and see where she lies. Not today, too busy. No, another day.

She had considered writing her memoirs, such was the vanity folk's interest in her story aroused, but there was altogether too much to withhold. Folk were suddenly interested in veterans of the International Brigades, and went round collecting them like curiosities. How did you give an honest account of public events without violating intimacies, giving yourself away? She had a horror of showing her heart and always had had. Besides, work remained to be done. Dora's dander was up over Iraq: she must take positive, focused action. There were modern ways to do it, this was what Dora was grasping. She'd been in London for the great march against the Iraq war. But marching up and down with placards was not going to achieve anything: he was too savagely cynical and self-righteously shameless. *He* let the peace movement demonstrate as a way of letting off steam harmlessly.

Wee man, I am not harmless, she threatened *him* in her mind and pinched his image between a giant thumb and finger like a louse. As you will find.

In Spain she had filched some anaesthetic and poured it on her lice to make them stop that crazy wriggling and biting. To make them fall asleep. So that she too could sleep. Nancy had been horrified. *Dora! Everyone's smoking and you could go up like a torch! Cremate us all! What were you thinking of?*

Well, that was long ago, she lullabyed to herself. Her great-granddaughter, Angelica, had lately asked: *What's the Spanish Civil War anyway, Nannan?* Then it came out that she did not, at seventeen, know what a civil war was. Hence was not conversant with the Russian, French, Irish, Rwandan or English civil wars. Dora, who had taken on intellectual battles that would have daunted anyone with a less than apocalyptic consciousness, quailed at the task of filling in Angelica on the whole of world history. Did she have time? Granted that these revolutions were all, rightly understood, phases in the one great Revolution of labour against capitalism, it was still necessary to supply the narrative. If she should succeed in restoring the amnesiac memory of the Age as manifested in Angelica, how could that leaky vessel be encouraged to retain the information? Great-granddaughterly innocence of the history of the world was, however, less irksome than Angelica's father Keir's polite lack of interest in his namesake, Keir Hardie.

If Rosa had been a political extremist, Rosa's children had been indifferent to politics to the point of utter gormlessness. More than that, Dora had recognised far too late that, with their rage and their railing and their impersonal, unmotherly passions, she and Rosa had turned the youngsters against their cause. They had literally bored the twin boys silly.

Rosa and Dora had drummed into the thumb-sucking cherubs their place and responsibility in the great plan. Keir and Karl had resembled those fatly smirking, vacuous Botticellian *putti* who reduce the most revolutionary of Renaissance works of art to smugness. Rosa's sons blanked out all political messages. Smiled round their thumbs. Dora had heard the infant Keir confide to his infant brother Karl that he *hated* Keir Hardie. He would like to *smack* him. Karl had not offered an opinion on Karl Marx, except in the yuppie life he went on to lead.

Happily, Angelica had, in turn, rebelled against her father's complacency.

'Why do you not look up the Spanish Civil War, Jelly, on Google?' she had suggested to Angelica.

'Cool,' Angelica had said.

And she'd phoned to say that not only was the Spanish Civil War on the web but, hey, Nannan was there, too! 'Famous you are, Nannan! A celebrity! I never knew you were a nurse. You never said. I'm well proud of you, Nannan!'

'I was never a nurse *per se*, Jelly dear. I was a hospital administrator.'

Risible to think of Dora nursing: she had never had the guts for it. She'd far rather have been fighting alongside Lachlan in the trenches. Oh, so much rather have taken the bullet for him. After the women's militias had been dissolved, early in the struggle, women had not been allowed to bear arms. Their role had been to mop up the blood the men shed. Up to the elbows in gore, they had been, at the final assault over the Ebro. Dora still hated to think of it, nearly seventy years later. Don't think of it then, she rallied herself.

Make tea, not war was the latest slogan.

Well, Dora thought, at least I can do that. Eirlys's doughnuts came to mind, and she swiftly and with relish demolished two. Sugar coated her chin and glazed her fingers with stickiness. She swigged it all down with the hot tea, so enjoyable: was this second childhood, when you enjoyed your food, at the very same time when your taste buds and nostrils were supposed by the quacks to be failing you? Indubitably not. (Mind, the quacks did my eyes proud, she acknowledged: off came the cataracts, to reveal the nap of a green velvet cushion, the gloss on a beetle's back.) To retire from a heroic life to a gentle hilltop with a picturesque view and neighbours who were chiefly middle-aged, pleasant and widowed – was this a comedown or a comeuppance? Or was it just a treat, the sweet course brought on after you had finished the bitter and the savoury?

She had sugar all down her sweater. Granules would embed themselves in the carpet and stick in her socks. *Aye, lassie, ye're a messy wean and no mistake.* Mother had sighed and made the best of her tempestuous daughter, 'my fiery particle', 'stormy petrel', names Dora would later bestow on her own terrifying daughter. Dad the Clyde trawlerman had never got over the communism of the traitorous bairn who called him to his face a lackey and lickspittle of capitalism, and rudely towered over him at fifteen. Ach, Dora thought, it had taken her so long, too long, to learn from Lachlan the tolerance and forbearance she might have shown to Dad's working-class conservatism. Finished and buried by forty-five, poor soul. And once he had been so proud of her (*apple of my eye!*), putting her through grammar school for all they could rarely eat butter and for all she was only a lassie. But she didn't want to think of Dad.

There was such a list of items not to think of! Dora put the plate and cup in the sink in a slovenly manner. She sucked the last of the sugar off her fingers (waste not, want not) and rinsed them under the cold tap. She would put her feet up and listen to music. She switched on the popular classics programme she had grown fond of. You never knew what music you'd be flooded with. Some fat warbler of Wagner, a delicate moment of Mozart, or, as now, the rich thrill of the strings in Dvořák's Cello Concerto. But this swept her back, as it always did, to Spain, to the beginning of the end, the Republicans' final breakthrough at the River Ebro, and the terror of the Fascist counter-offensive, with the loss of innumerable lives.

She had been working in a natural cave, the 'Cave of the Comrades', an ancillary ward to the huge hospital cave at La Bisbal de Falset. These natural wonders with their massive rocky overhangs had been used as emergency hospitals and medical storage facilities near the Front, allowing the wounded to be brought in with the least possible jolting. Metal bedsteads had stood at angles on the rock floor. The stench of putrefied human meat had spread over the countryside. She'd helped with the care of our boys, their boys: Republican or Fascist casualties were all just boys. Lights strung on wires in the otherwise pitch-black operating theatre had taken power from the ambulances; shadows had loomed as the lights swung. Someone had rigged up a wind-up gramophone and played over and over again two or three records, to cover the sounds of surgery and anguish. She remembered the beautiful torsos of tanned boy-amputees.

What to do with the limbs? There had been no furnace to burn them.

The dying had whispered into her ear things Dora hadn't wanted to hear. For Dora had been in demand because, with so many dying, and excellent Spanish- and Basque-speakers at a premium, she'd been needed to catch the last messages for sweethearts and mothers. Lachlan had been carried in on a stretcher and never spoke again.

At first she had not recognised her husband. His face had been shot away. Nancy had had to say, *Dora, dear, I think it's Lachlan. Don't panic.* But Dora had never been one to panic.

Dora had given blood until her lips were drained and white and she'd nearly fainted.

Giving blood had been the best experience of her life. The grand heroic gesture had always come easily. Comradeship, the highest emotion she had ever known, found its fulfilment in the gift of blood. Straight from her vein into the soldier's vein. Dora would sit on the uneven rock floor with her arm on the table, and watch the patient as his blueness became pallor, and the pallor blossomed into a rosy flush in his cheeks. All the nurses had done it.

And as the boy reddened, the lassie would whiten. They live on us, of course, from the off. The parasite creature in the womb, babe at the breast, leech-sucking our sap. And we in our turn were vampires, cadging blood from the ambulance and truck drivers. *Give me a pint, hen! Just one wee pint, a kiss for a pint of blood!* Oh, I could cajole then, though it has not been my custom.

But to Lachlan, of course, she had been unable to give blood. That hurt. Incompatible blood-group. Nancy gave my Lachlan a pint of hers, and I watched as their arms were attached by the red pipe. It did no good, he did not wake. I could not thank her, I spoke tart words to her and corrected her grammar. I could not look in her dear eyes, but she, I do believe, understood that, comprehended it. Nancy, of course, knew me, warts and all.

And Lachlan flew. The boy rushed up to the air like the birds above the river and the caves: you never see them drop. Because it was all so simple then: we in our heyday were on the grand highway of history, where all is black and white. Lachlan went in the Cause. I could not be sorry for him. As far as he knew, we had won.

Dora had been on every barricade for decades after that. And, she thought, I am preposterously irrational, for can I really have lived in envy of Nancy and Lachlan that they never lived to see our entry into the Doughnut Empire? No, for she had enjoyed – was still enjoying – life in so many ways, sensual and otherwise. Modest things now solicited her attention: the curlicues of vetch, a vixen and her cubs loping round the flats. She would stand at the back window and watch the cubs tumbling in summer, copper in the sun against the wooded slope behind The Eyrie, the vixen vigilant at the margin of the trees and bracken. Dora would observe the mother observing her. Later she would scent the fox as she emptied her rubbish into the wheelie bin. *Yes, you!*

Since the Wall had come down, she had lost a sense of purpose and gained a passion for ... what? Passive existence? She would not willingly surrender that. One could not help seeing those who had died before their time as, somehow, not quite grown up. Two of Nancy's three children were gone too. And Lachlan's, and my one precious bairn.

Tomorrow, however, she might well pay the seven-years-deferred visit to her daughter. Why not? So often she had nearly done so. And tomorrow she might very well find herself doing so quite calmly and rationally. It would not be high drama at all. Why should it be? After all, there was nothing there but well-trimmed turf and neat flower borders. She kept the future open, provisional, to give free will room to choose. The true Trot, as Dora had believed, is in a state of perpetual revolution: the self is ajar. And perhaps it is the case, she thought, that I have just practised *entryism*, as we liked to call it in the cell, into this genteel world of The Eyrie, this subdued, murmurous ante-chamber to a final quiet.

Water softly gurgling down a communal pipe. Mrs Dark that would be, washing up. A chirrup and churring of birds: Megan's flock gathering at her window to receive crumbs from her hands. A distant bell was sounded by the postman in the hermit Mr Powell's flat, agitating that poor soul to asthma, as the world reached in to the long hibernation of his life. Mr and Mrs Norton, that tender couple, were on their way across the forecourt, hand in hand, each supporting the other over the icy surface. She would visit Rosa. And who knew? When the time came, she might find a way to go herself which, like Samson, pulled down the temple of the Philistines upon them. The sense of election to some destiny beyond the rabble (but somehow on behalf of the people) was ingrained.

Knocking on the door: Eirlys again, wanting to know if Dora felt like a spin to Worm's Head, it was so crisp and lovely, the foam would be all lacy where it froze, and mind to wrap up well, woolly hats and mittens, yes, wear your Basque beret! And we might stop off by Joe Davies the Chip on the way back, for scrumptious they were, his fish and chips, and very warming to the stomach and inner woman.

2

This was the best kind of Sabbath, Eirlys thought. No chapel, a bracing walk along the peninsula at Worm's Head, fish and chips eaten with their fingers, followed by a companionable afternoon curled up with books on their laps. They sat at either side of Dora's magnificent double windows, and either read, drowsed or rested their eyes on the world beyond the pane. These companionable hours, laced with innumerable cups of tea, were precious to Eirlys. She felt the honour of being trusted by her neighbour to share her privacy. Not that Dora was ever anything but reserved. A solitary is Dora, a loner, she thought, and one respects and honours that. She didn't open the door of her fastness to all and sundry. And if people presumed, she favoured them with one of those aloof looks Eirlys had pledged herself never to incur, although the occasional lightning bolt had scathed her in her time. Dora was built to look down on people. Has the height for it, see! Eirlys thought and smiled. She could easily have tucked herself under Dora's arm. She felt the power of the woman even in extreme age.

Dora looked up and smiled, but Eirlys could see that she was half-blind to the world outside herself and the story. They were reading their way through Dickens. Not that they could keep pace, of course, for Eirlys in early retirement regarded herself as freer of obligation than Dora, who had her political struggle to attend to. So Eirlys had surged forwards with *Bleak House*, galloping on guiltily into the small hours. And besides, they acknowledged different reading principles. Dora's view was that not one word should be missed. She considered Eirlys a wanton, greedy reader. Do not fast forward, she insisted: you will miss something.

Eirlys plunged back down into her reading. Mrs Jellyby was presiding over a chaotic luncheon. Engrossed as Eirlys instantly became, her reading somehow included Dora. She'll drop off in a moment, she thought. It's about your time, *bach*, isn't it? Instead, Dora glanced up briefly, lowered her head and stealthily flicked through the pages.

'Dora!'

'What, Eirlys?'

'You're looking to see what happens!'

'Certainly not.'

'Yes, you are. You're cheating. Admit it! Don't you ever tell me off again for bolting. *Merch ddrug!*'

'I'm not a *merch ddrug*.'

'You are.'

'Not at all.'

Dora shrugged, grinned, then went back to her legitimate place in the novel and smoothed the pages. You could see the little girl in her.

A while later, Dora's shoulders drooped. Her body relaxed, one arm draped along the chair, the other hand on the book in her lap. One leg slid forward. She'd snooze now for twenty minutes or so. Eirlys would often nap at such times, too: she'd always been susceptible to other people's yawns. Instead she took the opportunity to sit and observe Dora unreproved. Silver-grey light picked out that marvellous head, its shock of white hair dramatic against the leather chair-back and the generally sombre, sepia character of the room, whose walls were lined with books, chiefly elderly and even antiquarian. The ceilings in these flats were lofty, so that Dora's considerable library climbed to a good height but still needed to overflow into the narrow corridor and hall, into Dora's bedroom and, slightly worryingly, into the kitchen area. Here books might share space with saucepans, and not only books but piles of dusty papers dating back, in some cases, three-quarters of a century. Eirlys worried about the likelihood of these promiscuous papers wafting down on to the gas stove. But on the few occasions when she had mentioned her concern, Dora had gruffly forbidden her fussing.

Dora jerked in her sleep and tilted a fraction sideways. The book was slipping from under her hand. It would make a bang when it fell. Eirlys reached out to catch it: such a shame for her friend to awaken from a nice nap. Too late. Dickens splayed his thousand pages on the carpet, but Dora did not waken. Several papers had escaped, which Eirlys retrieved and tucked back in between the leaves. She marked Dora's approximate place and laid the leather-bound volume on a side-table, then settled her own head back for a snooze.

When she came to, Dora was standing by the window, stretching.

'I've been watching over you, Eirlys. Sleeping like a baby.'

'Oh, dear. I hope I wasn't snoring.'

'Not at all. Babies don't snore.'

'Oh, good. You weren't either.'

'Aye, but I wasn't asleep.'

'By the way,' said Eirlys, 'your book fell down when you, um, weren't asleep. I hope I marked the right place.'

'Thank you, dear.'

Dora picked up and opened the book, revealing the papers the fall had disturbed. She examined them one by one – handwritten letters from Comrades, she said, but who on earth were they? She only half-remembered one of the senders. Written in the fifties and mostly requests for contributions, she said, or subs. Party business.

'Oh, yes?' said Eirlys, going through to the kitchen to make tea. She bit back her curiosity. Dora did not care to be questioned – interrogated, she had once called it – about her Communist past, and would clam up if pressed. Rarely she might offer you a glimpse, but only, like a star's light, if you did not look directly.

Eirlys allowed herself to enquire: 'Anything interesting?'

'No, not really. But who on earth was this George P? He seems to have known me very well. Can't place him at all. Dear, how young and pompous we were, how humourless. Such rodomontade! Well, here we come to it – aye, aye. George P wants twenty pounds for some cause or other. He'll be lucky! But the name doesn't ring a bell at all.'

'Doesn't the date give you a clue?' Eirlys asked, cutting cherry cake.

'I can't say that it does.'

And that was that. From the corner of her eye, Eirlys was aware of Dora reaching down another book, at random, to transfer the letters. Odd that she didn't throw them away, if they were so unimportant. Sheer habit, Eirlys supposed: the habit of storing private tokens so that, unexamined, they took on the character of secrets, even from oneself. But as Dora stuffed the papers into the new volume, out fell another letter. This time it was in an envelope. Every book on these walls, Eirlys thought, setting down the tray, is presumably full of memorabilia. The whole room is an external memory. She bent to pick up the new letter and, in the process of handing it to Dora, managed to spot that it was addressed to Miss D. Urquhart, c/o an address in Peckham. It was a fat letter, one of those personal letters people used to write, she thought, the kind you loved to receive, in the days when correspondence meant correspondence – before universal e-mail and phone calls thinned communication.

'But, Dora, this has never been opened,' she blurted.

'So it hasn't.'

That was all she said. But from the complicated look that accompanied her words, and the fetching of a deep breath, Eirlys had the idea that Dora might have been about to say more but had thought better of it. Instead she said that she must pay a visit to the *tŷ bach*: would Eirlys kindly note her flavoursome Welsh idiom. She took the letter out of the room with her and returned without it.

'Well now, Eirlys, where's that tea? And then I must get back to work.'

Eirlys made haste to leave. As she paused at the door, a car drew up and Dora peered out of the window.

'Eirlys,' Dora beckoned, 'over here. This must be the new resident's daughter perhaps? She looks very young.'

They looked down together. Someone in a purple hooded cardigan was stepping out of a black cab. The driver helped her with several cases and a giant backpack, which the newcomer could lift only with difficulty.

'I trust she's quiet,' said Dora.

'She looks quiet, doesn't she?'

'How can you possibly tell, when you have only had the opportunity to view the top of her pixie hood?'

'Oh, well,' Eirlys said comfortably. 'I live in hope.'

The youngster was fishing out a door key from her jeans pocket. As she raised her head, the hood fell back and revealed a flushed, animated face which, though fresh-complexioned, scarcely belonged to a person in her teens.

'Not the daughter, then,' Eirlys said. 'The resident herself. Whatever is the matter, Dora?'

Dora had staggered back, with a low yelp of shock. Both hands clutched one another at her chest, and Eirlys thought: *Her heart! Her heart!* She guided her down into a chair. Dora's face seemed to spasm and, as she leant her head back, her eyes brimmed. But she managed to flap at Eirlys and say with some asperity 'I'm perfectly fine, Eirlys, for goodness' *sake.*'

'What is it? Was it something out there?'

'Nothing. A wee pang.'

'What kind of pang, Dora?'

'Well, if you must know, a twinge of toothache. It's gone now.'

It hadn't looked like toothache but however could one tell? Dora, who had retained all her own teeth, possessed a strong person's hidden susceptibilities, but toothache was hardly the kind of thing you would make up. Should she ring, Eirlys asked, for an emergency appointment? Which tooth was it?

'No, no. I get these twinges now and again.'

Eirlys put out a concerned hand to Dora's rugged arm. She

was sitting motionless, drained. It was not often that you got these piercing recognitions that Dora was . . . Eirlys did not know how old, but certainly in her early nineties. You got used to seeing her as powerful and indestructible: it was partly her authoritative manner, partly her height and bearing, and partly the real physical vigour she retained. Eyes like an eagle's since the two cataract operations.

But of course some of this must surely be a front. There must come moments of unease, as now, when body and mind, living at altitude in the thin air of age, faltered. Which was to say, one must remind oneself that Dora was human like everyone else.

'Dora, lovely, just stay there until you recover. Do you feel faint?'

But her neighbour was already recovering. She brushed Eirlys's diffident hand off her sleeve and angled her craggy face against the window to take another look. The new resident had already entered the building and only her cases stood at the door. The two women listened as she laboured up the stairs with the giant rucksack and dragged it along the corridor to the flat next door. The key struggled in the lock. Then there were small sounds of a new tenant trying out a new space, footsteps murmuring from room to room, switches being experimentally turned on and off.

'No indeed,' said Dora. 'It can scarcely be the daughter.'

And this seemed to settle her nerves.

'Shall I go and introduce myself, Dora, do you think? Offer her a cup of tea?'

'Oh, Eirlys, let the lassie settle in. We should not be fussing her.'

Eirlys wondered if the young woman was on her own or whether she would be bringing along what people these days called a 'partner'. The second flats from the end were comfortably large enough for one, but two might be a squeeze. The builders had cunningly divided some of the more grandly spacious rooms, using partitions that scarcely deserved to be called walls. The party wall between Dora's and the newcomer's apartment was of this nature, as was the one Eirlys shared with the Nortons, directly below the newcomer – a fragile membrane compelling the residents on either side to quietly considerate habits. Lucky with the Nortons I am, she thought. Their television went off promptly each night at eleven. Even so, Eirlys had an intimate knowledge of their taste in programmes, and it was not at all what you would imagine.

Eirlys had been fond of Mrs Menelaus, who had lived in the flat the new tenant had just entered. A private and ladylike soul, she had kept herself to herself, but passed her neighbours with courteous cordiality if they happened to coincide over the post or the bringing in of milk. Poor Emma Menelaus had, during her last weeks, been bleached and shrunk by illness, so that her complexion was like chalk, the skin reminiscent of tissue paper. Eirlys had yearned to do things for her but Mrs Menelaus had refused all help until she could no longer walk, and by then it was too late. The flat had been in a shocking state; it had smelt. Dora had never complained about it and neither had Eirlys, though she had repeatedly rung Social Services. The residents accommodated themselves with tact to the propinquity of death, in all its mess and misery.

And when the rotund figure of Mr Presdee – known to Eirlys's family as Presdee the Death – and his boy came to take Mrs Menelaus away, Eirlys had suffered such a pang at the smallness of the figure on the stretcher.

Now the angular young woman padded about in the Menelaus flat. Of course, the girlie could not know that her predecessor had died there in the summer. The flat would not be tainted for her. Eirlys was glad there was a new person, and a youngster, too. It would be good to hear living movements over her head, provided of course that she was indeed considerate in her habits and did not, for instance, put down those wooden floorings that were forbidden by the terms of the lease and made you think there was someone tap-dancing over your head.

The look in Mrs Dark's pale eyes when Mrs Menelaus had come down on the stretcher had registered neither terror nor dismay, but a kind of social embarrassment, as if in the presence of a grievous *faux pas.* Something was being shown which they should be ashamed to witness: that had been the tenor of her wincing look. Eirlys had understood. Dora, on the other hand, affected to look down upon people's habit of dying as a weakness, a failure of control. Really, thought Eirlys, she is formidable. Dora must have run that school of hers with a rod of iron. Even though it was a radical school on the principles of some German chap whose rules were that there should be no rules.

Standing at her desk, Dora shuffled a pile of papers. Eirlys took the hint.

'I'll be off then, Dora. Thanks for such a splendid day. *Hedd yn y hwyr.*'

Peace in the evening. She blessed her friend with scraps of Welsh and Dora, who distrusted endearments in English, could not help but be charmed, her face softening. Something about that wry, sweet expression as Dora returned not only her farewell and thanks, but her blessing, too – *hedd yn y hwyr* – gave Eirlys deep pleasure.

Whatever is it about you, Dora Urquhart? Eirlys wondered as she returned to her own abode. The white shock of hair that Dora wore in a short, rather modern style had a genially tousled look. She didn't care a button for her appearance, with the net result that she could dress straight from the Tenovus shelf and still look remarkable. Was it simply that one knew her epic past? No, because strangers stopped in the street and stared. *They always have done,* Dora would say, and her vanity peeped out touchingly. *Oh, aye. I take no notice at all. You should have seen me,* she would boast, *when my hair was auburn.* Her eyes would light up and she'd roll the 'r' in 'auburn' with a peculiar relish, bringing a skirl from her native Glasgow. At fifty-one, Eirlys was conscious that her own hazel hair was going cloudy in patches, like a cataract on an ageing eye. She had mentioned this to Dora and added that she did so wish she had dramatic hair like Dora's. *Is that so, Eirlys?*

Not really, Eirlys now thought. There was too often that faint and saddening alloy of insincerity when one wished to be kind, to affirm the other person. Dora stood between her and mortality: as long as Dora was positioned there, you felt superstitiously safe, as if Dora were taking the buffeting of the storm for you. You felt young and vigorous. Quite nonsensical and egotistic, of course. Eirlys's greying mop told her that categorically every morning.

'Now then,' she addressed the massed plants that seemed to have taken over her living space. 'Drinks all round.'

Her favourite ritual: nurturing life in this host that she had gathered under her wing. Like her grandmother, Eirlys had green fingers but without the garden to go with them. Nevertheless, summer and winter, her plants seemed more than happy in the elegant and spacious bay window: the mild climate and the sheltered building were just what they liked. They created a green gloom within her rooms, altogether to Eirlys's taste.

She stood and looked at them for a long moment. The high ceilings were handy, as she could allow a couple of palms to get away. They spread their sharp leaves at the level of the picture rail and held a chatty dialogue with the frondy bamboos on Eirlys's curtains.

In a little while, when the newcomer had had a chance to find her bearings, Eirlys would go upstairs and knock, she promised herself, she would busybody just a tiny bit, see that the new resident was all right. She might want information about the cryptic stopcocks, for instance, or the whereabouts of the electricity meters, buried in the bowels of the building in a thick tangle of wires.

Eirlys tapped lightly on the door she still thought of as Mrs Menelaus's and stood well back to let herself be seen and appraised through the fish-eye lens to which Mrs Menelaus had always resorted even when she knew it was only Eirlys at the door; for after all, she'd once remarked, a woman alone can never be too sure. A man might so easily gain entrance to the building unbeknownst. People could be very careless, leaving the main door on the latch.

The newcomer greeted her with a welcoming grin. A lovely, open face, Eirlys thought. She registered a pale complexion and strikingly dark hair and eyes. A fraying sweater and jeans with a hole at the knee. By design. Of course, Eirlys thought: that is how she wants to look. It is a statement. Of? No idea. Something about society. Embarrassed, Eirlys launched into what even she perceived as a torrential gabble of introduction.

'Pardon? Sorry,' said the girl, 'but I don't understand Welsh.'

'But, darling!' Eirlys slowed right down and smiled. 'I'm not talking Welsh.'

'Oh, right. No, of course you're not.'

'I'm Eirlys. Your neighbour from downstairs.'

'Hannah. Hi, Ellis? Ayliss? Do come in anyway. Please.'

Eirlys, insisting she didn't want to intrude when Hannah was just getting sorted out, found herself ushered in to Emma Menelaus's world, complete with her dark Victorian furniture, for the flat had been taken furnished. Eirlys's eye took in the mahogany massiveness of it all, conker-brown, staining the airy room with its shadow. A Welsh dresser dominated the sitting room like an altar. It had belonged to Mrs Menelaus's grandparents, and had been the ageing granddaughter's treasure, despite the fact that it overwhelmed everything else. It had never been meant for a cramped modern apartment, as Mrs Menelaus had acknowledged, with that wistful look she had had, recalling perhaps some more spaciously proportioned world. In Mrs Menelaus's day the dresser had shone with a galaxy of bright suns, moons and stars, in the form of dynastic crockery, kept pristine. Now the gloomy dresser loured like a dusty monster. Nothing in the room had changed, yet the centre was empty.

Eirlys swayed a moment where she stood. This is it, she thought: one minute we're chirping away in our cages and the next minute we've flown. She looked out of the window into gathering twilight.

She hadn't many things of her own, Hannah explained, she wasn't bothered with owning stuff, so she was quite glad to be able to start out with the basics, though they were a touch gloomy perhaps. How had the lady who lived there before her ever managed to get it all in? She must have winched it in through the window with a crane.

'Actually I think that was how Mrs Menelaus did it.'

'Thought so.What was she like?'

'Oh, a kindly soul. But private. She kept herself to herself. We do generally – we shan't keep bothering you.'

'Oh, I won't bother you either, Eirlys. What a lovely name. How do you spell it then?'

Eirlys spelt her name, explaining that it was Welsh for 'snowdrop'. Had Hannah come far? From Bristol apparently. But this was a homecoming of sorts, Hannah went on eagerly: she came from West Wales, Carmarthenshire, originally. From the deep countryside, she said. Well, actually, a commune. They'd left when she was about six. Her father had come from Llangyfelach.

'Oh,' said Eirlys. 'Very near. So you're coming home. And your mum?'

The mother had died in a car accident when Hannah was eleven and she'd been brought up in Bristol by an aunt and uncle. Life has not been easy for her, Eirlys thought. She was impressed to learn that Hannah had a job in an engineering lab at the college. She had started but never completed a degree in engineering at Bristol, but she might take it up again here in Swansea. Eirlys made a mental note to tell Dora. Deep in Mrs Menelaus's best armchair, Eirlys could not seem to stop her eyes roving to the frayed sleeves of the sweater and mentally knitting them back up again.

Glancing round the bare walls, she noticed Mrs Menelaus's picture hooks minus the photographs of her parents and sister. And once you noticed this, you spotted pale patches, ghostly shadows of those photos. Buzz off now, she told herself.

'Well, there you are then. Why am I keeping you talking? I only came to ask if there was anything I could get you. Can I make you a cup of tea?'

The idea of a proper cup of tea and a piece of cherry cake as volubly described had great appeal.

'Are you fond of music, *bach*?' Eirlys asked on her way out.

'Well, quite fond. It depends. Are you?'

'Oh, we are all musical in my family – and poetry too, of course. Waldo, my cousin, is a considerable harpist. And his boy Ianto plays the xylophone lovely. But not here,' she added. 'In his own house, in one of the rooms where the noises don't carry. At a fairly early stage with the tympany he is. The Eyrie is a haven of quiet. You don't play an instrument yourself, dear?'

'Oh no.'

Not yet, the face lit up and seemed to say. Don't tempt me.

'Ah. There you are then. Well now, I'll bring you tea on a tray. No, don't you stir. You must be all in.'

Eirlys phoned up to Dora as soon as she got in to her own flat.

'Hallo, dear. Is your toothache better?'

Pause. Dora had forgotten it. Good sign. 'Oh, that. It was nothing. Well, Eirlys? Was there anything else?'

'Just to say I've met our young neighbour. And to assure you she is likely to be as quiet as a mouse and she does not play a musical instrument. Nothing to worry about.'

'I was not worrying.'

'No, but you might have been.'

'No, Eirlys. Were she to disturb my peace, I would take immediate steps to quell her.'

'Well, there's no need, I'm glad to say. Her name is Hannah, didn't catch the surname. She's an engineer and looking for her roots.'

'Well, good luck to her,' Dora said, with the suggestion of a sneer. 'Don't let me keep you, Eirlys.'

Eirlys put down the receiver and switched the kettle on. Bossy-boots, she thought, without rancour. Dora could be quite nasty when she felt like it. How terrible she must have been in the school playground to girls she didn't want to play with! Having occasionally but rarely met with greatness, Eirlys was content to abide in its shadow, recognising that it did not always look where it was going.

In this respect, she thought, I am a bit of a wife to Dora, and yet even the most uxorious husbands can underestimate their wives.

For example, did Dora know Eirlys had been in *prison*? No, she didn't! Well then! Eirlys exclaimed inwardly, pouring milk into a baby jug and adding tongs to the bowl of sugar lumps. And it was odd, but it was *because* she knew that Dora would be impressed by her jailbird history that Eirlys had from some scruple refrained from telling her, until the time when it would have been natural to convey that information had passed by. She had not made the confidence that might have been an easy way to acquire Dora's respect. Bur Dora was dismissive of Welsh nationalism, which she equated with fascism.

'Saunders Lewis!' Dora had once exploded. 'Do you know what he said after the bombing of Guernica?'

'Yes, I do.'

'Well then!'

Eirlys had held her tongue. She had refrained from saying that this was a long time ago, it was utterly out-of-date, that in the Sixties and Seventies most of the language protesters had been or become socialists. For Dora had been trembling with rage. To her, naturally enough, the wounds of Spain remained raw and fresh. Lewis, the Welsh nationalist leader, had toasted Franco as a 'fine Christian gentleman' just yesterday, as far as Dora was concerned. So Eirlys shut up, though there was much she could have said to correct the balance. Life was more subtle, more nuanced, than Dora could ever allow.

The courtship era of friendship, during which one laid down the foundations, had long been over. And so I have kept myself secret, Eirlys thought, and never told Dora of how I was there. There with Menna at every anniversary of the drowning of the village of Tryweryn to make a reservoir for Liverpool. Wild children we were, Dora, she informed her now, inwardly, as she cut *bara brith*. Up a TV mast I was, with Waldo. What about that then, Dora? Eirlys, the defacer of road signs, buttered the *bara brith* thick. No sense in stinting, and the girlie sorely needed feeding up.

Their young passion had been packed into the quest for a Welsh-language TV medium. And look what they'd got: S4C with the soaps and the pony and trap racing. Ah well, it was the principle. Hard now to recapture and yet impossible quite to renounce the elation of those days. And, as a matter of fact, she thoroughly enjoyed a good soap. Her mind flickered to the situation on *Pobol y Cwm* between Hywel and Ffion. A community based on infidelities and gossip, of popping-in and being thrown out.

Poor Dad. He had had a lot to bear with his girls being nationalists, Eirlys thought, and had borne it with loving if sombre forbearance. She stood holding him in her mind, wishing, as so often, that she could express her gratitude. Was gratitude, when you came down to it, the greatest passion we can know? His daughters' generation's acts of civil disobedience were perhaps less terrible to the teetotal innocent than their taste for wine and the state of Eirlys's hair. He'd had a curious career, moving from the steelworks at Hafod to the Independent ministry and then, on some issue of conscience too abstruse for the young Eirlys to fathom, and never discussed in the family, back to manual labour in a canning factory at the docks. So of course Dad had understood perfectly well that sometimes the most respectable chapel folk must stand as martyrs in a sacred cause, though he could not for the life of him see that the Welsh tongue merited such a title.

She had not understood how he could say this. It was their mother tongue. Eirlys would fire up, shout, storm. *Traitor! Dad, how can you? They've tried to kill our language. Our language is us! Sacred, of course it's sacred! It's our* mother*!*

It was, aye, the tongue of Pantycelyn and of the Bishop Morgan Bible, her father had acknowledged, but it was only a *language* after all. The more furious she became, the more dryly monotonous his tone.

Slow of speech, sober of temper, he assured her that he spoke in a spirit of respect, of course, veneration even, for Hebrew and Welsh, as she must know (his forehead rumpled with wrinkles, which Eirlys's fingers had yearned to reach out and smooth), were his twin darlings. But at the same time, she'd been riled by his preachy, long-winded sentences.

'But, *cariad*, Hebrew itself is only a language.'

'Oh God!' she'd rage. 'Oh God, oh God!'

'Oh God indeed. It is a dress, a vesture,' he said. 'Language is a dark glass, through which we see darkly. But your hair now, Eirlys! Down to your waist! What is the significance of such an excess of hair, might I ask? Eve had such hair? Ah, I see. But I am bound to wonder whether that was because she lacked scissors? We are not in that happy garden now, I think?'

Hairstyles, she had explained to him, were also a language. His own hair, so neatly trimmed and parted like a schoolboy's, was making a statement.

Dad had allowed himself a wan smile. 'What there is of it,' he'd replied.

And Mam had called, 'How you can bear to torment your father, Eirlys, as soon as he's in the door? Come in by here, madam, and peel the carrots.'

But Dad had called back, 'Oh no, Eirlys is not tormenting me. We are discussing the iconography of our hair and whether it is a sacred language.'

The long, messy hair of the newcomer, Hannah, was clearly making a far more modern statement. Whatever could that be? Eirlys reached round, head back, and tried to touch her own mane, as she used to. Impossible, of course. Yet how odd it was that the girl you had been – wild, aflame – was still lodged in you somewhere. Buried in fat, she thought. A sleeping incendiary.

In time the hair had been cropped. Eirlys had gradually ceased hurling herself against policemen twice her size, screaming choice abuse. Her life had narrowed. She'd studied Welsh but then changed to Social Work at the college in Abertawe, and graduated with first class honours. So proud of her on that day, Dad and Mam had been: the first ever Harries girl to take a degree. Then had come social work itself, with its deep satisfactions and exactions. The husband she hadn't married and the babies that hadn't come. The boyfriends who'd married mutual friends, or moved away and lost touch. Parents growing elderly and becoming gentle living wraiths, to whom she had been able to offer the care of the unattached daughter. Their gratitude. The knowledge upon which she rested after they joined one another in the earth: that she had done her best by those who had done well by her.

Eirlys would not say that she had had an unfulfilling life, no. The marvellous chatty weave of family. She practised an ethic of feeding, or so Dora said. Feed my sheep, said the Bible. Christ had cooked up something wonderful out of five loaves and two small fishes. In that case, though, you'll have to explain, Eirlys pointed out to herself, why you left your vocation in social work and dodged up here where no one speaks the language you would have died for! Your nearest and dearest have to make an excursion to find you, rather than popping in, yet here she was, stuffing strangers with goodies. It must be pathological. Never mind.

Out Eirlys stepped with the tray and there scurried little Megan, in her slippers that came up over her thin ankles like boots and her pretty, pale hair that had faded less than her mind. Like a light bulb on the blink, her mind pulsed with fitful beams of awareness. Eirlys checked the catch on the front door, perching the tray on one splayed hand like a butler in a film. Megan must not be allowed to get out and wander off. The quiet soul could become lost or be run over as easily as a child. And generally she seemed to know her danger, for she would haunt the doorstep when she did find the door ajar. Hesitantly she would look round for guidance, and could be led back in with no trouble at all, sometimes offering a perfectly sensible word or two about the weather.

Perhaps Megan was also perpetually on her best behaviour for fear of her son-in-law, Hugh, for whom the habitually charitable Eirlys could find little to say that was positive. Hugh had the moral odour of a man who had never received his due from the world. A man whose wife's mother owed him an inheritance.

He had made the investment of mending Megan's fridge door when it fell off, to save the cost of a call-out. He had installed a gas leak detector. He came regularly with his spouse on the Sabbath, pre-prandially, and delivered Megan some kind of droning homily of an hour's duration, whilst drinking sherry at her expense. And so far he had received, in recompense for these dutiful acts, only the rather poor interest of her growing fear. Dora had analysed the situation thus to Eirlys. It would have been excellent to be able to disagree.

Megan chirruped, 'Oh, Eirlys, what a heavenly tray!'

'It's for our new neighbour, Megan. Nice, polite young lady, just moved in.'

'Look how lovely it's set out. Such a pretty tray cloth. Well! A picture is that. Don't mind me, dear, I'm just off to the—'

'Now, lovely, back you go to the nice warm room. Chilly it is out there, brrr.'

'Brrr,' agreed Megan. 'To the Post Office.'

'Leave your mail by here, my love. I'll post it for you, isn't it? Go in now by the fire.'

Megan had brought out a handful of pages ripped from magazines, in lieu of post.

'I've had my tea,' she said, and disappeared.

A good conversation, Eirlys thought. Oh bless her, it's sad to see a sharp mind go soft. Megan had worked for the Inland Revenue at Tŷ Nant in the compliance office, and doubtless had terrified many a taxpayer in her time. Eirlys herself had once refused to pay her tax and recalled being savaged by a compliance officer, but that had been because the so-called government prohibited her from declaring her earnings in the tongue of Owain Glyn Dwr and not only required her to hand them over to the Conqueror to fund his occupation of her native land, but insisted that she submit to this injustice in her second language.

3

As soon as the little Welsh lady had gone, Hannah started wolfing the dark, faintly bitter bread, swilling it down with tea. Sweet person, Eirlys. Too sugary perhaps: so much niceness couldn't be sincere? She was probably a mass murderer underneath. Hannah hoped she wasn't expected to operate a delivery service in response. They'd be disappointed if so, because she planned to be herself here, even if that meant they thought she was sociopathic. Should have said no to the tray. But you couldn't get a word in edgewise, with the beaky little mouth going like that, blah-de-blah, while the greedy eyes licked at everything.

Perhaps that was how Welsh people were though – a bit cloying, a bit all over you? The taxi driver had been just the same, terribly soft in his manner although he was lovely. But then he'd said he was a Brummie. And the guys who'd got on the train at Neath – but they were Arab refugees. So maybe the place just does that to you. It marshmallows you. And I could do with sweetening, Hannah thought. Barry had certainly thought so. The mass murderer was probably even now filling in the old dear behind the party wall who didn't want her to play the xylophone indoors. She pictured her as a lady with a taste for tattle and flower-arranging.

My pad, my territory, mine, she thought, pottering round, opening drawers and cupboards. Odd smells of otherness. Darker patches of wallpaper showed where the dead lady's pictures had once hung. Up in the corners near the ceiling, a small city of spiders' webs had escaped the eye of the landlady and the vacuum cleaner nozzle. Fine by her. Fellow creatures. Doing no harm. In their own world. She'd never minded insects. And the days of living in a DIY palace were over. At last! Unbelievable. She wanted to punch the air. She'd torn herself free and run to this fortress on a hill that Barry would never scale. Her own mess. Clean dirt.

And a good stiff mattress too: she threw herself down. Whistled with pure joy at having her own bed. What was more sensuous and even erotic than your own bed? To spread yourself like a starfish in a cool sea of linen! Sleep when you like, wake when you like. Total bloody luxury, she thought, lying on her back, head on her folded arms. No one to gurn about grubby sheets and complain they hadn't been ironed. No one to wake randy and whining at six in the morning, though of course the poor guy had long given up hope of satisfaction in that department. She raised her feet one at a time and waggled them about to admire the ankle-boots she'd bought specially for her escape.

Of course, she wouldn't stay. She'd take off when she was ready. When I've found you and seen the world you chose over me and Mum, she said to the father who'd drifted away like smoke when they were still at the commune. A shiver ran down Hannah's spine. She looked out of the window: her real father was there, in the twilight, now very close at hand. She'd traced him to Llangyfelach through the electoral register and the telephone directory. He'd been there at least three years ago. She'd found his street on a website where aerial photos let you zoom into any address in the world. She'd seen his roof.

But the heavy brown furniture of the dead woman loomed at Hannah and she suddenly felt terrified, as if she were making the worst mistake of her life – laying herself open to being the needy little girl her father had left.

What have you done? she asked herself. What have you laid yourself open to doing?

That was it: she must never, ever go back to being the person she'd been before she met Barry. So take what you find here calmly, she told herself. Before, she'd had no boundaries and flowed trippily from one guy to another, taking blissy stuff and waking up in surprising places with surprising people, feeling see-through. Offering her private, most intimate self to be handled like meat. No more abortions, ever. She'd take care of herself now. She knew how to.

Hannah had never had a taste for property. The dead woman's furniture would suit her as well as anything. As Barry had said to Lara and Sophie in a bitter moment, your stepmother doesn't know her recliners from her three-piece suites. The motherless girls had raised their lips in a silent snarl. Hannah had done one back, just as nasty or nastier. Probably the same childish misery had spurted in all three breasts. After all, they were nearly the same generation – Sophie fourteen when Hannah had arrived nearly four years ago, and Lara not quite ten.

Nothing Hannah could do on the domestic front could ever satisfy them. *She's a veggie*, Barry had explained to the girls. *Her heart isn't in gravy*. At the mention of a vegetable, they would speed out of the room gagging, clutching their throats.

Can't blame them. I'd have killed me, she thought, if I'd been them. A twenty-two-year-old kid installed in their mother's place? What did I expect but their loathing? The girls were shot of her now. Well, Lara at least; Sophie was at uni. Hannah minded about Lara. But she'll be glad I've gone. She'll have him to herself. Will that be good for her? He can be lovely, she thought, when he knows you need him. Poor Barry. There was little if any harm in him.

Strange sounds came from outside as if someone were trying to throttle a cat. Unearthly screaming, but frighteningly human, too. She threw up the sash to listen, letting in the ice and salt of the air.

The uproar had stopped but, putting on her jacket, Hannah went out to explore anyway. She'd always loved the dark. How long since she'd roamed alone at night, always feeling so safe? Safer out here than with people any day. As soon as she stepped out of the main door, the security system detected a presence and floodlight drenched her. Halfway down the steep slope, she turned to look back. The Eyrie reared up silver-grey in the night, the strange pillars and architraves around the balconies casting complicated shadows, the vanes on the three tall gables gleaming. But when the light switched itself off, the building became a black shadow in which the warm yellow lights in people's windows showed Hannah the private worlds of the dwellers, going on behind closed or open curtains. It gave her pleasure to see them. Just as she was querying why that was, and realising that it was being on the outside looking in that pleased her – being free of what in her mind she called 'all that' – Hannah saw that in the flat next to hers the old lady was on her balcony looking out, resting on her elbows, cupping her face in her hands. Perhaps she too had heard the animals cries.

Presently the lady ducked back in. The moon was full and the stars above the wooded ridge behind The Eyrie seemed close and over-large. Hannah's breath misted in the air. So quiet, no traffic at all, so that when another creature cried out – was it an owl, a barn owl? – it haunted the whole basin of the valley with a dramatic echo.

Hannah moved across the moonlit forecourt to the edge of the black wood, where she was sure the sounds had come from. An owl certainly, she knew, as it called again, or rather a pair, calling to one another. They sounded so like babies crying. She stepped in under the canopy of the firs. It was pitch-black. She shut her eyes tight to accommodate them to this denser darkness and, standing there, caught minute rustlings and soughings and the snapping of twigs. Birds churred in their sleep.

Further in, the dark wood became a dappled place. Moonlit tracks threaded past and through rhododendron bushes, and the waxy leaves glimmered. As a girl she'd made dens in the rhododendrons with the other kids. It all flooded back, with a leap of the spirit. You could keep house there, outside the edgy world of the grown-ups. And there'd been a tree-house. Her heart bounced. She hadn't thought of it for years. I've never been afraid in the honest out-of-doors, Hannah thought, and proclaimed this fact to the person in her mind who was shaking his head and remonstrating: *Come back in now, dear, it's time.* As she stopped to breathe in a scent of resin and some kind of musky odour, the owl called again but at a distance. It had flown out across its domain and homed in, perhaps, on some shrew or mouse. Had heard its terrified heartbeat *pockapocka* from high up because owls don't see their prey, do they, their sensational hearing maps their aerial pounce.

She crashed steeply uphill through bracken, then stood still, for it absolutely stank here. She laughed out loud. A real stench, ripe and rank and feral, of fox pee. I know you, my friend, she thought: vixen on heat, aren't you? Just as she was thinking this, all hell broke loose down below her – the wailing shriek of the female and the snarl of the male, fighting-mating by the dustbins in the full light of the security lights because they didn't care, did they, at that stage, and, look, there they were in the tie. She'd never seen it before. Locked in together, tied together at the swollen root, and now the dogfox brought his back leg over the vixen's rump and the two were left standing there like prats back to back, giving the odd tug, as they might have to do for an hour or more.

Feeling her way over a fallen tree-trunk she'd seen from the flat, she knew pretty well where she was now: not far from the top. She'd just go on so that she could say she'd done it. She had to clamber hand over hand up limestone rocks, the cold spasming in her hands. She'd no gloves and the denim jacket was far too light. Then the ground levelled out. The stand of firs was more widely spaced and Hannah walked through easily to the other side.

For miles the silvered gravestones stretched away, on a gentle downward slope. Milk-white stone angels with their backs to Hannah cast their shadows over the burials. Some pointed up to the starry sky, others down to the earth. Great globes of urns and tall towers topped with crosses crowded together, and an angel with one hand played the violin. Through them all a path wound like a black river, down which Hannah, in absolute wonder, began to walk.

4

The lass's face had given Dora a pang. In the angular features, the jutting jaw and especially in the peculiar and disconcerting eyes, Rosa had scrambled up from under the ground, putting her scattered self together, rising from her own ashes. Recognition had thrilled through Dora, racing the length of her nervous system in a flash, so that she had experienced the recognition as a kind of electric shock in all her body at once. Not just in her eyes. She had seen Rosa through the palms of her hands, in the arches of her feet.

The face of the newcomer had looked up. Without focus. Those dark, liquid eyes.

A rush of joy; then staggering back as if from a blow, for Dora could not physically afford this excess of feeling. All strong emotion must convert into opinion, principle, irony.

The nervous system, she now thought, twisting her scarf round her neck, for it was a bitter day, resembled a tree. We walk around with a species of uprooted tree inside us. This is scientific. And the extremities are like roots that tingle and twinge. She must get out and walk off this nonsense.

Of course one saw Rosa everywhere, always had. Nothing remarkable about that. She let herself out, locked the door and fled downstairs rather fast, to avoid confronting Rosa's likeness again. Trust Eirlys to insist on extending the tea caddy and the biscuit tin to the newcomer. Who would turn out to look nothing like Rosa; such sightings, which had once been commonplace, never did. She flitted past Eirlys's door and escaped into the burningly cold air.

Dora and Oystermouth had nothing in common. Oystermouth with its genteel pensioners drinking coffee; its tourists on the lookout for beer and trinkets; its surfing shops. Why would a self-respecting Scot-and-Trot wish to spend her final, important years in such a trite spot? Naturally Keir and Karl believed, with sinking hearts, that their grandmother had come to Wales to be near *them* and, though she believed in frankness, even to the point of crudity, she had not disabused them. They were, in any case, terrified of and embarrassed by her, and made it clear that they led stressful lives – but please, call us in an emergency, oh yes, do. We know you are very independent. Keir's wife, Tessa, took a different line and oozed: *Oh, darling, do come round more often; we never see you. Come for supper/cocktails/a barbecue.*

And of course, folk mainly thought that Dora had retired to Swansea because of its associations with Spain and socialism. She had visited the great plaque made of Welsh coal, slate and steel above the entrance to the Miners' Library at Hendrefoilan, where thirty-three men were commemorated for sacrificing their lives 'in support of the heroic struggle of the Spanish Republic against fascism'. She could hardly say that she had not been moved. Too moved: the tide of grief had begun to rear, bringing with it a knowledge she had always suppressed, that Lachlan's life had been thrown away. Food for powder he had been, in the last mad push. She had not come here to dwell on this.

She started the car. Don't look back. You might see the false Rosa at Emma Menelaus's window. Of course, one did glance up at the last minute. Happily, there was no face looking out.

The *great*-grandchildren, on the other hand – now that was a different matter. That was pure romance on both sides. Stars in their eyes whenever they saw one another, and the knowledge in the tall, slender and rather odd Angelica, the most Doraesque of Dora's kin, that in being close to her Nannan she was touching her own deep history. Touching also something of her future: a way to grasp and tackle it. Yet there was little of Rosa, so far as

Dora could see, in the lass. Jelly was lissom and anarchic, with a turbulence altogether solipsistic. She chased her own tail and danced with her shadow. At seventeen, she lived covered in light and superficial irony, like cheap glitter. She was obsessed with the tatty paste jewels she wore at her navel, and the matter to which she had so far given the deepest thought was the question of breast-enhancement. Nevertheless, there was a kinship there between them and, to butter or cheer Nannan up, Jelly could become quite ecological.

Dora drove down the steep hill to the twin beaches of Rotherslade and Langland and her heart cautiously lifted at the sight of the sea, dour and grey-green like tarnished pewter. Almost an ugly brew in this raw light, as if some almighty smoker in the sky had emptied out his ashtray into it. Tide halfway out. The sea, as soon as she got out of the car, boomed softly from cliffs to cliffs.

A stick-man was walking his stick-dog way out on the khaki beach, throwing, she thought, a stick-stick for it to catch.

The Rosa-impersonator receded. So did the claustrophobia of the flats. Dora walked down onto the beach, as near to the foaming, sudsy tide-line as she could get. Out there on the high waves sat gulls – or, no, were they seals? Human, like the silkies of her mother's tales? – which then climbed on to boards, for they were neither gulls nor seals but surfers, who perched transiently in attitudes of graceful swagger on their surfboards, playing the waves, only to collapse. Out there the manes of the breakers trailed a crest of spray, blown back by the wind as the tide surged in. Dora stood still to watch the horses of the sea, then, chilled, clambered up onto the cliff-path leading around the headland to Caswell, relishing the buffeting of the air, which was almost as achingly sharp today as Morayshire, where she'd founded the school. She had insisted on outdoor pursuits (not silly ball games, of course) as part of the pupils' training. For Dora herself had grown up spartan and tough, a running lass without a spare ounce of flesh. A tree-climber. An athlete swooping on the ropes her brother had fixed high in an elm in the park. An outdoor lassie. Not made to be cooped up indoors with a bunch of old biddies.

When the bracken was dead it made a fine sight, rust-coloured, a field of corrosion. But her mood had darkened. For whenever she sighted Rosa, she thought of her own death. What would she do if she became immobile or lost her focus like wee Megan and could no longer stride out here in her own good company, with the sea-wind challenging her hardihood and her head snug in its Basque cap that Keir had compared unfavourably with a frisbee? Nowadays nobody knew what a Basque cap stood for. Yet she was proud of wearing it, even in a world where nobody knew. She pulled the peak low over her forehead. Ignoramuses. Doubtless, folk took her for an eccentric golfer. She strode out, head high, wearing the uniform of Liberty, the veteran of a forgotten war, like those Japanese soldiers who had lived in caves on islands for years after Hiroshima, true to the god-emperor, waiting for the Yanks who, of course, were by that time busy elsewhere.

Keir in his lemon-yellow tea-cosy hat with a bobbing pompom! Accusing me of wearing a silly hat! Ach.

Dora stopped in her tracks. But whatever will I do when my time comes? The sky loured and she flinched. Nobody was playing on the golf links. Only the surfers remained fanatical and fearless. What will I do? For Dora had as yet made neither preparations nor accommodation. Other folk did, she was aware; she saw them prepare for the blow before the blow came. That had never been her way.

It was chilly if you stopped. Well then, do not stop. Simple as that. She dug her gloved hands into the pockets of her donkey-jacket and continued round the point, but was met by such a blast that she turned and scuttled back the way she had come. Bundling herself into the car, she turned for home.

She was lucky, for she had managed to miss all the neighbours. Settling down on the settee, she turned on the television. And there *he* was, the Prime Minister. She could not forgive the man. Had she womanned the barricades for *that* narcissistic smiler, that holy Joe with the honeyed tongue? She was at a loss for words, and not, please note, because she was tending to forgetfulness and had mislaid her reading specs (which would, of course, turn up), but because this wretched lawyer had devalued the currency of words. Truly a case for gelding. There was too much testosterone about, and probably a good thing that modern plastics were feminising men. Yet that proliferation of plastic, itself the product of testosterone-crazed thinking, was polluting our world, so some other mode must be found.

Reason?

Tried that.

A buzz on the door. It was Angelica, the sweetheart. Dora's heart rose as Jelly came sashaying in, wearing a fur-trimmed jacket over jeans that left her midriff bare. But Jelly was still in the midst of the palaver of a passionate but empty chat with her friend on her mobile phone. She swooped on Nannan with a kiss and a wink. Carried on chattering into the phone. Dora continued to listen to the Prime Minister's speech.

He was himself a weapon of mass destruction. She wondered if the courteous Emma Menelaus had ever heard her through the wall, ranting at the TV. Well, the new lassie would have to get used to it.

'He can't hear you, Nannan,' Jelly paused in her conversation to advise.

'I know *that*, Jelly! It's a television set.'

'It's just the way you tell him off, it's as if he could hear. Look, gotta go, I'm at my Nannan's, catch ya later,' she said into the phone.

'Don't worry, I'm not *that* far gone.'

'No, Nannan, I didn't mean—'

'These are serious matters, Angelica.'

Angelica read the weather of her Nannan's face. 'Oh, dear,' said the girl. 'Nannan, you know something?' She stretched out her hand to Dora and it hung there, suspended.

'I may do,' said Dora cautiously, though she permitted the hand to find rest in her firm grip.

'Nannan, I love you absolutely to bits,' said the seventeen-year-old with that candid sweetness they had nowadays, their power to be unafraid of intimacy and endearment. Tears had risen, to Dora's shame. She blushed. The tender, stroppy girl, with her violet-blue eyes beneath the strong, squarish eyebrows, broke every rule in the grid-like code of manners in which Dora had been raised. Angelica poured softly through the grid like a cloud of scent, saying, *I love you to bits.*

Simply that. Not fearful of these words at all – words that were almost terrible in their nakedness. Dora had rarely uttered them, even to Lachlan, though she had opened herself to him.

Talk flowed blessedly between Dora and Angelica. An hour went by so delightfully, then another, and yet you wondered afterwards what on earth had been said. Then Angelica's mobile rang and she started yet another gabbled chat about where she would meet so-and-so, when, and where they would buy strappy shoes – 'No! Pink ones!' – and a burst of giggles. Jelly would phone Tally and then Tally would phone Sam, then she'd ring back and confirm, and at the end, 'Love ya loads. Bye.'

Was it too easy then? Dora wondered, waving the lovely creature with the bare midriff off from her window, all this 'I love you to bits'? Was it the equivalent of the fatuous refrain of the boy-cashier at the Co-op bleating, 'Have a nice day,' at which she raised her eyebrows and delivered a look of bale? And yet Jelly's words and the tingle of a kissed cheek clung about Dora's consciousness for many hours, and brought to her lips a foolish smile.

It was not totally impossible, she thought, catching sight of her reflection in the double-glazing, that the boy in the supermarket did tepidly hope that I would enjoy my day. But her present smirk reminded her of *him*. The Prime Minister. Idiotic. The Tesco laddie had been programmed by his outfit to express the fathomlessly insincere wish that she, a woman with nothing pertinent to himself but a wallet stuffed with tenners, should return to that emporium of capitalism and lighten the wallet again.

Hence it was just and reasonable that Dora should have favoured him with a wee grimace in return. Not that she had anything against him, save that he was mass-produced.

'You'll never guess,' said Eirlys.

'I'm sure you're right.'

'Well, the new young lady –'

Dora yawned. She picked up the papers she'd been working on and tapped them on the desk so that they fell into place.

'– is a sort of engineer, as I mentioned yesterday.'

Dora was interested, despite herself.

'But the thing is, she can do plumbing, apparently. If we need an odd job man in an emergency—'

'Person.'

'Pardon, dear?'

'Odd job person or odd job woman.'

'Of course.'

Eirlys was humouring her, and it did irk Dora to find her generation so casual with language. Neither parsing nor feminism seemed to have penetrated to the South Wales of her friend's childhood, but it could not be helped. Dora looked grim. Eirlys simply smiled and babbled on.

'Well, there's useful, I thought, but Mrs Dark raised the issue of whether she's Corgi-registered, see, not to her face, of course, but fair dos, Mrs Dark has a point there, and you couldn't ask her to tackle your boiler if it broke down on Christmas Day, but for drains and suchlike, Dora, say your overflow got clogged, she could be asked to have a look, couldn't she?'

Dora said she would bear it in mind. The possession of these skills did whet her curiosity. She had often urged her girls at the Gutheim Fellowship to opt for careers in the sciences, and not just maths or biology either. She had nourished visions of her girls building a new world, climbing about fearlessly in white steel hats on scaffolding, both material and ideological. Designing irrigation systems for deserts. Planning and building homes for the shelterless. She did not despise art, only artiness. But a pair of working hands: this was a lass's strength and resource.

'Got a job at the college she has. In the engineering labs. Working for Doctor Price. She's to be his technician and build the scaffolding for the experiments. And, oh, you should see her toolbox! Keeps it lovely, she does.'

Dora could see that Eirlys's easily-moved affections had been kindled. What was the young person's name again? Dora asked.

'Did I not say? Hannah. I don't know her surname.'

No, of course Dora had never expected a Rosa, nor was she disappointed or relieved. Dora was not superstitious.

'Well, I suppose we'd better invite her in for a drink,' she said.

Eirlys hurried to obey.

The way to disperse your ghosts was by confronting them. And yet Dora was unwilling to kill the illusion. Not just yet. Rosa had appeared to her many times over the years, glimpsed in the posture of some lassie in a queue or at the wheel of a car. Once Dora had got on a London bus and ridden behind a young woman all the way to Fulham, aware, of course, that there was in reality only the most tenuous resemblance to her daughter, if indeed any at all. But the spell which Dora cast over her own perception was, for that hour, worth the inevitable disappointment when the false Rosa turned in her seat or rose to leave. Such willed delusions made Dora's heart glow with the conviction, not that Rosa was alive in the here-and-now – she was not *mad* – but that Rosa had once existed and might so easily have been here now, a living presence on the earth, going about her business, though not as young as the look-alikes, of course. Always Dora's heart latched on to the young. She could scarcely imagine her daughter ageing.

Now Dora rid herself in advance of the delusion. She gave her mind to making arrangements for the delivery of the powerful, expensive, state-of-the-art computer she had ordered. Then she began to clear a space for it on her desk amongst the debris of papers. What she really needed was a secretary. But then one would have to put up with the presence of a stranger in one's own territory.

Eirlys was chattering to the girl in the corridor. Dora could hear them discussing keys. This one was for the back door, leading to the washing lines and the bike shed, Eirlys was explaining, and this was the key to the electricity meter cupboard, and this ... goodness, whatever was this for? No idea, she said, but keep it anyway because you might find a spare door that needs unlocking. So many keys were out of date, she concluded, but you never knew. Now she was knocking and calling to Dora, who said, 'Come through.'

As Eirlys ushered the newcomer into the flat, Dora, having resigned herself to putting down her book, removed her reading glasses. She stood up to shake hands and, taking the smaller hand in her right, covered it with her left, and could not for a long moment let go, thrown off balance so that she staggered and nearly fell, and her heart skipped a beat, and her soul veered in the push-me-pull-you of the eyes which belonged, without a shadow of a doubt, to Rosa.

5

The old woman looked up from where she was sitting at the edge of a pool of lamplight, her hair an amazing and beautiful tousle of silver. She looked serene and rather stately, setting a bookmark between the pages of her book, closing it and laying it aside, her high-cheekboned face a map of fine wrinkles. She was wearing a loose woollen sweater of pale blue, a blue that picked up the strong colour of her eyes.

But as she got to her feet and held out her hand, a spasm seemed to shake her body, and Hannah feared for a moment that she would fall. At the same time her face twisted and she lunged towards Hannah, who rushed forward and tried to steady her. She was tall. And how powerful her grip was: the hand that was grasping Hannah's squeezed so that her knuckles crunched painfully, for the old lady didn't let go, she seemed to be tugging Hannah to and fro. While Hannah was asking herself, Is she having a seizure?, the other hand came clamping down over hers and the woman seemed to want to say something.

'Dora! Dora, *cariad*!' Eirlys was saying, hands on the old woman's arm and back, trying to guide her gently down into a chair. But she resisted, would not be guided, and her eyes swam with sudden tears, she leaned down towards Hannah's face with puckered lips, and in a spirit of what seemed timidity or fear, seemed to want to kiss Hannah on the mouth but turned aside at the last moment and touched her cheek with her lips. The stranger's skin on Hannah's was surprisingly soft.

'Hallo,' said Hannah. 'I'm Hannah Francis. From next door.'

She reached over and kissed the lady back. Never one to be

afraid of endearments and risky caresses, she smiled into the stranger's anguish. She took her hand again, to show that she hadn't recoiled.

'My dear,' said the old woman, looking down at the hand that lay in hers. 'Where have you been?' she asked gently.

Hannah was bewildered. 'Just in my flat,' she said. 'I've been unpacking. Oh, and I've been down to the village and bought some basic items.'

'No,' said the lady. 'I don't mean that. Never mind.'

She passed a hand, with its thick, blue, forking veins, over her eyes.

Eirlys said, 'It's all right, Dora.'

'Of course it is. Perfectly normal.'

She allowed Eirlys to settle her back into her chair, begging her not to fuss – she was quite all right, she'd been deep in her book. And when one is deep in a book, she explained, it is rather like being in a dream, and to be startled out of a particularly choice passage is like being woken up – one is not sure for a moment which world is which.

'I mean,' she went on, 'the world in the book cannot be true.'

'True in a different sense,' said Eirlys.

'Aye, aye,' said the old woman crossly, 'I know all that. I've read my Plato.'

'Oh, I know what you mean about reading,' Hannah jumped in. 'I am *gone* when I'm in a book. My father used to read to me every night before bed. I wouldn't sleep without it. Even now I need to read before I can drop off.'

She had not remembered that about her father for such a long time. He would carry her upstairs on his back, her arms around his neck, her head on his shoulder. But when he left them, doped-out Mum didn't take over. Hannah had a sudden memory of Mum lying on the bed as Joni Mitchell sang 'Green' in the background. Hannah was Little Green. Mum was the child who'd made her. Child with a child pretending. Hannah remembered the queasy feeling of not wanting to be Little Green.

'It's nice that you are a reader,' said Eirlys. 'Dora and I read together, and sometimes we drive each other mad by reading out our favourite passages.'

Would Hannah like beer or wine? the Welsh lady wanted to know. They could offer a few nibbles, as people called them nowadays, but if Hannah wanted something more substantial, just say the word, she could put together some sandwiches, no problem.

'Oh no, really, I'm fine,' Hannah said. 'And I don't drink anything stronger than orange juice, if you've got it.'

She was aware as they talked that the old woman had taken out a handkerchief and was wiping her lips delicately at the corners. She was gathering herself, composing her features.

'Was that you out there last night?' she asked when she was ready. 'When the cats were fighting?'

'Yes, but they weren't cats. It was foxes mating.'

'How do you know?'

'Saw them!'

'In the middle of winter?'

'That's when they do it. And then the pups are born in March.'

'I saw you from my window.'

'I saw you, too.'

'You went into the wood, in the dark.'

'Yes, but you could see in the moonlight. I climbed up the scarp. I'd heard an owl, a barn owl I think it must have been, and then I saw the foxes.'

'I didn't see you come out of the trees,' said the lady, and for the first time in the conversation she held Hannah's eyes. But her underlip quivered and she looked away.

'No, I went over the top. Then I came back by Limekiln Lane.'

She didn't want to say anything about what she'd seen then: it was too like a dream or vision, hers alone.

Eirlys said that, oh yes, Oystermouth Cemetery was over there, a most historical place, at least by daylight. She wouldn't go wandering around there in the dark herself. No lamp-posts, see! No, of course she didn't believe in ghosts! But foxes were another matter. Eirlys often watched the vixen in the summer with the young ones. Magical they were. Hard to think of them as pests.

She handed Dora a glass of red wine and poured orange juice for Hannah.

The old lady's strange contortions had gone now: she sat back and rested her eyes on Hannah carefully, taking her in. Her gaze held a dreamy, melting expression and her attention made it seem as if the small talk now engineered by Eirlys was the most fascinating conversation in the world. Hannah looked round the room – simple furniture, very comfortable, an old-fashioned desk with rows of intriguing drawers. But the books! The walls were covered to the ceiling in books. It was like being in a library and, good grief, there were books in the kitchen on shelves where bottles of spice ought to have stood. What would Barry have said about that? A choking thought. It was brilliant. He would be shocked to his marrow. A spotlight in one corner burnished the lettering on leather covers and Hannah leaned over to read the titles.

'You are welcome to browse,' Dora said. 'Please do. Come whenever you like. You are welcome to borrow any of my books.'

'They look interesting.'

'They do? You can tell just from the covers?' Dora asked in a caustic tone, sitting up straighter, looking more lively.

'Oh, well, I don't know. What a stupid thing to say. But I love books. I love the feel and the smell of them in my hands. What kind of books are they?'

'Political, historical, legal, philosophical and some science.'

'Pretty heavy books then.'

Eirlys laughed. 'The removal men – sorry, Dora, removal people – thought so.'

'They saw them from a difficult angle, poor souls.'

First the drinks; then interrogation by Eirlys, obviously Chief Tattler of The Eyrie. The old lady went quiet and took no part in the conversation. She hardly seemed to hear what was being said but stole glances at Hannah, as if sipping at her.

Having asked about Bristol and seeing that Hannah didn't want to discuss where she'd come from, Eirlys chattered about some relatives she had there. Her kinship group had apparently overflowed Wales and colonised the Marches and the West Country. And the nice thing was that the whole tribe would soon be gathering for a wedding in Swansea. So many names, all very Welsh. Did Eirlys speak Welsh? Silly question! Eirlys had, well, worked for *y famiaith, yr hen iaith*, she said. The old language, Eirlys translated, the mother tongue, which was once prohibited by law, did Hannah know that? Purring tabby, she is, thought Hannah, watching her neighbour lick herself with pleasure at the memory of her deeds in the battle for the old language.

But Hannah's own people had been Welsh-speaking, she knew from the censuses. They'd been marrying and breeding in Llangyfelach until 1901, and were perhaps still there, living in the same network of streets, multitudes of them, a close, cosy huddle like Eirlys's, waiting for her. Like spiders on a web. Her father had returned to Quarry Street some twenty years ago. And if she turned up on his doorstep now, she might find not just Dad but bondings beyond bondings. Leaning forward, she listened attentively to Eirlys, prompting her with questions. So many third cousins, now she came to think of it, and, oh, of course, the godchildren and people who called Eirlys auntie, although she was not strictly their aunt by blood, but then she had sometimes wondered how defining blood ought to be, given that we are all members one of another, as the Bible put it.

'Quite right. Karl Marx in another dialect,' Dora chipped in.

'Really?'

'Certainly. As Aneurin Bevan would have told you.'

'Darling Nye,' said Eirlys sentimentally. 'He was the man. Anyway, we hope you will be very happy here, Hannah, and I have told dear Dora about your plumbing and odd-job-person skills, so we shall bear that in mind in an emergency.'

'Sure, I'd be glad to help.'

And so she would, Hannah realised, and saying so gave her a buzz. 'Any time,' she added, and felt strong beside these women too dainty or too brainy to tell a stopcock from a washer. Barry shrivelled and puckered like a balloon. *See, I can do things,* she had told him. *I don't have to pretend to be incapable so that you can feel manly.*

How long had the two women been living in the flats? Dora for seven years; Eirlys since The Eyrie had been renovated thirteen years ago. She had been the first person to occupy a flat here, she said. Before that it was derelict.

'Where you are sitting now, Hannah,' she said, 'birds were nesting. Imagine. And Dora's window, I seem to remember, was the main entry point for the pigeons. How would Tom Ching have liked that, Dora? But then, what would he have thought about the likes of us taking over his holiday home?'

She turned to Hannah and explained. Tom Ching had belonged to one of the Cornish dynasties that made their pile through copper and arsenic refining in Swansea. When the industrialists had started building mansions around the bay, away from the toxic copper fumes, Ching had converted a gentry house, *Nyth Eryr* – only he rebuilt it in the fashionable Gothic style, hence the quaint crenellations and heraldic mouldings. And when Menna and Eirlys were girls, they used to come cycling here, Eirlys told them, her face lighting up so that Dora smiled fondly. By that time the house was boarded up, and they'd clamber in and play games in their private den. Then there'd been a fire and it was all blackened. At the last moment, a property developer had bought up the land and the ruin and got permission to convert it into apartments.

'You should have seen them, dear, the trees all around,' she said. 'Centuries to grow and half an hour to kill.'

There was a Welsh poem about that, she recalled, she must ask Waldo. For her cousin Waldo, she said with reverence, had the entire corpus of Welsh poetry by heart.

Hannah found that a look had passed between herself and Dora, a look of abashed complicity that said: *Remind us to be out when Waldo calls, in case he takes it upon himself to declaim an epic.*

'Is the *Mabinogion* a poem?' asked Dora. 'It is very long.'

'No, not strictly, Dora dear. We can ask Waldo about that, he will know.'

Dora gave a little squeak, which she turned into a cough. Hannah thought, she has a sense of humour, and as they smiled at one another, she saw that Dora's teeth were wonderful, only slightly dingy, and they were all her own. At the same time, she saw quite clearly that Dora was remarkable in some way.

'Oh, listen to me gabbling on,' said Eirlys. 'How are you, Dora?'

'Fine. Enjoying the thought of inheriting Tom Ching's ill-gotten gains. And enjoying the company of a young person.'

'Yes, it is nice,' Eirlys agreed.

'Oh, but I do not mean that I do not enjoy your company, dear Eirlys,' said Dora. 'Nor to imply that you are *old* company. To me you are quite a youngling still. Green and growing.'

'I'm not that young,' Hannah said. 'I'm twenty-six.'

'Quite a codger.' Dora laughed like a girl.

'But most of us here are on the elderly side,' Eirlys went on. Mrs Dark of Sketty was among the earliest residents, and Mr Powell of Pontardulais, whom one rarely saw, as he was a hermit. It had taken her ten years to realise he liked it like that. He did not want cakes brought or errands done. Some people don't, she acknowledged doubtfully.

It must have seemed a long ten years to Mr Powell, Hannah thought, always having to flee Eirlys's cake-tin.

Eirlys said, 'I often wonder what he does up there.'

'And what does he do?'

'Smokes. His cleaners don't stay long. *Gets in your hair terrible*, one of them said to me. But apparently he attributes his long life to the gaspers. Reckons it tans the lungs like leather – lot of nonsense. Bit of a fire hazard, I'd have thought. I mean, what if he smokes in bed and falls asleep?'

Then there were Mr and Mrs Max Norton, such a lovely, harmonious couple, bless them. There was also dear little Megan. And Mrs Menelaus, of course, who'd occupied Hannah's flat, she had been one of the original residents.

'What was she like?' Hannah asked.

'Oh, hard to say. She wore lilac gloves. I think that sums her up,' Eirlys said, after a musing pause. Eirlys had really admired the way Mrs Menelaus drew off her gloves, one finger at a time. So ladylike.

Dora harrumphed and did not bother to conceal it with a cough.

'Now, now, Dora,' said Eirlys. 'Lovely she was, Emma Menelaus.'

'Oh, certainly she was. Mrs Menelaus was a good person. Her lilac gloves I have no opinion on. But I had great respect for her, she had a Trojan quality, and a kindness to her. She is missed.'

Dora had been angling peeps at Hannah. She'd felt them hover at her cheeks, like ghosts of the kiss with which the old woman had greeted her.

'Anyway, Hannah dear, you shall settle this for us,' Eirlys went on. 'What do you call your work: workmanship or workpersonship? Do you want to be a good workman or a good workperson or workwoman?'

'I don't mind, Eirlys, either is fine.' She ducked the question. 'But I would like to do my work honestly and not bodge it.'

When she had moved in, Eirlys went on, she'd been the youngest person here, but time had crept up on her.

Hannah stood on Trewyddfa Hill, high above Llangyfelach. A punishing ten-mile bike ride inland from The Eyrie into Swansea's industrial heartland. She had ridden from plenty into poverty, from the haves to the have-nots. She leaned her bike against a tree and sat in a lather of sweat on a low wall. Far below her lay the panoramic grids of streets John Morris and Thomas Ching had built for their copper, steel and tinplate workers a couple of centuries before, substantially unaltered since the capitalists, in a spirit of enlightened self-interest, had laid out the model villages. Hannah took out her binoculars and put them to her eyes. She spied out her father's territory and that of her forebears back 150 years.

It was not difficult. She'd found an aerial view on some

software Barry had bought for his computer – a programme called 'Earth' in which you could zoom in on any house on the planet. Coming closer and closer, you had the illusion that the person you were interested in would pop out of his front door at any moment and catch your eye as you hovered like a hawk above him, ready to drop. But the satellite photos had been taken a while back, and, in any case, you could never get as close as you wanted. Everything went blurred. Seducing and thwarting, the programme betrayed its early promise.

Quarry Road in the Chingtown area was easily located. The copper baron had built on a rational plan, with terraces at right angles to one another. She counted her way along from the gabled pub at one end of the terrace to the fifteenth house, which was her father's. And, moving across the street and counting three and four along towards the Calvinist Methodist chapel at the far end, she located the adjoining houses of her great-grandparents and great-aunts. These people, whom she had neither met nor heard of before starting her search, had lived intensely in her imagination since she'd begun to study the censuses and order birth, marriage and death certificates. The Francises and Lloyds had become not only real to her, but present, as if they inhabited a parallel here and now, although she was quite aware that they were in their graves; indeed knew the plot numbers in Morriston Cemetery, and would visit them with flowers.

Hannah put down the binoculars and the view retreated into the distance: the industrial park where the steelworks and pits had been, spired with high chimney stacks that belched black smoke out across the valley; the steep town and the tower of the beautiful cathedral of dissent, *Tabernacl*, from this vantage point small as a toy. The immense skies boiled with smoky clouds to the east, clearing to blue in the west.

Hannah could go down now, this minute, tap on that door and say, *I am your daughter.* There was a biblical feel to the tale. But it would not be like that. Take it slowly. Once you recognised the reality, the world you had cherished in your imagination must shrivel away.

Hannah had tried and failed to embrace a living man in all his reality, warts and all: Barry had been too known. What had there been left to find out about Barry? He had no secret or private places, as far as she could tell. He was a decent bloke, who loved football and washed the car without fail on Sunday mornings. Generous with money, proud of his young wife, the handsome, middle-aged family man had become as dull and stale to her as last week's bread. But perhaps such boredom was wholesome? Perhaps it was what normal people settled for, to keep them earthed. Now that she was on the long-planned verge of rediscovering her dad, Hannah distrusted the impulse. This thrill over Jack Francis – wasn't it only his being out of reach, in another world, that lit her up when she picked up a clue here, a clue there?

And he had done her wrong. How would she forgive this? How would he forgive his daughter for turning up with her demand that he acknowledge her and – it followed – his guilt? If he shut the door on her, that would be in keeping with most of what she knew about him. And yet he had read to her at night and sat on her bed singing folk songs, strumming his guitar. He had blown smoke rings for her to wear on her wrists like dissolving bracelets. He was also that person and she did not want to corrupt that memory.

Oh, but I've done bad things in my turn, Hannah thought, to Lara and Sophie. Poor girls. They'd been right to hate her. So why not write to them? *No. No letters can atone for what you did and didn't do. Just don't bother. We don't want to hear from you. Ever.*

6

Eirlys's naughty niece, Aeronwy, had just left the flat – well, they had all gone, Tom and Tilda and their brood, with Waldo and his son. But even though the tinies were little monkeys, it was the fourteen-year-old's presence you felt as she accused Tom and Tilda of being Dracula and Frankenstein, knicker-crapping parents who would never let her do *anything*, she was a laughing stock, all her mates were allowed to, but her! oh no! as soon as she mentioned anything, Hitler and Stalin forbade it. Because Aeronwy was at an operatic age and went in for the big aria, with vibrato like Madame Patti's, departure offstage was also memorably concussive. The silence Aeronwy had left behind rang in Eirlys's ears after her niece crashed out of the front door and plunged down the stairs.

Now it was dispersed as Aeron emerged from the building and stropped off, followed by her braying elders. Eirlys watched the lanky beauty cover the forecourt with economical strides and kick Tom's front wheel, to his rage. This issued in a loud recitative between father and daughter that was diverting to the residents, some of whom were lured out onto their balconies. She caught sight of Hannah Francis, her head in a towel-turban up on Dora's balcony, her arms folded, looking on with an open mouth.

Had Hannah really been washing her hair in Dora's basin? Eirlys could not imagine this. Probably she'd just wandered in to say hello. Dear Hannah had been here for, what, two months now, and a pleasant girl she was. Something lost and wistful in her at times, but so vivid and energetic. You could tell the time by her going off on her bike to work, rain or shine. And at weekends she'd disappear on the bike for whole days, *searching for her roots*, Eirlys supposed. She wondered if Hannah had found any. Yesterday she'd said she intended to learn Welsh. Seemed to think this could be done in a few months. Eirlys had promised to chat to her *yn Gymraeg*.

In the what?

In Welsh, darling.

Oh, thanks! I can't wait.

A sweet girl, and such dramatic dark looks. But what had made Dora open her heart so wide to her? Now Hannah was removing the turban, which she draped around her shoulders, running her fingers through her wet hair. Eirlys watched her turn to call something in to Dora, who came out on the balcony to join her and, look, had her arm loosely around the girl's shoulders. Eirlys gazed up at them, searching for the n'th time to see what on earth it was in Hannah that called forth Dora's devotion, for one could call it nothing less.

Dora's feeling burned too brightly. Wouldn't it burn her out? Didn't you have to eke out your strength at that age? Occasionally there were hectic spots on her cheeks, something Eirlys did not like to see. Great plans she had, Dora said, political plans! These seemed to call for the most powerful and expensive kind of computer you could get, together with a personal tutor. Another phase in her war against Terror, said Dora, by which she meant *him*, the Dear Leader, the destroyer of our liberties, the warmonger. There was less time for comfortable reading sessions together. Dora had become rather bogged down in *Bleak House*, she confessed. Dickens' heroines were, honestly, such twerps! Dora wanted to shake Esther Summerson till she rattled. Eirlys had suggested Dora try a bit of judicious skipping, expecting wrath. Dora had only replied mildly, 'Don't worry, my lassie, I'll come back to it.'

Aeronwy, who had been lured into the car, where heated words were clearly being exchanged, now leapt out again. Whoops, thought Eirlys, and watched Aeron stamp round to the front and stick her chewing gum to the light, before ambling off down the forecourt, flapping her hands and going, 'Yeah, yeah, whatever.'

Tom was out, too, snarling about bolshy girls and little madams.

Well, that is how families are, Eirlys thought. We have to take the bad with the good, dear. Although I do think (with all humility, mind) that I'd have managed Aeronwy a bit more skilfully than Tilda.

If she were mine, she thought, Aeron would be a tidy girl. At least, I like to think so. She mopped up a pale pool of posset which the baby had spouted onto the settee. Tactful I'd have been, and not taken the bait. Aeronwy, God love her, only wants a hug and a kiss, a bit of petting and listening to, and perhaps some sign that you understand she is her own unique self, not a baby Tom or Tilda, so cut her some slack. Naturally she doesn't want to study her Welsh irregular verbs or come in by nine p.m. How could she? Eirlys put her face up close to the sofa and sniffed the fabric: a bit smelly still, bless the babe. She dabbed again. There you are, damp but clean.

Sitting in the emptied flat, glad and sorry that they had gone, Eirlys let the quiet fall around her in a honey-coloured reverie. Morning sunlight filtered through her curtains and turned them golden. Saturdays were always a time of special peace. She shared this peace with her weighty little Buddha, whose presence was always a source of calm. She took his body's cold neutrality into her hands and let him dictate her breathing. Poor Dad would never have understood the Buddha. What a shock to the kindly, narrow man it had been in the Sixties when they'd all begun to 'hang loose'. Glad I am, Eirlys thought, that I never let him see quite how loose I hung.

And whatever would he have made of mutinous Aeronwy?

See, I am rather like you, Aeron, and have been tempestuous in my way. But I had causes, and I do wish you had some of your own.

Having grown up in the wake of war, poverty and famine, Eirlys had heard her uncles hacking with silicosis alongside the other miners and steelmen in the wards at Morriston Hospital.

So is it any wonder, she inwardly asked her niece, that we went around with serious, passionate faces, with our Gwenallt in our hands: 'I never thought I should hear how two of my friends/ Spewed out the dirty red of their lungs into a bucket.' Uncle Wyn and Uncle Gwyn went that way. The early funerals, with the horses and the crêpe. The coughing. And somehow, darling, for me the Welsh language was all bound in with this coughing and the history of this coughing. How could you understand this – and how could you possibly imagine how Waldo's annotated copy of the *Communist Manifesto*, set, as he says, as a poem to our people, which he's prohibited by pompous old Tom from showing you, is all to do with this coughing? – when you have known and seen no want except the hunger for a Big Mac? Nor would I ever want you to.

But perhaps she would take Aeron to Tryweryn. A drowned village stirs the imagination.

And yet a drowned village is also held to be picturesque.

Kicking the wheel wearing only thin trainers must have given Aeronwy a sore foot. She'd be hopping round now, God love her, saying she couldn't walk. Sometimes, mind, Eirlys was startled by a kindred impulse to scrape a pound coin along Tom's perfect paintwork, so infatuated was he with his wretched motor. Lovely boy he was, though, she reminded herself.

Looking out, she saw Dora and Hannah cross the forecourt and get into Dora's car. Laughing together. I am turning into a net-curtain-peeper, she thought. All that is missing is the nets.

Someone – Max Norton from number fourteen, was it? – shuffled past Eirlys's window with his black bag for the dustbin. Max and Ruth: so easy to anglicise her name, she had said, except for the pronunciation of that difficult 'R'. Max had met Ruth on the streets of a Hamburg suburb in 1945 and had brought her back to Wales where she'd spent over fifty years working on her English 'R'. One could not honestly congratulate her on it; the guttural in-the-back-of-her-throat 'R', Eirlys thought, is the fatal stigma that betrays us as foreign. But the happiness of Max and

Ruth was transparent. Nothing foreign there. Their quiet flame lit but failed to warm The Eyrie. Husband and wife cleaved to one another, it was touching, it was funny and sweet, but what would they do without one another? When they were cloven? What then? she all but defied them. Perhaps they are all too aware of parting and seize the day. He (frail, after his heart attack) would convey her (frail, with her replacement hip) on small and stately outings or errands and there was something in his attentive bearing towards his wife that at once pleased and saddened Eirlys.

All of us here are singletons. You are twins.

Whispers reached you of other people's lives, each in their separate pod. We live so close to one another's privacies, she thought, opening the curtains and looking out to make sure Max made it back safely from the treacherous muddy patch beside the bins – and yes, there he was, yoo-hooing and giving her window a friendly little tap with the knuckle of his wedding-ringed finger as he came by. But he made a point of not turning his face towards the window to pry. For they had jointly to ensure one another's privacy. That was a responsibility just as imperative as keeping the drains nice and insuring the fabric. The walls sometimes seemed transparent, and you must keep yourself to yourself as if you lived in a glass honeycomb. Through the partition, a neighbour might be pulling on his pants a metre away or, pale with pain, leaning up in bed on one arthritic elbow to take a sip of water. And the folk often so frail, so that it was hard to shrug off the claim that made itself felt when one thought of the human need banked up all around. Should she not go and knock? Ask if all was well? Perhaps it is my foible that I see through the walls, Eirlys thought, and these urges get me into busybody mode. But no one likes a busybody.

Now here were Max and Ruth making their slow progress to the car for their outing.

Eirlys sipped her coffee and considered baking brown wholemeal bread. The delicate aroma. Later she would bake. In her time, Emma had enjoyed the little treats Eirlys had left outside her door. Surely the Buddha, who warned against desire and fear, would have had nothing against such small gestures, which pleased Eirlys and cost her nothing?

How sad it had been when Emma Menelaus went. Eirlys took the pressure of that thought and did not turn away from it. She had seen Mrs Dark turning away when she was confronted with the coffin borne down the stairs by Presdee the Death. In her mind's eye, she saw Mrs Dark standing there in her venerable and crisply ironed navy dress, her body twisting away.

Of course, Mrs Dark was old enough to feel that the passing of the senior woman had brought her one step nearer to the exit sign. Mrs Dark, whose Christian name was unknown, lived alone, trying not to await the coming of Presdee the Death. Such reclusive souls they mostly are, thought Eirlys, widowed or divorced, building their dignity daily, and Red Dora at the centre like a glamorous bird of prey with that beaky nose and those talons, warding off the approach of Presdee the Death. Dora, like Eirlys, had family around her – the slinky, sashaying great-granddaughter, Angelica, being her obvious favourite. Good God, Eirlys thought, imagine if Angelica and Aeronwy ever got together! The Anarchist-Syndicalist Alliance! There had been A-S people at college in her own day, to whom she'd been transiently attracted.

Sometimes researchers and people Eirlys thought of as pilgrims turned up wanting an interview with Red Dora. You could spot them in the forecourt, scanning The Eyrie as if it were a cathedral. They were writing their Ph.D. thesis or were members of a Communist cell in Pennsylvania: was this really *the* Red Dora who'd served in Spain? Who was arrested in '56 for her egg-attack on Anthony Eden over Suez? Who was on the barricades in Paris in '68? and with the miners in '84? *That* Red Dora?

Oh, could we see her? Which is her window? What can you tell us about her? Eirlys never told them a thing. She'd say she didn't know, had never heard of Dora Urquhart – *How did you spell it, then? No, sorry* – or fibbed and said that Dora was away. White lies, her father had told them, are lies all the same. But Eirlys could not agree. White lies were admissible when you were standing between the caged lion and the gawpers at the zoo.

In the afternoon she took delivery of a crate for Dora. Of course, it was the computer, and there were subsidiary packages, which she could see from the box held printer, scanner and so forth. She urged the delivery man, who had hinted that it was not his job, to carry the package upstairs.

'I am just trying to work out how you expect Miss Urquhart to lug that ton weight upstairs?' Eirlys said pleasantly.

'Not supposed to carry indoors, am I? Sorry.'

Poor little Megan was shuffling out of her door, too, making for the burly delivery man. 'Oh,' she said. 'Is it for me?'

'It's for Miss Urquhart but unfortunately she won't ever be getting it,' said Eirlys. 'Because, young man, she's ninety-two, so her carrying capacities are a bit limited.'

'Well, I'm seventy-six,' said Megan, pained. 'Or sixty-seven. That doesn't mean I can't have a parcel,' she pouted. She seemed convinced the parcel must be for her, because her desire for a parcel was so strong.

'I mean, how is she to carry it? I'd take it myself, but I don't think it and I would fit on the stairs.'

The delivery man, blushing, hefted up the crate and took it upstairs. 'No probs, darling,' he said, and came loping back down, several steps at a time.

'Was it for me?' Megan queried.

'No, dear, it's for Dora.'

'Is it Christmas?'

'No, had Christmas just a couple of months ago, didn't we?'

Eirlys's tapping on Dora's door brought no response. She tapped louder and laid her ear against the wood. She had not heard her go out. She left the huge package wedged in the narrow corridor.

Megan was still fussing expectantly at the foot of the staircase. She was losing her mind so quietly, and in such a sober and subdued manner, that it was easy to avoid noticing that she was creeping downhill. Megan made no commotion at all, but at times one could feel a profound vigilance emanating from her soft, haphazard flutterings. Her eyes tracked you to deduce whether you could spy her fear that she had lost some vital bearings. She spoke with an assumed lightness, almost pretending to a flimsiness she didn't have, for Megan's calling as a tax inspector had required plenty of marbles.

Megan scented baking through the open door of Eirlys's flat, something eggy and lemony, with a hint of cinnamon.

'Tasty treats in the air!' Megan said. And as she said it so simply and plainly, the anxiety and false front fell away and she smiled pleasantly, the right kind of smile, as she seemed to realise herself. Eirlys could have wept for her and she returned to her own fastness with a sense of trouble that skittered with tiny insect legs round her stomach. Look what could happen when you weren't looking: something intimately programmed into the cells of your brain – into *you* – which had been there from the beginning. At the same time, yawning now and turning on the kettle, Eirlys didn't find it plausible that such decay could consume her.

'Angelica has kindly offered to begin my tuition,' Dora explained. 'She is my mentor. My e-mentor. Then she will hand me over to a professional.'

Eirlys, Hannah and Dora sat and looked at the screen of the computer, which, on its desk with modem, printer and scanner, seemed to take up most of the room in the kitchen area not already occupied by the overflow of Dora's monstrous library. Eirlys had never seen a computer so lordly. It was a huge, sleek, silver creature, state-of-the-art, rectangular with rounded edges, covered with a kind of silver mesh.

'Why didn't you get a laptop, Dora?'

'I wanted maximum power and memory. For my final fling.'

'Where do you sit to play on it?'

'Work, Eirlys. It is not a play station. On an office chair. It hasn't come yet.'

Eirlys wondered what Dora hoped to achieve with this computer. She recalled that Angelica of the tongue-stud and the nose-ring had been heard egging Dora on to come surfing.

Surfing the net. Of course. That was something of a relief! One did not like the idea of Dora, a child in some respects, accepting a dare to plunge into the winter sea in a wetsuit. Eirlys had had enough of her computer at work to last a lifetime. The forty e-mails that had pinged at her every morning, demanding this or that, had sometimes made her feel murderous. And that couldn't be good for you, feeling homicidal every morning. In fact, those aggressive pings all on their own might have precipitated Eirlys's breakdown and early retirement.

'I shall be able to keep tabs on *him* now,' Dora was saying, clicking her mouse decisively.

'Who on, Dora?' Hannah asked, and Eirlys flinched. A-ha! Done it now, she thought.

'Forgive me, dear, but I think you mean on *whom*. Your otherwise excellent education did not teach you the minutiae of parsing – either that, or you have no Latin. Do you have Latin? Well, that is not your fault. Of course, classics are lost to us in any case, for *he* has thrown them away.'

'Whom has thrown what away?'

Hannah never seemed remotely afraid of riling Dora. And Dora was extremely rilable. Hannah's antennae were perhaps a little coarse, Eirlys thought. Although, actually, she could get away with anything, for Dora had angled up into Hannah's face a look of sheer, amused affection. She is in love! thought Eirlys.

'Now you are teasing me.' Dora's lips puckered but she chuckled, too.

'Am I?'

Still clicking the mouse, Dora explained the circumstances under which Hannah might and might not use the nominative and accusative of the pronoun, unless, of course, she wished to turn *him* into a verb: the verb 'to Prime-Minister'. Yes, Dora said, there should indeed be coined such a verb.

The man has *Prime-Ministered* democracy, he has *Prime-*

Ministered language, he has *Prime-Ministered* the climate and *Prime-Ministered* the Middle East by air, sea and land.

There was a scuffling noise from the path below.

'See what that is,' said Dora.

Megan's head bobbed rapidly along the path. It was followed by a balding, middle-aged man and his blonde wife, clearly in pursuit, and lastly by Mrs Dark, offering support, should it be needed. Hannah, Eirlys and Dora stood at the window, as Megan's daughter and son-in-law chased her round the wheelie bins and into the car park. They were small people, well-matched, but neither fit nor particularly diplomatic, for Megan was the most biddable person in the world and, though easy to alarm, slow to panic.

'Whatever are they about?'

Dora opened the window.

'Shall I go and help?'

Dora thought no: there was already a netball team out there. 'Silly fools, what have they said to get her so het up?'

The whole block had become animated: Max and Ruth Norton in their top-floor flat opened their window and peered out at the circus; doubtless Mr Powell had paused in whatever he did to while the smoky days away, to take up position.

Megan had dodged behind the Norton car and was haring along the wall dividing the car park from the wooded slope. She was proving remarkably agile. Eirlys's heart screwed up at the concentration on her powdered face. Something had parted company from itself in Megan's mind. Panic rushed Megan along, the hare running before the hounds of kin.

Eirlys went down to negotiate but could do little to control the chase. Seeing her appear, Hugh jabbed with his finger where he wanted her to dispose herself.

'Cover the drive, woman! Over there. Cover the exit! Don't let her run down into the traffic.'

'If you stop chasing her, she'll stop running.'

But Eirlys could see the point in making sure Megan kept safely within the grounds of The Eyrie, and so took up her designated position. Megan dashed between the wheelie bins and the residents' cars, and Eirlys thought of rounders at school, a game she had especially disliked because of the numerous opportunities for humiliation it offered.

What if Megan falls? she thought. She will break something. It will be *your fault*, Mr Son-in-Law. She walked away from her base towards her neighbour, softly speaking her name and saying it was all right, don't be frightened, you are safe, no one shall hurt you, darling.

Then Dora whistled and everyone stopped where they were. Eirlys recognised the sound. Dora had kept a whistle from her days as Principal of the Gutheim Fellowship, and now found a use for it in seeing off unsolicited phone calls about insurance or double glazing. She blew a blast from her window and clapped her hands.

'Oh, look!' Megan pointed. She let Eirlys and her daughter approach her. 'There's Dora! Darling Dora, she's up there, everything will be all right now. How did she get up there?'

It was magnificent, Eirlys thought afterwards, when the whole playground had been cleared and the pursuers dispatched by a few princely words from Dora on her balcony.

'They want to put her in a rest home,' she told Dora. 'She doesn't want to go.'

'No, of course not.'

'She can manage here a good while yet – she just needs support. Someone coming in every day.'

'You worked with Social Services,' said Dora. 'Have you contacts you could alert?'

'I could have a try. Apparently, Hugh and Mary are off to Mallorca, and they can't keep an eye out any longer.'

'Aye,' said Dora, her hawk-eye severe. 'There's the brutality of folk for you. Invading Spain.'

'I told them quite clearly not to agitate her. We don't want the poor soul running out in front of a lorry, do we?'

'There are worse ways of going.'

A short pause. Dora stood always on the graveward side of

you. Good gracious, of course the woman did not fancy herself in love. She was far beyond last flings. She was holding off the sky.

'I think we could do more – well, I could,' Eirlys went on, 'to make sure she is safe. I mean, popping in. And perhaps you, too, Hannah, if you've time.'

'Sure. Glad to. We could have a rota.'

'I doubt if I shall do much popping.' Dora turned back to the computer and lost herself among the fish circling in the screen-saver aquarium.

'Oh dear, no, I wouldn't expect you to.'

As she left, Eirlys knew that she would look in on their neighbour but that Dora never would. She would control events from a distance, rather than come in close. Who could imagine Dora with, say, a baby? And yet she had borne a child, hadn't she – the mother of Keir and Karl, those plump, amiable men who occasionally visited, but of whom Dora never spoke except to say that they had had a Maoist father and unfortunate names. We should have called them Nemesis and Lucre, she observed.

Eirlys saw them and their wives making occasional duty visits, which they alternated for economy's sake. You never saw Keir and Karl at the same time. There was no love lost, evidently. Yet Eirlys had intuited fear on both sides. What had become of their mother, Dora's daughter?

Megan would need tactful vigilance. Eirlys started as she meant to go on and, with Hannah, looked in on their neighbour. The two visitors had departed, and the incident seemed to have left little impression on Megan, who was chewing a mouthful of lemon cake and remarking how she would love a little dog – a poodle, say, or a chihuahua.

'We're not allowed dogs,' Eirlys reminded her. 'It's in the charter.'

'No, I was only *saying*. I just do like animals. Not bossy, see.'

'Well, that's true,' said Hannah. 'I like animals, too. I don't eat them. I don't eat anything with a face.'

Eirlys had never thought of meat in that light. She could

respect the point of view, though she had been brought up in a household where you had to eat everything – face and brains and giblets – and be thankful.

As she returned to her own flat, Eirlys met Max Norton with a chamois leather in his hand. There was a blemish on his bumper, he said, and he hoped it was just that, not something more sinister such as a scratch that would have to be painted out; he hoped no boys on skateboards had been making free with the car park, he went on, which, as everybody knew and the notice said for those who could *read*, was private property. Eirlys said she was sure this could not be the case, though every Saturday night without fail, the same group of boys came rolling home singing, and battered the bollard on the roundabout with the same good humour, the same berserk compulsion, and who could say that they did not come up to the flats and administer a modicum of social justice to Max's red Volvo?

7

Hannah stood on Trewyddfa Hill, looking down over the miles of slate roofs, as she'd done on many Sundays. She'd cycled the whole area, making it her own. It had become her custom to have a bite to eat in a burger bar that had once been a baker's shop owned by the Francises over a century ago. She'd attended a service in Welsh at Moriah Independent chapel where generations of her people had married. By and by she'd begun to feel at home. Hannah had walked every street but one.

It was not exactly a matter of plucking up courage; she had courage. Loving Dora had brought her such strength. Hannah could call it no less than love, for affection was too weak a word.

Dora would do anything for her. She would do anything for Dora. It was as simple as that. But there were mornings when Hannah woke in Mrs Menelaus's death bed in terror, hearing Dora through the wall. Moving about. Coughing. She coughed worryingly first thing in the morning. But not for too long. Soon the coughing would stop and Hannah would calm down. I could tap on Dora's wall, she would think, or Dora could tap on mine, if we ever needed to. Like political prisoners in their cells. We've told one another that, heaps of times: *Tap on the wall if you want me.*

But what if Dora died behind that wall?

And die she must. This year, next year.

Hannah could bless even these spasms of apprehension: they belonged to a love that had met her out of the blue, and the gift would outlive Dora herself, the giver. It was for life.

But she had said nothing to Dora about her quest. Dora didn't poke about in her private life, and Hannah had the feeling that Dora would not approve.

Freewheeling down the hill, she entered Quarry Street. On the steep, terraced hill, the smell of late breakfasts of bacon and egg was on the air. Black bags for the bin men lay outside each door. The street was deserted except for a couple loading a removal van towards the top end, where a cluster of worshippers stood outside the chapel.

Nobody answered Hannah's knock. She walked around to the passage at the back of the terrace, and counted her way along the cramped backyards to where a small, dark boy was on his knees with a white rabbit, plucked from a wire netting cage and gripped between his two hands. The creature pulsed and quivered, head retracted, ears down. The way he held it made her see the boy's power to hurt it, really hurt it.

'Hi,' she said over the wall. The backyard was paved and bisected by a washing line heavy with clothes.

'Hi.'

'Like your rabbit.'

'Mopsy she is. Had her for my birthday.'

'Wow. She's gorgeous. I was wondering – does the Francis family live here?'

He screwed up his eyes against the sun. Said nothing. Grey-green eyes. Dark hair cut close to the head. Some milk teeth missing. Perhaps he hadn't understood her English accent.

A harassed-looking woman peered out of the door. A small, strong figure in shirt and jeans, her hair a mass of corkscrew curls. 'Who's that?' she asked the boy.

'Don't know. Is it time?'

'Yes, we're late. Chop-chop.'

'Oh, *Mam*.'

'Just come.'

'Can we go to Oxwich?'

'No, it's Caswell on Sundays, as you very well know.'

'Hi,' said the woman to Hannah, who had not moved. She

signalled with her eyes: *Want something? Then clear off.* Then she turned to the child. 'Put Mopsy away now, Jake. Oh, for goodness' sake, your bloody *shoes*! Look at you! We're meant to be there by now, aren't we?'

She threw a pair of trainers into the yard. They landed with a clump. Went back into the house. A man who was, no, not Hannah's father, someone else, came out and, scooping up the rabbit in one hand, replaced it in the hutch.

But perhaps, Hannah thought, quite unstrung, turning to push her bike away up the path, that *was* her father. She trembled from head to foot.

She retraced her steps. The man was tall and tanned, early middle-aged perhaps, with a stubbly balding head, wearing cut-off denim shorts and a white T-shirt, the same as the mam.

'Excuse me.'

He turned. 'Oh, hi.'

Was it him? She could not ask. The boy, Jake, rushing round the yard with spread arms, pretending to be an aeroplane, came to a halt and stared at her.

'I'm looking for Jack Francis,' Hannah said. 'Does he live here?'

'Go in, Jake,' said the guy. 'I said, go *in*. It's all right. Everything's fine. I'll be through.'

Afterwards she walked the foreshore at the Slip. The tide was far out, leaving khaki-coloured sand at the edge of the bay and further out a wilderness of mud and rocks. Slicks of standing water reflected the enormous light. Hannah picked her way out to where a sunken boat had been revealed, beached years ago half in and half out of the mud, its timbers leached and corrupted by the salt water, yet still holding the perfect shape of a boat and offering the illusion that it could be dredged up and floated away.

She took out her mobile and thought of texting Lara.

Hannah had a half-brother, but Jack Francis had left with some tart and moved away. No, the man didn't know where to – did she know he'd been inside? – and quite honestly Siân and Jake were better off without him, but if she caught up with him before the CSA did, remind him he owed them a few quid in maintenance, like, thousands, but they'd pay to be rid of the bastard, and why did she want to know anyway?

She hadn't said. Well, sorry he couldn't help her, the man had said, but don't come round here looking for him again.

Hannah perched on a rock next to the rotten boat. A man with a red plastic bucket was collecting mussels and winkles out on the gleaming flats. Further out again, a woman was walking steadily towards the sea. Tiny fish ghosted among the shallows of a rock pool. She sat so still that a rock pipit foraging among the stones hopped close by.

The comfort was, she and Lara were now back in touch. Two or three times a day they texted.

What Jack had done to her and Jake, she had done to Barry's girls. Well, something like that, but no way as bad. She remembered moments of peace and closeness with them when, in illness or the griefs little ones had, Lara would creep close to her for want of anyone better. Earachy nights with the child. Being a human hot water bottle for her. Pushing her squealingly high on swings. Baking sponge cakes, four hands in the eggy, sugary bowl. All that. And she'd thrown it away. But the miracle was that a fortnight ago Lara had made contact, without Barry's knowledge. Every day they told one another some little fact or other. For instance, Lara said she was about to buy a new top. She wondered what colour it would be.

Hannah had a half-brother, then? It was a novel, raw thought. Something to keep to herself until she knew the safe way to respond.

8

Bones forgot their dryness; sap rose. Your roots twinged and tingled with vivid life, and with that vitality came old imperatives charged with fresh conviction. In other words, in came illusion. Dora knew in her heart of hearts that she was dreaming. Summer outside; summer inside. The windows stood wide open night and day. Nobody in the real world gets these second chances, Dora chided herself, soaking in the bath and looking forward to the day ahead. The computer lassie was coming again this afternoon. An evening walk with Hannah. Dora sang in the bath and it sounded rather good with the echo. Never had had much sense of pitch, of course, but *never too late!* she thought, and launched into 'The Red Flag'. She flew it while she soaped her back with the sponge, daring tyrants and despots, and inwardly promising her neighbours that she would pipe down after just one more chorus.

Lugging herself up after a long, sensual soak, Dora began to towel dry. She caught sight of half her face in the steamy bathroom mirror and it pleased her. The warmth and wet had plumped her up like a baby. In her heart she stood to her full height, in her prime of life, spreading her wings and beating them with a thunderclap.

However arbitrary the attraction that had initially drawn her to Hannah, it had done Dora immeasurable good. Hannah was capable and unconventional. Well, but so were many others, to whom Dora did not feel herself drawn. And then again, the lassie knew nothing much and ached to learn; her mind was an unstocked garden that offered rich soil, for she was serious, solemn even, in her covetousness of explanation. Dora loved the look of her very still face when she began talking of Spain or the Hungarian Rising, breathing shallow, with a peculiar intentness. Parched land soaks in the rain. Unlike dear flibbertigibbet Jelly, Hannah was old enough to know she'd missed something alarmingly big – such as the whole of world history – and was anxious to make good on the deficit.

How the young woman stirred Dora's emotions. Reaching in her hand, Hannah touched the quick of what Dora knew to be her motherhood. There were times when Dora winced back, into irony or cantankerousness, with the squeamish anticipation that some membrane, stretched to the point of rupture, was about to give. She'd catch herself on the verge of calling Hannah by Rosa's name, and it would come to her that she never even thought of visiting Rosa's grave nowadays.

I feel as if I've only just woken up, Hannah had told Dora with a startled look. *I'm learning all this so late on.*

Well, never mind, Sleeping Beauty. There's time, Dora had replied (though was there time? Not as much as the spendthrift young assumed. And such cosy words felt odd to Dora, who did not deal in blandishments).

Her hand had stolen out, more or less of its own accord, and one finger had gently stroked the oval face. Electric sparks! She'd swiftly withdrawn it. Hannah had noticed nothing amiss. She'd perched on the old camel pouffe, stuffed with newspapers thirty years out of date, in an abstract reverie, her pale face framed by dark hair, pondering the world she'd awoken to.

And Dora exerted her charm and ingenuity to pique the girl's attention. Why not open up the pouffe and read those papers? she'd suggested. Time-travel back to the pre-Thatcher Seventies? A glitter in the girl's face had answered her, and they'd found themselves disembowelling the pouffe, tearing the past from its innards in handfuls, laughing like maenads. After a good read, they'd stuffed the papers back in.

About Hannah herself Dora knew little and never pried. She'd been raised by hippies, deserted by her father, had never finished her degree but had lived with some boyfriend in Bristol and come here to work and look for her roots. This was the sum of Dora's knowledge. Hannah would tell her more if and when she chose to. But there was something self-regarding in her love for the lassie, Dora suspected, a familiar contaminant. She did not particularly want to know about Hannah-before-Dora.

The girl borrowed books, did her homework and had made up her mind to be Green Hannah rather than Red Hannah. Communism wasn't her thing. Her reasons? In all their photographs, Lenin and Trotsky were snarling and thrashing their arms up and down like Hitler. Dora disapproved of this utterly sloppy way of arguing, but now that this had been pointed out, she couldn't help noticing it, too.

Hannah would cruise Dora's bookshelves, fingering jackets, drawing out a volume to part the covers and smell the paper. The scent of paper is so interesting, she said, it tells you so much. Dora was constantly trying to give the books to Hannah. If she'd had her way, her shelves would have been considerably lightened. What did Dora want all these tomes for? She almost begged the lassie to relieve her of them. For after all, she said, I can always come in to you if I want to consult them. Hannah was adamant: there was no room in her little pad.

'Well, they are yours when you are in a position to house them. You are very welcome,' Dora remembered saying. 'More than welcome.'

In her infatuation, Dora thought of rewriting her will. A grain of bourgeois caution and the aloof look on Angelica's face when she bumped into Hannah deterred her. It would be the action of a silly old fool.

So she tried to benefit Hannah piecemeal. A book is never complete, Dora had always believed, until the reader has responded. Hannah was fascinated by Dora's marginalia. For instance, look what you've pencilled here (it had been Engels' book on the Manchester working poor). Taking the opened volume from Hannah, Dora had recognised that she'd pencilled, sixty-odd years ago, quite a love-note to Friedrich Engels.

Crammed the margins of several pages with microscopic verbiage, pocked with exclamation marks. Embarrassing, and yet touching, too.

And, Hannah had said, *you or someone else has plonked a cup of coffee down on the page and, if you turn over, there's a pipe burn. An ember.* She and the lassie had gazed at the burn. *You never smoked a pipe, did you, Dora?*

Lachlan's ember, that would have been. Her young husband, for the first time in many years, was clearly present in her mind. They had been known to one another in Glasgow, attending the same Party meetings and rallies. But Lachlan had been eight years the elder, and not until they had both gravitated to London and met up working in the offices of a small, left-wing publisher in Peckham had they become close, then inseparable, then lovers. She remembered that pipe stuck in the corner of his mouth: he'd thought it made him look like a wise young owl, bless him. The round specs of a myopic intellectual; large, thoughtful grey eyes, with such a gentleness in them. Two silky wings of fair hair flopping either side. The ember could be dated with some precision. Winter of 1936, the year of their marriage; the year before Lachlan went out to Spain and Dora followed under the auspices of Spanish Medical Aid.

They'd lived in shabby, beatific lodgings in the East End of London. She remembered the roil of grubby, sex-scented sheets, limbs tangled with limbs, a menthol glow between the legs, peppermint kisses, the potty beneath the bed they'd piss in and chat, since shyness and shame were for the bourgeoisie, not for them. And the sleeps then were like none ever since.

It had all come back with a hot roaring sensation in her ears, when Hannah noticed the ember-mark on the book. At the same time, Dora remembered the existence of an unopened letter from Lachlan that had fallen out of a book one afternoon with Eirlys. She'd hidden it from herself in her bedside cabinet.

Dora shook her head. She'd never smoked a pipe, no, she had told Hannah. Cigars, though, certainly. Not the big Castro ones;

the wee cigarillo ones. *But you will take at least this one book, won't you?*

And Hannah must have gathered from Dora's tone that she should not turn this gift down. She'd accepted. Closing Engels very softly, she had held him to her breast, where, God knows, the dear man belongs. But Dora had felt sad for Hannah. Her isolation and the way she held the book, for all her flamboyant clothes, suggested nuns and celibacy. For a moment it was as if Dora, who'd practised free love and experienced multiple orgasms before there was a name for them, was the youngster and Hannah the post-orgasmic nonagenarian. (Not, of course, that one had to be post-orgasmic, only that a humble sparkler succeeded the Catherine Wheel.)

What was it Angelica was always shouting down the mobile phone to her friends? *Get a life!* She would read that letter from Lachlan. Dora's heart beat high into her throat. Why delay a minute longer? How could she have left it sealed for nearly sixty years? Had she not the normal ration of curiosity? But no, it was not that. She had been afraid – and she was still so afraid that she pushed the letter to the back of her mind again.

Yesterday Hannah, cruising the shelves and straightening up a spine here, a spillage of papers there, had detected a thoroughly bizarre likeness. *Oh! Look at you in this photo, Dora! How regal you were. When was it taken?* Dora had shouted with laughter. It was not herself but Comrade Trotsky, taken in his youth. His dandy-shock of dark curls crested in a coiffure that added at least four inches to his height. *Not you? Oh, I can see that now. Goodness, he's got a small tache, whatever was I thinking of?*

Hannah had blushed beetroot-red. Dora had not been abashed but, to tease Hannah, had given her a straight look, making it worse. When Hannah had gone, the renegade Trot had picked up Trotsky and considered the man. The manikin rather. So much the creature of his age. Clay feet not allowed to show. Still, one ought to have intuited them. Millions dead. Hard words, hard deeds. Yet Trotsky had been a god in her firmament, taking away all of Jesus's shine. And oh, the tears for his crucifixion.

Well, never mind all that. Out of the bathroom, kettle on, curtains open. Check up on the world. The fresh sensation of something about to be revealed seldom let her down these days. Another glorious morning, and she'd left the windows wide open all night, so that clouds of perfume from the lavender and thyme banks filled the living room. Her appetite was quick for light and space, her curiosity always in bud for well-nigh everything. For instance, this mob of birds now rising from the castle ruin. What had frightened them?

Had the postman been? The paper boy? Hannah would have left by now for work. And as usual at this time in the morning, they were coaxing Megan into the ambulance for her attendance at the daycare centre, a male nurse and the ambulance driver, a bonny lass with pink cheeks who was keeping up a patter of chat, her palm cupping Megan's elbow.

'In you hop, there's a darling,' the nurse was probably saying, and Megan, turning, beamed.

The glowing smile skimmed above the fussing of her helpers towards Dora, standing at the window in her T-shirt. She caught and returned the smile before her neighbour turned away and boarded the ambulance.

Yet something was different, that was for sure. Megan was bundled up in a linen coat and a hat and a silk scarf, done up like a parcel, despite the humid weather, as if she were being captured for a church congregation. And the son-in-law and daughter were here, too, wearing baseball caps and lifting some cases out, with many groans at the weight.

Ah, that's it, then, Dora thought. That's the way the wind blows.

As she turned away, the living room dimmed and darkness filled the chamber behind her eyes. She felt a premonition of being tottery and defeated.

Goodbye then, farewell, poor soul, she said inwardly, and whether it was Megan or her future self who floated out from shore, she could scarcely have said. She was at least twenty years the elder. She could have been Megan's mother.

The voice outside was Eirlys's, enquiring of the baseball caps what was going on. How useful to have a gently professional manner, thought Dora, and some grasp of the law on these matters. Eirlys was offering the opinion that Mum might manage very well if someone came in every day and just, you know, checked.

Dora thought she heard a rumble of 'nosy parker'. She returned to the window.

Hugh Thomas bristled and said that Megan had her own social worker, thanks very much, and her own GP, adding that the district nurses were no good at all, the care-package was a disgrace, the NHS was a joke and the world had too many do-gooders in it by half.

Eirlys said she was sorry to hear that and had not meant to interfere, only she was fond of Megan.

Querulously, the wife bleated that they had to stay in Mallorca, you see, because of her health, she'd almost suffered a nervous breakdown, with the stress, and she hoped Eirlys didn't think—

'Oh, no,' said Eirlys. 'I didn't think—'

'Do come on, Mary. The ambulance needs to get going.'

Dora could hear Hugh slamming the boot shut on Megan's cases. She could imagine the wife scuttling round at her master's voice, taking refuge in his irritation. How useful husbands were if you wished to disclaim all responsibility for yourself and your actions. Even a wee baldy with a paunch, a grey tache, a T-shirt advertising Hawaii and palm trees, and long white socks. What a refuge for women of flabby will.

'Gone then, has she?' Dora put her nose out as Eirlys came upstairs.

'Afraid so.'

'I heard you remonstrating.'

'No business to do so, as I was smartly told.'

'I gathered. Come in. If you've time.'

'They're going to let the flat out,' Eirlys said. 'To cover her expenses. Such a pity. But you know, darling, it was coming. Coming it was, a long time.'

'I didn't think she was so very confused,' Dora said.

'More than she let on. I was quite fearful for her safety. Perhaps you didn't see it so much, being upstairs, but the poor sweetheart, I was afraid she'd just take off like a little bird and get flattened by one of those fast cars by there.'

They looked out over the shrubs and the lavender bank at the street. Young men with naked torsos were towing speedboats, using the road as a short cut to avoid the crawling traffic of the coast road. You could hear the mechanised beat of their music throbbing through The Eyrie every so often. No thought of speed limits, for what were limits to these immortals? And the snarl of motorbikes.

'Flattened she could have been,' Eirlys went on, 'by that lot. Easy. At least where she's gone she won't be flattened.'

Dora raised her eyebrows eloquently.

They thought they'd netted a tenant for Mum's flat already, reported the Baseball Caps, returning the following week to clean. The husband was now wearing his cap backwards and his face was flushed and moist, though whether from drink or jogging was not clear.

'That was extraordinarily quick,' Dora said.

'Well, not really. We've had it on the market for several weeks, since the decision was taken, and quite simply, it's a seller's – or a landlord's – market. You ladies are sitting on a small goldmine.'

Dora held her peace, trenchantly.

'We had to do it, you know, Miss Urquhart,' pleaded the wife. 'It was the only thing. I need the sun for my health. Of course we'll be popping back.'

'And what kind of person is your prospective tenant-to-be?'

'A terribly sweet little chap. I thought so, didn't you, Hugh? Hugh did think so. He was very taken.'

'Quite a tall chap, I'd have thought. I don't know why you're calling him little. A lot taller than you, for instance, Mary, though not quite the stature of Miss Urquhart perhaps.'

'But he was nice?'

Hugh was testing the catch on one of the communal windows, finding it wanting and hiding this from the others in case it required attention or cash. After all, as the sole rooster in the hen coop (for all the men here were clearly considered by him to be pitiful crocks), he would be appealed to, to set it right, despite everything that had to be done to secure the Mallorcan property, and no doubt those Spanish estate agents were thieves and shysters – and then there was the custom of his Sabbath drinkies and nap, which he was unprepared to forgo, whatever the hassle – and his turned back mutely told this tale to Dora. What caused women to live with such men? Was it the Sexual Urge? Dora looked the wan Mary up and down, and could not easily imagine this. Or was it a sort of politeness? There were all these men around going spare. Or was it that they did it because everyone else did it? *Sign here please*, and a lady willingly obliged.

Hugh, completing his fiddling with the window-hasp, remarked upon jerry-building, and grunted at his wife.

'Was that a yes or a no?' Dora asked.

'To what, dear lady?'

'To your wife's question.'

'Which was?'

'I was just saying, darling, what a pleasant fellow he seemed. The young man who came about the flat.'

'I wouldn't call him young.'

'Well, but nice?'

'I'll call him anything you want, nice and even young, as long as he pays his rent on time. That's my sole concern as far as Mother's tenant is concerned.'

'And how is dear Megan?' Eirlys asked.

'Fine, yes.'

'You think she'll settle in, then?'

'Oh, we think so,' fluttered the wife. 'She's doing very well, considering. No, really, she is. We went traipsing round at least ten places. You can't be too careful. In choosing for your loved-ones. Of course, you have to pay for quality.'

'*She* does. *She* pays,' said Dora.

'Perhaps we could go and visit?' Eirlys suggested.

'Oh no. No point,' said Hugh. 'She wouldn't recognise you. Some days she doesn't even know who I am.'

'You do surprise me there,' said Eirlys. 'She always recognises me.'

Whichever way you looked at it, thought Dora (and that must be with a heavy heart), poor Megan must be better off not knowing that she has a son-in-law like Hugh. To obscure Hugh in a cloud of unknowing might indeed count as a blessing if you had been burdened with such a relative for several decades. If you had been expected to simper at him, coo over him, greet his jests and anecdotes as novelties, and not only fetch him cups of tea but watch him devour platefuls of your cakes, and smile and smile, till you were nothing but a comic mask. It could not have been good for Megan's mental health.

Back indoors, Dora took a deep breath. She opened the drawer of her bedside cabinet and drew out Lachlan's letter. She stood holding it in both hands. The doorbell rang. She placed it in her pocket and let Rachel in for her lesson.

Angelica's boyfriend had been able to introduce Dora to 'the best IT talent in the valleys' – a young woman with an old-fashioned look like a flyweight boxer. Skinny knees protruded from Rae's baggy shorts. She slicked back her oiled hair and bobbed her head as she ducked and wove at the screen, explaining the intricacies of computing. Would Miss Urquhart be up for learning how to build a computer? Then, you know, if anything should go wrong, you can be your own technician and do an upgrade, she said, observing that Dora seemed to follow her explanations better than most of her mature pupils.

'Glazed they goes, early on. You sees their eyes come over all vacant. Then that's it. You've lost them. Pitiful it is,' Rae continued, and pulled the back off the magnificent silver monster, showing that it was mostly an empty box. 'Mind, the young ones is no better. Thinks they knows it all. But you, Miss Urquhart, you got a head on you, man. So go for it.'

So Dora did go for it. Keeping always at the forefront of

her mind her quest for *him* – *him* the bomber of Baghdad, *him* the destroyer of democracy – she'd entered the box with the labyrinth, its unthinkable tangle of pathways, and trained for one last political act. She was still unsure what this would entail.

'Rachel,' she said, 'ideally I would like you to teach me everything you know.'

'All of it?'

'Aye, my dear. Are you, for instance, conversant with hacking?'

Rae's giggle implied a guess that Miss Urquhart might not know the meaning of the term.

'I am serious.'

'Well, Miss Urquhart, everyone asks us that when they starts. But you needs to know passwords and all sorts if you wants to hack. Do you really want to hack? I don't think so.'

'Where can we find the passwords?'

Evidently an ignorant question. Rae suggested, diplomatically, 'Let's walk before we runs, is it?'

She had no problem with criminality, Rae insisted: if a student wished to hack or phish, when they had raised their IT skills to that standard, up to them it was. Sundays were out, though, and to Dora's query as to whether she was a sabbatarian, Rae replied that, nah, she 'had to' go clubbing. That apparently made Rae a sabbatarian by default since 'wasted' she was on Sundays. She took stuff but only recreationally, she said; still, it was important to socialise. Otherwise she was at Dora's disposal.

'Don't take stuff, Rachel. There is no dignity in it. I've seen them vomiting in caravans. And you need to keep your fine mind honed.'

Dora did not speak as one shocked, though it was indeed shocking to see programmes about the drugs people took: but she knew you lost the young person's trust and interest if you criticised the drug of choice.

'I know a fine mind when I see one. That is why I am employing you, Rachel, to work seven days a week, for a handsome remuneration. Sometimes morning, sometimes afternoon, as suits you best.'

'Can't do it, to be honest with you. I've got my commitments, haven't I?'

But they had cruised together into all manner of forbidden places. This afternoon Dora and Rae listened in to a closed forum belonging to the US military. The soldiers' exchange of views on the 'ragheads' was at first impenetrable; then Dora began to guess the words and had a keen image of fresh-faced young men, hormones pumping. Some of the men were girls, she gathered. So young.

But they had been around for thousands of years. They were never going to evolve. And whose fault was that? Once, she and her comrades had known. Get rid of capitalist-imperialism and the People would do the rest.

They left the website. Rae, sensitive to Dora's weariness, said she would leave it there for the time being. But, as ever, she had a little cyber-treat to leave behind.

'I'm not tired,' Dora said, though she was. The business with Megan had depressed her. 'What's the treat?'

Rae took Dora to a government website, and left her to find her way to the treat.

'No clues,' she said. 'You'll know when you reaches it.'

Indeed, it took no time at all to find her own name. Your name calls out to you excitedly, whoever is taking it in vain. Here was Dora's MI5 record, which, she saw, had been released under the new Information Act. 'Secret Service File on Dorothea ('Dora') Urquhart', she read. There followed an explanation for the public: Dora Urquhart was a longstanding member of the British Communist Party from the 1930s who worked at the National Organisation in the 1950s. Oh, *was* she? Dora fumed. Presumably the boobies had not troubled to check up on whether she was safely underground. Beneath her eleven files were papers pertaining to Eric Blair, alias George Orwell.

Oh, Nannan, you are really, really famous! she remembered Jelly prattling. *Me and Sam are so impressed.*

Aye, but famous for what?

She opened the files and began to download and print. Her spine was a chain of small consecutive pains and a printed version would be easier to read. The yield was a prodigious heap of pages, photocopies of typewritten reports on the minutiae of her movements, starting in January 1950 when she'd been living in that flat in Putney.

'SECRET,' read Dora.

She learned that on 2 January she had gone to lunch with a man addressed as Brian. But 'on listening back,' the spook went on, 'the reference to Brian might not have been the same man'.

The following day she had been followed to lunch at the Bedford Café with a woman (unknown). Dora had eaten egg and chips from 12.45 until 1.20 p.m. Then she had taken a number forty-two bus, carrying a green shoulder bag. She laughed out loud. She had so enjoyed giving the spooks the slip as they spied on each small excursion, however routine, storing it all up for their superiors. She was fascinated, having never kept a diary. So the State had obliged by keeping one for her! It even possessed an archive of photographs.

Now the daily woman, 'Betty Evans', was in their sights. Her times of arrival and departure were to be recorded. The wrong name, of course: they were hopeless duffers. Beryl was the name of the woman, Dora was now so glad to recall, for she had been a rock to her.

There was a Ford car parked outside Dora's house, a spook reported. Yellow and black. Dora couldn't remember any such car. Probably it had had nothing to do with her. She went to the window and peered out. In the radiant evening, a few late gardeners tended the allotments on the hill. Nobody was out there watching. They didn't even know Dora was still alive, for goodness' sake – alive and active! The spooks themselves were probably underground by now. Dull days they must have spent shadowing her, for most of what she had done in those years before starting the school had been purely administrative.

Hannah knocked and put her head round the door. Would

Dora like a pizza and/or a walk around the front? It was such a lovely evening.

'No, dear, I won't tonight, if you don't mind. But shall we swim tomorrow? Rotherslade?'

'Sure, looking forward to it. Everything all right?'

'Fine, fine.'

As soon as Hannah had gone, Dora returned to the papers, to 10 January.

'During the evening,' he wrote, 'she and her daughter could be seen having their meal but Dora did not leave the house again.'

The page quivered in her hands. An undreamt-of sighting of Rosa.

Here she was, a wee soul of eleven or twelve. Dora stood with the spook outside the glowing window on the rainy January street. In the frame were a red-haired mother and a dark child, eating together, breaking the crusty loaves and dipping them in, perhaps, that delicious vegetable soup Beryl used to make. Talking over the day, shiny-eyed, beneath that lamp shaped like a flower that had hung over the small round table.

We were all in all to one another, Dora thought, all in all.

And the dark-haired sprite of a girl took form again, so dramatic in her looks and ways, chatting away in the knowledge that every word would be savoured and cherished. But at the same time, the white-haired Dora remained outside with the spook, looking in.

Dora foraged ahead. One February evening the phone-tapper heard her joking and laughing with Peter K about her propensity for ferreting things out, and then: 'Dora called to her daughter in the next room.'

Another precious fragment.

She saw herself turn away from the phone conversation and call out small words of enquiry or affection or banter to 'Comrade Daughter'. And what would the invisible Rosa be up to in that antechamber? What time had it been? 18.35, the tapper told her. So it would have been: 'Are you doing your homework,

Comrade Daughter?' And Rosa, kneeling up inky-fingered at the table in her grey school tunic, would reply, 'Doing it now, Comrade Mother!' or 'Done it, Comrade Mother!'

More, Dora must have more. She wished the record would never end, with its thrilling shards of revelation.

Ah! Nancy was putting Rosa to bed and reading her a story, Dora was telling Peter K on the phone. Nancy she had dearly loved. And Lachlan had loved her. Even so, we made up, she thought: we were fast friends, Nan and I. Beyond forgiveness there had been a new bond, woven of their love for Lachlan. Nancy, who'd only had six or seven years left to live when she had been putting Rosa to bed, had been more than a sister to Dora.

But now, oh no, in March 1950, Rosa was ill in bed. The doctor had been called. Don't let it be polio. Dora could not, would not, go out and leave her. 'The Party can rot!' she yelled down the phone to Peter K.

That overwhelming fear you had when your child was sick welled up in Dora now, fifty years on. Sheer, visceral terror. How glad Dora was, though, to see that she'd insisted on staying with the child throughout her illness. (Not polio. Not diphtheria.) The tappers, who never commented, only recorded, manifested mild amazement at Dora's devotion. 'It seemed as though Dora were being persuaded to go back against her will,' the tapper reported. 'She said in no uncertain terms she did not want a mother's help.'

But now it was June and Rosa was better. All was sunshine. Mother and child were seen dancing in an upper room.

A woman believed to be Dora was out and about. She was tucking into a three course lunch at Bianchi's Italian restaurant, Soho, with a man suspected to be Russian, working with TASS. Dora's spook – at an adjacent table enjoying a parallel meal at government expense – wasn't sitting near enough to hear, so he inventoried the subject's physical characteristics. 'The man was about 5ft 4in, slight build, low forehead, very dark hair, profuse and brushed neatly with a left-hand parting, wearing a gabardine.

His teeth were small and tightly packed,' she read. 'The woman believed to be Dora Urquhart wore a camel woollen top coat, amply cut. She wore a cheap brand of silk stockings. They ate a large meal and some sort of dark wine, which was served in a curious long-stemmed flask the like of which source had not seen before.' They talked in an undertone. Occasionally there was laughter. The supposed Dora showed a number of snapshots to the alleged Russian. 'It may be,' admitted the spook, 'that I took a mouthful at that moment and thus missed seeing it – but I did not see the photographs returned to Dora, although I remember Dora replacing her wallet in her navy-blue zip-fastened handbag.'

Wilf Giles, of course. She'd shown him her snaps of a working holiday in Paris with Rosa. How bored poor Wilf had been and how polite. He'd died of cancer in the Eighties.

The irony of it! The spooks had faithfully kept precious memories that had escaped Dora. Aye, but keep some for tomorrow, she warned herself. Don't read it all now. She put the papers away in her desk drawer and went out on to the balcony. Mrs Dark had long since retired for the night and the small sounds from her flat above had ceased. Hannah was perhaps reading in bed. Megan's flat was dark. The lassie had been driven out from under her own rooftree by vulture chicks. The light in Eirlys's bay window, she saw, was still on, shedding its glow on the path and a ring of bushes outside. Eirlys had no children. Dora could hear her television purring away. Owls were calling.

It was in the margins that you had to look, Dora thought, for crumbs to sustain you. She seemed to hang suspended, like a pearl of dew quivering on a leaf. Saturated in dream, Dora stood on the balcony and took courage, looking west, into the dark, towards the garden where Rosa's ashes lay.

9

Thrift and thyme grew amongst the lush greenery that crowned the cliffs leading to Rotherslade Bay. 'Oh, and mallow,' said Eirlys, 'which benefits so greatly from the gull droppings. So lucky we are!' she exclaimed as she pointed out the plants.

She didn't walk, she *pottered* along. She was driving Hannah up the wall. People in a state of grace could be so damned annoying.

She can't help it, thought Hannah, taking in the drifts of tall pink mallow she'd never have noticed without Eirlys. There's bugger-all she can do about it: she just can't help being lovely and appreciative. She's a dock leaf to our nettles. Hannah smiled and took Eirlys's arm as the path momentarily widened, hoping that Eirlys would pick up pace now that the beach was in view.

The aching scent of gorse and broom pulsed in the heat as they walked round the cliff path. It was almost too sweet, like a drug. And look! Eirlys exclaimed, bending to a tiny purple-flowered plant with curlicues like an Elizabethan signature: vetch. And down there, look now, samphire that Oystermouth folk used to pickle and eat! Cook it with olive oil and lemon juice, she advised Hannah, and add a sprinkle or two of Parmesan. It's succulent and tangy in salads, though, she said, if you can't be bothered to cook.

Eirlys stood still and gazed round at this world of hidden balm and blessing – the turquoise sky, the blue-green sea, the three rows of green and white beach huts, the pebbled path – amazed, as if she were viewing it all for the first time.

'Swim, Eirlys dear!' said Dora. 'Ice cream! Sunbathing!'

Looking down, they could see the matchstick folk on the beach, playing cricket, climbing rocks, collapsed on towels or bobbing in the sea. A girl was whacking a boy with bladderwrack. On the stepped wall leading down to the sand, rows of tanned Gower folk basked, looking out to sea and complaining about the eyesore of the block of luxury flats the Council had allowed some racketeer to build on the cliff top.

'Ach! The vulture chicks on our beach! Surely they should be back in the Costa del Sol by now?' Dora said grumpily, as she clambered down over the bank of coloured pebbles, supported in the most tactful way by Eirlys on the one hand and Hannah on the other. 'Ignore them, do,' she ordered her courtiers.

But Eirlys, of course, must wave to the Thomases and pass the time of day, ruled as she was by a polite God, whose heaven was a tea party with Welsh cakes.

'Come over and sit with us,' Mary called. 'Masses of room! We'll be a little outpost of The Eyrie.'

'Over my fucking dead body,' hissed Hannah. 'Sorry, Eirlys, but I am *not* sitting with them.'

She and Dora, as one, started walking towards the caves at the southern edge.

Eirlys called out to Mary as they passed that they couldn't take the full sunshine and would be better off in the shadow of the rock. Once they settled on a spot, she laid out the rug, anchoring it with stones at three corners and the picnic box at the fourth.

'Look at them,' said Hannah. 'Honestly.'

'We shall not look at them,' Dora said. 'We shall pretend they don't exist.'

'Haven't they heard of skin cancer? They're almost the colour of my wardrobe. Remind me of a seal and a walrus. Know what I mean?'

The sea! Dora must go in, now! she said.

She was a child in her appetites, thought Hannah, smiling. She lounged back on one elbow in the warm sand. Dora shed her garments for the plunge, and she and Eirlys padded down, hand in hand, towards the incoming tide. They seemed to vanish into light, the glassy shallows of the sea. Like queens passing.

Eirlys in her cuddly plumpness and Dora in her skeletal magnificence had stepped out of their clothes without undue modesty. Hannah folded a tent-like dress and a pair of pedal-pushers fastened by a secret safety pin, and tucked them in her bag, as she had done for Lara and Sophie in Cornwall not so long ago.

She texted Lara: told her she was on the beach, toasting in the sun.

The girls' eyes had glittered like the sea as they'd dragged their dad towards it. Rotherslade thronged with their sparky look-alikes. Twin Sophies squealed and pranced on tiptoe down to the water, and a teenaged Lara, brown as a hazelnut, cantered down the beach, her mane bound in a bouncing topknot. This Lara yelled in Welsh – or Polish, it might have been, for all Hannah knew – waved back to shore and made urgent signs by the curving bend of her body that it was cold, brilliant it was, come *in*!

Hannah had never let on to Barry and the girls that she adored danger and surfing and water-skis. Had lagged smiling on the water's edge with the towels. For after that third, casually undertaken abortion, Hannah had changed. She'd been ashamed of her body, afraid of it. She'd covered up, despite being the person who'd slept around on the walking tour in Crete, all the way from Kastelli to Siteia. She'd walked, a loner in her tiny skirt, the sacred path at Knossos, with her hair down to her waist, allowed some young Greek to fuck her in a poppy-field. She'd never let on. Barry had thought her prim. He had assured her that there was nothing wrong with a modest bikini.

Perhaps, if she had caught up with her dad again, he'd only have moved on. Well, *fuck you*, she thought. *So boring. Such a disappointment. Always repeating yourself.* But the half-brother, that was a different thing. A powerful feeling surged up. Hannah had no idea what to do about it.

Lara texted back. It was not fair! She was in Asda. *She* wanted to be on the beach.

So come, Hannah texted.

Nobody's invited me.

I'm inviting you now.

Are you serious?

I am serious. Speak later. Will try to sort it with your dad.

Hannah peeled off her top and shorts; took to her heels and struck out in a crawl past Dora, floating on her back in a porpoise elysium just beyond the point where the lazy waves toppled.

Dora saw Hannah shoot past in a thrash of white water. She had once loved to freestyle, and even to butterfly (that would have showed them!), but knew she should stick to her gentle breast stroke. She chatted with an old gentleman bobbing around in a rubber ring. After a while he was towed ashore on a string by his grandson. Eirlys said she was going in now and Dora accompanied her.

Towelling one's toes was a knack Dora didn't seem to have. The swim itself was at once bracing and enervating, but the drying off of a moist body with sand in its crannies was tedious. And, she thought, with the sun fierce upon her head and back, boiling her brain rather, that the sense of omnipotence that drove her into the sea as if she were still a girl would finish her off one day.

Basque cap? Here it is. The most efficient sunhat on the beach, she thought, as she brought the peak down over her eyes. She was aware of Hugh semaphoring.

'Ignore those two lemons,' she reminded Eirlys. 'Or I will go home. Something our political leaders haven't managed to spoil yet,' she said, 'the sea.'

'They're working on it,' said Hannah.

'Ah now, I don't know about that,' said Eirlys. 'Fair dos. Used to be badly polluted by here. Cleaned up a treat.'

Dora felt the yen to inveigh on Green issues rising like a wave. Even on a beach? With dipped ginger biscuits and the sea so serenely rising and falling, rising and falling? On a beach, hedonism was not only licensed but proper. Instead of inveighing, the resolute sybarite clumped her sandals together to clear the sand.

'Hallo,' said Mary, appearing beside them. 'Anyone want a cuppa? Hugh's off up to the café for drinks and he would be glad to get you ladies something.'

'Treats on me!' Hugh bellowed preposterously, and sunbathers poked their heads up like turtles to see what was going on.

'We've brought a flask with us, thanks.'

'Oh, of course.' Mary was disappointed. She lingered a few feet away, and clearly would have been glad of a cosy natter with someone other than her husband. 'It's the one thing we miss, you know, in Spain,' she said. 'A proper cuppa. A *dysgled*, that is in Welsh,' she said to Eirlys. 'Welsh for a cuppa, isn't it? *Dysgled o de!*'

'It is indeed.'

'I did it at school. But I've forgotten everything except the cup that cheers.' Mary sat down on an edge of the blanket and stared at the sea.

'You're very brown,' said Hannah.

'It's the sun!'

'They say you ought to be careful. I always cover up.'

'I never do.'

'Oh. Why is that?'

'It's the culture, see. The sun is full of vitamin D, in any case. And once you're a nice healthy brown colour, this is what Hugh says, you're safe from the destructive rays. It's like a hide, he says.'

'I think you're mad,' said Hannah.

'Oh, now, Hannah. She doesn't mean anything rude, Mary,' said Eirlys, pouring oil on the waters. 'She's just concerned for you.'

'No offence taken,' said Mary huffily.

'Right.'

'Do you not believe in global warming, Mary?' asked Dora.

'She doesn't, as a matter of fact.' Hugh appeared with two

cardboard cups of tea. 'Squash up, darlings,' he said. 'Room for a little one. Global warming is unproven. Fact. Scientists disagree on it. Fact. The jury is still out on that one.'

Dora did not move. Hannah evacuated the blanket and sat temperamentally on the sand.

'Plenty of room,' said Eirlys unhappily.

'*Hola*,' said Hugh.

'*Iechyd da!*' said Mary.

'How's your tea?'

'A tiny bit stewed.'

'Oh, well, dear, I'll get you another one,' Hugh said. He seemed nettled but not with Mary.

He was hurting, thought Dora, in his chivalry.

'Only a teeny bit. It's fine.'

'Well, if you're sure.'

'How's your mum?' Eirlys asked.

'She's well, thank you. We are really pleased with the set-up,' Mary responded lightly, and then bounced the question across to Hugh, with a gesture of her head.

'Just the job,' he said. 'Fine and dandy.'

He rolled over, placing the cup in a dip in the sand, and spoke in praise of the expatriate life. He seemed to be addressing the whole assembled beach.

'You people over here in England,' he proclaimed, 'you don't know what you're missing.'

'Wales,' Eirlys corrected him. 'But about Megan. If you could just give us her address?'

'Oh, I beg your pardon. Land of Mary's fathers! Mind, we've got Welsh expats living in the same condominium. You never meet a foreigner, apart from the Welsh.'

'A foreigner?' asked Eirlys.

'He means Spaniards,' Hannah said. 'Don't you, Hugh?'

'I tell a lie,' Hugh replied. 'We have some German neighbours. Multicultural, that's us! The Cymrics and the Jerries, but hardly a dago in sight. Where we live, Brits outnumber the natives – it's true. Yes, yes, Eirlys, I'll write the address down, don't worry.' He patted the pockets of his shorts. 'No pencil, no paper. Remind me when we get to the car, Mary.'

Dora rummaged around in her bag. Never went anywhere without pen and paper. There must be one in here somewhere. No. She felt around in the many zippable pockets of her trousers. No pen but here was the letter from Lachlan, which she'd been transferring from drawer to bag to pocket in the last few days. This really must stop.

Hugh was praising Spain for not being Bradford or Dover. Had the ladies been to Dover recently? No, exactly. If they had, they would have found illegal immigrants everywhere. Don't get him wrong – nothing against Johnny Foreigner. But it was a funny thing, he couldn't help thinking, when the British Isles had been forced to emigrate lock, stock and barrel to Spain!

Nobody spoke. Mary drew a heart in the sand and stuck an arrow through it.

'Only joking. I am learning Spanish.'

'He is,' said Mary. 'He can converse fluently with the native population.'

'I can imagine,' said Hannah.

'It's an easy language, mind, no particular virtue in that,' Hugh said, 'compared with Welsh. Could never get on with the jolly old *Cymraeg*.'

Eirlys said nothing. She poured more tea, handed round sandwiches and did not take the bait. Dora could see her gloomily wondering how they were going to roll him off the blanket. How many stones of blubbery maleness had he deposited on Eirlys's territory? How many million words were waiting to pour out of that gasbag mouth? She stared at his mouth as it worked and the small, bright eyes above it. Would the sky fall on Hugh if he stopped speaking for a moment?

'Come out and visit us!' said Mary. 'I mean it! Don't I, Hugh?'

'Of course. The more the merrier. But you'd have to acclimatise. You might get the bug. Want to come out and start up a Spanish Eyrie!'

And he was off again. About the redhot property market and

how there'd been a bonanza in recent years; did they know how much money was released from British homes to buy a slice of Spain? Fifty-seven billion pounds!

'But don't you miss Wales?' asked Eirlys. 'And what about when you need a dental appointment?'

'We'll come back to Swansea,' Mary said. 'Course, we have to keep popping to and fro anyway. We have responsibilities.'

'Let me guess! You don't fancy Costa life then, Eirlys?' Hugh asked. 'Two swimming pools we have. No jellyfish in *there.* It's a lifestyle choice, you see, that's how we look at it, over and above the investment factor. And the golf!'

'I don't play golf,' said Mary morosely.

'No, well, I don't either, dear. But we might want to some day. Have you ever been to Spain, Dora?'

Had Dora ever been to Spain?

Dora looked like thunder. She pulled down her sunglasses and gazed her persecutor in the eyes, through the gap between the peak of her cap and the top of the sunglasses. She had learned in her time to aim and shoot a rifle. Precision-focus, no tremble, hit him dead-centre in the forehead, just above the bridge of the nose. She had stunned hecklers in crowds and big booby boys and giddy girls in schoolrooms with this look. Hugh seemed to feel the force of the glare, for he rubbed at his forehead and gave a little 'hem'.

'Have *I* ever been to Spain? Yes, but I am wondering,' retorted Dora in a torrent of Spanish, 'whether *you* have ever been? And whether you are aware that this goldrush of international package tourism was initiated by none other than the fascist dictator, General Franco?'

'What's she saying, Eirlys?' Mary fluttered. 'What's she said to Hugh about Franco? Hugh doesn't approve of Franco, Dora. Anyway he's dead, surely? Isn't Franco dead, Hugh? I'm certain he's dead.'

'Well, well! Dora speaks the Espagnol! Very fluently too, jolly good, Dora, muchas gracias! You put us all to shame,' Hugh rallied.

He was shaken. Had got the gist. Unworthy of me, perhaps, thought Dora, to strike at such a very soft target. She watched him straddle and grope his way to his feet. Suspects he's an unhandsome, uncouth specimen, of course. Hence all the boastful braying. I see you, Hugh, I see you.

'Best toddle off,' he said to Mary. 'Leave these good ladies to the Costa del Mumbles.'

'But before you toddle,' Hannah said, 'you didn't really say how Megan is.'

'And the address? Well, what's the name of the place, for God's sake? We can easily look it up.'

'I'll write it down and leave it in the foyer,' said Hugh. 'How's that?'

'Perhaps Megan would care to visit Spain?' Dora suggested maliciously. 'Had you thought to invite her?'

'Oh, no, Dora,' Mary said solemnly. 'She couldn't. She's ailing. Even when she was in her right mind, she couldn't have stood the sun.'

Count me out of this, Dora thought, lying back and pulling her cap over her whole face. Blank the ninnies out. The darkly fusty interior of the Basque cap provided a pod with tiny pinholes through which the glare weakly needled. As the foe abandoned the beach, Eirlys and Hannah were exclaiming in whispers about them, despite Eirlys's scruples about speaking ill of ruffians.

Dora would not visit Megan. Far too painful. The others could go for her. And in any case, she thought to herself, I do not have the human touch, do I? Otherwise known as smalltalk. So what possible use could I be to Megan? I'm retired anyway. An old carthorse out to grass.

'How about another swim?' Hannah suggested.

'You two go,' Dora murmured. 'I'm going to retire to the cave for a wee snooze.'

She sat at the mouth of the shallow triangular cave the waves had scooped out of the limestone. Its dank chill soothed her skin. She took out Lachlan's letter. It had been sent before Dora embarked for Spain but had arrived after her departure. And on her return nearly two years later, her younger self had presumably buried it in a book, unable to bear reading it.

There was one sheet of paper, covered on both sides with Lachlan's large, hasty scrawl.

It was about cigarettes. How they were to be sent by separate post, not with her letters. In their boxes, or they all got flattened. He was smoking a flat one now. If Dora could manage it, would she send *lots.* He didn't mind the grub, it was OK, he'd had an orange the other day and he quite liked the canned stew, which was just as well, as that was all he was going to get! It was the fags he missed. And the Spanish ones he couldn't get on with – too bitter. Tell Mam and Dad, he said, and all our friends, to send as many Woodies as possible but *not with a proper letter* as the censors stole them – well, Davey had got a stiff rebuke from the censor (by post of course!) the other day ('*we never steal fags!*'), so Lachlan had better say here that someone! – *not the censors!* – steals the men's fags. And, Dora, bring my piccolo recorder, he said, the one that drives you mad when I play the sea shanties. Still no sign of action, he said, but plenty of rumours. He ended: '*When* are you coming to me? Any news? *Salud!* Your pal Lachlan.'

What had she expected?

The sea lapped, and gulls and children called. Dora sat in her cold nook and considered her feelings. Was she disappointed that it was not a love letter? Full of passionate exclamation?

She looked at the date. The week before the slaughter at Brunete.

Fatigue overcame her. Dora replaced the letter in the envelope and, returning to their little pad, lay back and surrendered to the sun, allowing it to relax the joints of her hips and shoulders. That's the way: let go.

She let her mind wander back to the byre by the Ebro, the first week of September 1938. The last time she had seen him alive. Walls three feet thick would have held off the inferno of heat and given them a cool space, except that most of the roof had been lost in bombing. Flies had droned and the smell of fire had mingled with dung. The farm had lain on a changing frontier. Up to three months before, the farm had been in the Republic. As Franco's army swept forward, it had changed hands. The farmer had retired to the byre, his house being in ruins, installing whatever bits of furniture he could salvage. Now, with the Republican push across the Ebro, the byre had returned to the Republic, but the Republican farmer had gone.

The war had left them the miracle of this sofa and a day and a half of privacy. A ramshackle, grey-brown object, seething with lice, once covered in scarlet velvet, the sofa must have been left out in sun and rain, and perhaps been used to store olives: it reeked of oil and sacks.

Lachlan and Dora were gods. Itching, dirt-encrusted, emaciated gods.

'Lousy wee sofa!' he'd said.

'Do you not like it?'

'Aye, I like it well.'

'Not much room.'

'Who needs room?'

She'd shifted, between the dirty, sweating ecstasy of the half-asleep man and the sofa-back. Their sweaty skins had come apart with a sucking sound. Thirty-six hours, all to themselves, between Lachlan's discharge from hospital with a light leg wound and his return to the Front.

Splayed on the couch: two in one. Roasting hot. Whispering. Crickets had shrilled behind the sofa. A lizard had scurried across the wall, paused, seeming to tick.

He'd asked Dora to be true to him. Ah, but he hadn't been true to her. It had cost Dora dear. He had loved, did love, would love elsewhere. The thing with Nancy. And several others; he'd never tried to hide this, for deceit, they agreed, was the only poison. Love must be free. There'd been no casual flings in those days. All emotions and connections had been raised by the nearness of death to the level of eternal gestures. She'd so feared the Nancy in Lachlan's brain. And his innocence and idealism had had such glamour, as when he'd got hold of that old flute and played it to the echoes in the ruined cathedral. Dora had been shocked at her mean and low possessiveness, for a person's sex could never be a chattel. Yet now at the Front, in that inferno of carnage at Terra Alta, the Heights of Death, Lachlan had had the right to ask for fidelity.

'What I really want,' he'd said, 'is to grow radish and lettuce in our back garden. And new tatties. Don't laugh.'

She hadn't. He'd read his Tolstoy and coveted the role of Levin swishing a scythe in the wheat-field. More Levin than Lenin in you, my man, if the truth were known.

'That is the sum total of my ambition in this world after we have halted fascism. Because I believe,' he'd said, after Dora had promised, 'that that is what we are fighting for. For each family's right to eat lettuce and new tatties, and peas straight from the pod.'

She had returned to the byre after he'd left her. The roofless room had seemed like an antechamber to heaven. She'd sat on the dead settee, with the life that would be Rosa inside her.

Gull-keenings and babies mewing, over-heated under beach-canopies. Half-opening her eyes, Dora found herself casqued in her cap. Heard the murmured chat of Hannah and Eirlys. Thought of the stretching-out of the decades since Spain, so that you could never be certain of the integrity of your memory. I was only nineteen, she thought. How much of it had she invented? Not the byre, not the sofa, not Rosa. And she had taken from Lachlan a leaven of his good qualities. He had taught her a measure of tolerance, that was beyond dispute. He'd pointed out that, in her rancour against Calvinism, she sounded quite Calvinist. *Reprobating people and damning them to hell, when they are just simple, ordinary folk – puzzled, like you and me.* He had said it so inoffensively but the young Dora, who had been in the right, she knew everything on every subject, had gone quiet and refused to hold Lachlan's hand.

Not to hold his hand. To waste the chance to link hands, palm to palm, when they would have to spend eternity apart, and given the manifest absurdity of God, that did mean for ever. And when they'd gone off to be gallant in Spain, and the worst had happened that could happen, and she had come back alone, Dora – after the first tempest of grief – had taken sips of the bitter medicine of tolerance, the temperate spirit that moved in him.

A hopeless fighter, Lachlan had been anyway. One arm of his specs had been taped on. Poor coordination between left and right hands. He had thrown his life away. The Republican generals had squandered the lives of thousands of boys in that desperate last push. Dora, questing back to where Lachlan lay stranded, with the Second World War, the Cold War, the Korean War, the Vietnam War and now two Middle Eastern Wars standing between them like mountain ranges, felt she could make little out. What had he been like then, really, this grave, tender young idealist? Or rather, how would Lachlan have turned out? For he had been in bud; still, in his mid-twenties, an open question. The lettuce and tatties would never have satisfied the dreamy veteran of Spain. She'd never have been enough for Lachlan.

Never. And perhaps he would have been killed later, in the Hitler War.

If he could be here now, in the same time-zone, an ancient bag of bones on Rotherslade Bay, sucking at an ice cream, deaf as a post, how would that have been? Dora, in that case, could scarcely have been the Dora she was, a person who had evolved in the wake of his death: wife to no man; her own master. But she had brought with her some vital gifts that came from him. These kernels of goodness amongst the mind's trash-can of vanities.

'Are you awake under there, Dora?'

'I have not been asleep.'

'I believe you,' said Eirlys.

'Good swim?' Dora asked, sitting up.

'Brilliant. We want to know if you'd like a Ninety-nine?'

'Definitely.'

'You'll have to take your hat off to eat it.'

She did enjoy an ice cream. There was something about sitting with your friends on the beach, licking and nibbling away at a chocolate flake, which put everything in perspective.

But there was a disgraceful figure conducting a barbecue high on the rocks. The stink of charred animal billowed out, interfering with the beach population's legitimate enjoyment. Look at him, there in his cut-off jeans and a cowboy hat, with a reddish beard, waving like a semaphorist who has lost his flags. And with him a girl young enough to be his daughter, prodding some burnt offering on the impious altar. Surely the beach would rise up and chase them away?

'Do look at that!' Dora pointed him out to Eirlys.

But Eirlys leapt up and semaphored back, yelling, 'Frying tonight, are we?'

The tolerant beach smiled.

'That's Waldo. My cousin. You've met him. He has the soul of a poet.'

'And how does that manifest itself?'

Eirlys looked puzzled. 'Well, dear, in poetry. And he plays the harmonica lovely, Dora. He can keep it up for hours.'

Dora felt faint. 'That would be a treat indeed.'

'He's come within a hair's breadth of winning the crown at the Eisteddfod,' said Eirlys. 'His mam is rightly proud. When he was a boy, Waldo could give you a cheeky answer in regular *cynghanedd*.'

'And who's the girlfriend? The lassie with the black sausage?'

'Oh, that's not his girlfriend, Dora: Rhiannon, our niece, that is. And there's his boy, Ianto.'

Waldo was a modest man, she added, but in point of fact he was a member of the Gorsedd. Dora felt irritated at the thought of the fatuous druid or bard or whatever he was pageanting about in wind and rain wearing a sheet with a flock of his cronies.

A stream of new people was arriving, chattering and laughing their way down the steps to the beach; Eirlys appeared not only to know them all, but to wish to introduce her friends to every one.

'Beauties they are. Fresh Welsh fish,' Waldo was saying. 'Nothing better in the world.'

On a rock, he displayed sea-bass caught off Mumbles Pier, which he described as noble. Their eyes were dulled by a viscous film. He said he'd been singing but his son had begged him not to. The stench of burnt fish rose into the air. Dora coughed and moved upwind.

The Harries had gathered from Hafod and Ystalyfera to Llandysul. Eirlys made a complex of introductions. As Eirlys explained the family connections, Dora realised that Eirlys's relatives mated for life so that, if they changed partner, the first was somehow still attached to the web. There were Patagonians, Germans and a Welsh-American family from Miami. Hi. Oh, *hi*! great to see you. *Sut mae, cariad! Sut wyt ti? Schönes Wetter, oder?* In this colourful and eclectic crowd, Eirlys appeared to be in her element, holding several conversations at once in the Dragon's two tongues, while she helped undress a chubby tot, who then waddled off towards the sea, peeing as he went.

Dora munched burnt fish and found it surprisingly tasty.

Like a gull she looked down on the little world, her heart hovering in total calm. She had chosen to look back at Rosa and Lachlan. She had not been struck down. The last line of Lachlan's letter echoed strangely in her mind: *When are you coming to see me?* And Rosa, whose resting place remained unvisited, asked the same question: *When are you coming to see me?*

Dora gave her attention to Eirlys and her relatives. Something about her effortful cheerfulness made Dora ask herself: *But is she happy?*

Hannah, full of vigour and life, was cartwheeling on the hard sand with the kids. Dora watched her build a sandcastle. A magnificent construction, castellated and towered. Hannah threw a high-arched bridge over the moat and engineered flying buttresses. The little ones brought buckets of water to wet the sand, and painstakingly decorated the walls with shells. Then a sun-wearied girl sat, plonk, on Hannah's lap, slipped her thumb into her mouth and fell asleep. Dora watched the tender way Hannah rocked the child.

There were things Dora would like to ask Hannah to do for her. All in good time, she thought. Hannah will surely do for me whatever I ask.

The urchins abandoned the baroque fortifications of Harries Castle and all hared off to the sea, kicking up sand with their heels.

The tot in Hannah's lap awoke, flushed, squirmed, bawled for Mam and removed. Hannah came over to Dora and took her hand.

'How are you doing, Dora? Have you had enough?'

'Oh, I'm fine. You are a fine cartwheeler.'

'I saw you building the castle with the kiddies,' Eirlys said. 'Lovely that is. Having such a nice time, aren't we? Are you having a nice time? Did you have some fish? Veggieburgers? Waldo! Is there anything left for my Hannah? And nothing with eyes, mind!'

Eirlys needed everyone to be having a lovely time every moment of every day.

'I think he's writing me a haiku,' said Eirlys. 'Spoil me rotten, do my family. God love them.'

She turned upon Dora and Hannah lonely, baffled eyes. '*Haul a hwyl a haf*,' she said. 'Sun and fun and summer.'

10

An egg always slipped down lovely.

Bacon was a flavoursome meat, and healthy if you crisped the fat and dried it on kitchen paper. One must always eat breakfast, with plenty of nutrition balanced by the fibre component. Seen in this light, a cooked breakfast, grilled or poached perhaps, began to take on a fibrous character in the mind.

Eirlys lolled back against her pillows with that magical first cup of tea. Thursday, and Mr Powell, the hermit, had gone out for his weekly shop with his hood up as usual, his jute bag in one hand and a dog-lead in the other. Why the dog-lead, Eirlys could never begin to guess. She always gave him time to make his getaway if she saw the blur of his camouflage jacket at the outer door, or caught sight of him scurrying up the forecourt. Poor boy. What had he lost?

She had an idea the rest of the residents stood aside for him, too. A corporate tact prevailed every Thursday morning.

At least a fortnight had gone by since they had accosted the Thomases on the beach, and Eirlys still did not have Megan's address. That day, surrounded by her kin and the dearest friends a woman could have, Eirlys had felt more wretched than she could explain. She'd felt sick to the stomach, and perhaps it had been the heat or Waldo's fish, but she'd shivered and her skin had gone to gooseflesh. She'd thought: *In the midst of life, we are in death.* And she had irrationally wanted to reach out to Megan and draw her back to The Eyrie, as if that would somehow secure her too. Since then, there'd been a family wedding, which – thank heaven – was over.

No tenants had appeared for Megan's flat. Hugh and Mary had left, as far as one could ascertain by taking an unobtrusive peek through Megan's window, much but not all of her furniture. Local boys on their binge night out had taken down the 'To Let' sign and heaved it into the next-door garden. She had seen one toss it like a caber. Had to laugh, bless him.

She too had practised vandalism in her time. The sight of the boy giving the 'To Let' sign the heave-ho brought back irresistibly her own days of activism. Slender then I was, she thought, as you ought to be for acts of civil disobedience. Not that she'd been a particularly effective saboteur. *Off to do a job*, the comrades had said. She and Menna and the whole gang of workers. She'd worn a pair of denim dungarees for work. Inconvenient when you needed a pee, mind. So, pee before you leave. Into the van. Roar off. All out at the designated road sign. At an earlier stage in the campaign they had daubed signposts with green paint so as to obliterate the Imperialists' anglicised place-names; when this had no effect they would carry the signposts off in the back of the van. This had been where she'd shown the full extent of her ineptitude. Didn't have the muscle for uprooting posts. Straining and dragging at them, arms out of their sockets, Eirlys had been a feeble vandal. Fair dos, mind, she reassured herself, I was great at painting out the English names: my artistic streak coming out there.

She swigged the last of the tea and lay down again. They'd won. But when you'd won, you found a world where the complexities, the ambivalences, hit you bang in the eye. Wales had been a man's world. Dinosaur attitudes to women, to sex. Anoraks, fumed her sister. Cavemen. Then she'd settled down and had five children, now all regular performers at the Eisteddfod.

More troubling was the awareness that the Just never inherit the earth. Never. The poor ye have always with you. Always. It was shameful. After your victory, you came onto a plateau in the foothills of Dora's world.

And here she was in Little England, cut off much of the time from her language, among monoglots. How dear Dora had bristled when Eirlys had thoughtlessly referred to her as a monoglot. Quite right, too. How insensitive, how ignorant of her. Eirlys chafed at the memory and hoped that Dora had forgotten. *Are Spanish, Russian, French, Basque, Italian – oh and a sprinkling of German and Yiddish – not languages, then, Eirlys? You do surprise me.*

I could have crawled down a crack in the floorboards, she thought, recalling the bruised women of Pucklechurch, their scorn for the ranting middle-class youngsters who were using the prison as a protest hotel. A political education they had given Eirlys.

She would scatter blueberries on her muesli, she thought. That is both healthy and delicious. But did she eat to live or live to eat? She loved her food. Simply loved it. The satin of liquids on her tongue, and what was more fragrant than newly baked bread?

When she got up, an automaton took Eirlys's place. The automaton ignored resolutions made under the quilt. Pat of lard in the frying pan, pricked sausage under the grill, soon to be joined by several rashers of streaky. One beef tomato sliced down the middle; two eggs hit the fat, but look, Eirlys, you are not altogether lost, she told herself. The bread originally selected for frying is virtuously slotted in the toaster for afterwards, to be eaten with home-made orange marmalade.

Sheer sensuality was breakfast. Eirlys shook off her slippers and propped her feet up on the coffee table, the tray on her lap. Dad had said we should enjoy our food, having thanked the Giver. As a small girl, Eirlys had thought he must mean Mam. Who else? She ate her fill, washed up and cleaned her teeth.

The cooked breakfast was instantly a matter of regret. More than regret: mortification. Eirlys flopped, bloated, in front of the TV. It was as if someone who didn't like her very much had force-fed her a mass of gunk guaranteed to kill her.

The day was finished. She might as well continue as she had started, shovelling in chips and ice cream and that gorgeous walnut or lemon cake she had promised herself to take to Megan's. Except they didn't know the address. Dora had said she would ring round every damn Home in Glamorgan to locate her.

There was a screech of brakes, a thudding of rock music. In our private car park? She strode to the window, and doubtless Dora and Hannah and the Nortons did the same, and Mrs Dark, so that if the block of flats had been a ship, it would have heeled over as the crew scampered to starboard. An anxious face peeped from each porthole.

Two young men sat in an open-topped, metallic-blue sports car, elbows flung out over the doors. Tattoos on their arms. Drum and bass thudding from a stereo. The driver was pointing over, presumably to Megan's flat.

Perhaps they would go away. Perhaps they were just looking.

Eirlys did not think Megan's flat would suit a pair of young males. And surely Hugh and Mary would realise that lady tenants were more domesticated and careful of other people's property, in the way a landlord would wish. One could imagine those two doing one hundred sit-ups in a sweaty gym. For muscles on them they had, tanned and lean. They'd switched off the music when Hugh and Mary turned up.

Eirlys bustled out and waylaid them in the hall, as Hugh, at his most amiable, shepherded the men in. On closer inspection, they seemed less youthful than she'd supposed: she put them down in her mind as old thirty-nines or young forty-fives. Manly men.

Hugh and Mary were not best pleased to see Eirlys in the hall, announcing that the residents wanted to visit Mary's mother and barring the way to the front door. They had no option but to introduce Mr Jones and Mr Sanderson: '*Voilà!*' Here were their new tenants. Well, yes, technically Mother's tenants, acknowledged Hugh, but who was left to do all the donkey-work? Muggins, of course.

At whose expense was Hugh conducting his Mallorcan lifestyle? Eirlys wondered.

Hannah arrived and was introduced. They attacked Hugh about Megan from either side.

No need at all, according to Hugh, to go fussing round his mother-in-law. Give the poor woman a chance, he said.

'A chance for?'

'Oh, he means to settle in,' said Mary. 'Mum's only been there for two or three weeks, hasn't she?'

Mary had been pretty once, and one could sometimes see a wraith of that young girl who had been so very naive and sweet, and fond, perhaps, of kittens, in the small figure in the flowered skirt and childish hair parted at one side. Her tan was so bronzed and perfect that one would imagine she took it from a bottle. But it was real. And it revealed how smooth and unlined her skin was. Older than me, thought Eirlys, by at least a couple of years, and look how well preserved she is. Mary would always have been a good girl. Earnestly wanting to be seen to do the right thing.

Mary had once confided that Megan had been a tartar of a mother, with a tendency to smack her daughter's legs. As a tax inspector, she had exercised a tyrannical hold over Mary's collection of threepenny bits in her red metal savings box. So it was not surprising that they were less close than they might have been. But, Mary said, she had forgiven Mum fully and freely, and wanted to do right by Megan.

'Mum needs to get her bearings, see. And perhaps it is a tiny bit early to visit yet. It might make her, well, hanker, mightn't it? What do you think, Hugh?'

Hugh was caught between his natural desire to shut Eirlys up and his need to ingratiate himself with his new tenants.

'Whatever you think, dear. The water meter is just outside, it is very simple to check it.'

'Hugh, you promised down at the beach to let me have Megan's address,' Eirlys said. 'You know very well we would never impose on Megan. Mary, if she looks weary or confused, I will skedaddle. Word of honour.'

She brought pen and paper, and took down the name and

address. Mary revealed it hesitantly, as if offering Eirlys damning evidence. She feels bad about her mam, thought Eirlys. Well, it's natural. Not easy for a women like Mary to take a course of action that obviously benefits herself. She smiled into the brown face. Ah yes, Myrrh Lodge: she knew of it.

Sandy Sanderson said he could smell something appetising. Now what was it? Bacon! There was nothing he liked more than the smell of bacon. Got your juices going.

'That's the scent of my breakfast,' Eirlys said.

'Lovely. Full English! My favourite.'

Eirlys remembered a cookery book her mother had owned, entitled *The Right Way To His Heart*, which had been left over from the austerity of the war and explained to the newlywed how toad in the hole could be an aphrodisiac within marriage.

'We are very quiet folk here,' said Eirlys. 'We do so much value that.'

'Noise,' said Hannah, 'we can't stand it.'

'I don't think there's anything more important, do you, Mary?' asked Eirlys.

'Oh, no.'

'And do they know about no pets?'

'I'm sure they wouldn't expect to bring pets.'

'No way.'

'Well, that's good,' said Eirlys comfortably. 'I just thought I'd mention it.'

'Of course.'

'Oh, do come *on*, Mary.'

Walking away, Hugh muttered something about the potty old Welsh dears and the anorexic youngster: they would not cause any trouble. Harmless spinsters, most of them, he said. They would doubtless meet Dora Urquhart. She was a real card.

'Why does Mary stay with him? Why would any woman?' asked Hannah, after they had gone.

'I suppose she chose him,' Eirlys said mildly. 'Once. The young men seemed all right, didn't you think?'

'Young? They were ancient!'

'To you, maybe.'

'Oh, but Eirlys, what about "Do come *on*, Mary!" What if she'd rather be, well, on the sea front, beach-combing?'

Eirlys vaguely considered whether Mary would like to be beach-combing. She did not think so. Not on her own, surely. Wouldn't Mary look up from the shells and driftwood and find the sky too enormous and alien above her? Wouldn't she look round for Hugh? His nagging and strutting would be a familiar comfort, like some filthy old gardening anorak on a known peg.

Then again, what did she, Eirlys, know of Mary? Had they ever had a real conversation? And would conversation be permitted by the omnipresent Hugh?

'Marriage,' she said, 'is a bit of a three-legged race, I suppose. You and I wouldn't really know, would we?'

She could have married either of two young men, Gareth or Daniel. Which one should she have chosen? How would they have grown old together? Crookedly twisted or twining together in a lovely way? Both had partnered her in protests and Gareth had gone on to great things in the National Assembly and was now the Minister responsible for Rugby. She'd seen him on television last week, opening a National Rugby Culture Centre in Cardiff. His curly hair had greyed now. His speech had started well: plenty of jokes, gusts of audience laughter. After this, a monstrous garrulity set in; the listeners appeared concussed. You glib old droner, Eirlys had thought, and burst out laughing.

Once, she'd loved listening to Gareth's eloquence and had even fed it as a girl, sitting on the floor between his legs in front of a two-bar electric fire, asking little questions and thinking herself in heaven.

No, she did not think that would have been an easy marriage, with Gareth the Tongue. And Danny, of course, had gone to the subcontinent of India. To the province of Khasia, to research into the Welsh missionaries of the nineteenth century. That would have fed her appetite for life. Except that he had gone with her best friend Betsi.

But she would have loved children. Her own babies. Apart

from anything else, it would have freed her from the duties – or exactions – of the childless auntie.

'Well,' said Hannah, 'I wouldn't put up with him. I just wouldn't. I'd be off like a bloody shot. Arsehole.'

Eirlys drove with Hannah to the address near Neath given by Mary. It was a large modern building built of reddish brick. The well-tended gardens were surrounded by chestnuts and limes, and pampas grass with its creamy plumes.

Megan did not appear surprised to see them, but was politely at a loss to know where she had met them before. Her room at Myrrh Lodge was small but comfortable, and Eirlys was relieved to see that the Thomases had found Mary's mother a more than halfway decent place to end her days. Staff were abundant and wore uniforms that keyed into the four wings, themed in bright colours for instant recognition. Megan was in the House of Light. Eirlys was speechless but Megan had found means to adapt. If she positioned herself with her back to the wall the colour of egg-yolk, she need only be assaulted by lemon-yellow on two sides and could rest her eyes on magnolia on the third. The Manager had explained that the rooms had recently been redecorated in line with the whole chain of Homes across the country. It appeared that each room was allegorical and that Megan had been lodged in a room which would bathe the occupant in a simulation of perpetual sunlight.

To live in a world where the sun never set might have daunted Eirlys, she thought, but Megan addressed it in an oblique and subtle way by keeping the lights switched off and the curtains nearly shut. In this womblike dimness she received her puzzling guests with subdued cordiality.

'Do sit down,' Megan said. 'On the chairs provided.'

That was another nice touch, Eirlys thought, that there were articles of furniture she recognised from the flat. And, still looking on the bright side, Eirlys insisted to herself as she wedged her beam-end into the elegant but narrow chair, Megan's nearest and dearest had relieved her of the burden of their bullying presence and would be taking themselves off to Mallorca. Family, yes, was all. Almost always.

Peering at Megan through the gloom, Eirlys's heart gave a peculiar twist. What a little mouse-person Megan was. Her face with its pointed chin was a pale triangle with glittering eyes. Really you could have got two of Megan into one of Eirlys, but it was not her size or timidity that snatched at Eirlys's heart. It was Megan's slippers.

She tried not to look at them. Hannah was chatting away, holding Megan's hand and telling her about the car journey; how they had to come the long way round West Cross because of a diversion, and how stuffy and sticky the weather was.

Megan asked, 'Where did you go in the car?'

'We came here, to see you.'

Megan compressed her lips and shook her head slightly; something, she seemed to indicate, was very much out of order about their proceedings. Then she stopped, as if to remind herself that she should not be so rude as to show incredulity at a person claiming to have come here in a car.

Eirlys asked Megan how she liked it here. Had she settled? Were the people kind? She unwrapped the purple, red and white freesias she had brought and arranged them, not very artistically, in a vase that was too big. The white blooms made a pale patch of luminescence in the curtained gloom.

Eirlys thought: For what crime are we sent away to die in an alien prison? To a cell in the House of Light? The door closed in your face against familiar people and places. You just have to serve your sentence. As she, gamely, is doing.

'Lovely scent, Megan,' she said. 'The scent of freesias I just adore.'

'Dora!' exclaimed Megan. She clapped her hands, shot up and looked exultantly at the door.

Eirlys and Hannah stared at one another and then followed her gaze.

'Do you mean the *door*?' asked Eirlys. She wondered what she could find to say about the door.

'No, dear,' Megan corrected her. 'I adore Dora. Dora, I think, is there. Behind the door.'

Eirlys tried not to look at the unbearable slippers with Megan's spindly ankles growing out of them; tried and failed. The slippers were beautiful. A deep midnight blue, of some satiny fabric, silvered with tiny moons and stars. Way too big for Megan's feet. She had to shuffle when she wanted to move.

She has her feet plunged in the firmament, thought Eirlys. Dad's voice echoed about the visionary Woman of the Book of Revelation clothed with the Sun and with the Moon under her feet.

'Why do you say that, Megan, *cariad*?'

'What?'

'That Dora is here.'

'Well, isn't she?'

'I don't think so.'

'I can hear her coming.'

Footsteps were nearing Megan's room. All three stared at the door, but it was only a carer with a tray of tea and a plate of assorted biscuits. Not the cheapest biscuits either, a good sign, thought Eirlys, her antennae still in working order. Hannah looked quite unstrung.

'Oh, lovely tea!' said Megan ingratiatingly to the carer. 'We shall all have tea. Sugar lumps! Take two biscuits each, everyone, because the plate goes out ... I'll tell you why in a minute.'

'Feeds the birds,' mouthed the carer.

'No, I don't. Don't be a fibber.'

Dora had evidently fled from Megan's mind but for Eirlys she was still oddly present. A superstitious thought flashed through her mind that, if Megan was 'seeing' Dora, Dora might somehow be on her way. Packing her bags.

The limes had bled sticky sap on to the windscreen and Eirlys was forced to scrub at it with a chamois. The heat inside the car was stifling so they opened the doors to try to cool things down.

'The burning fiery furnace,' Eirlys said. 'Never mind, get in. We'll soon cool down, once we get moving.'

'That was so weird about Dora,' said Hannah, strapping herself into the the car. 'It was like a haunting. But you can't be haunted by someone who's still alive, can you?'

'Dora *is* memorable, isn't she?'

'Don't say that.'

'Why not?'

'Oh, I don't know. Puts her in the past.'

'I know how fond you are of her,' said Eirlys. 'And she is of you.'

'Oh, and you, Eirlys. Do you think she will visit Megan?'

'Not really. Do you?'

'Not sure. I don't know her as well as you do, Eirlys,' Hannah conceded. 'It seems to me she might do anything. And you can't predict what she'll do by what she's done in the past. God, I'm done in, aren't you? I really thought Dora was there. Perhaps we should tell her what Megan said about her, to give her a chance to come and visit?'

Eirlys drove through the city centre, inching forward between bumper-to-bumper cars: digging up the roads the Council was, as usual. She wanted to get home and shut herself in her flat to have a good cry. How lucky she was to have a space to cry in. Many people didn't have that luxury. They had to lock themselves in the loo if they needed to bawl.

'We can ask Dora.'

But Eirlys had seen by the expression on Dora's face when they'd mooted the visit that wild horses wouldn't drag her to visit Megan. She'd got a huge whiff of Dora's fear. Dora did not, under any circumstances, wish to peep behind the door and see what might lie ahead. And why should she? Dora had done so much with her life; she had paid her dues over and over again. The great mercy and reckless courage she had exercised in Spain, and since then, were not available to her for the little calamities of daily life. And it was not that Dora cared too little for her fellows but that she had cared too much.

'But, Eirlys, didn't you think the whole thing was weird?' Hannah persisted.

'Not really. How do you mean? I thought it was fundamentally a good, well-run establishment and I was relieved. They've done their homework and spent some money on it. Pleased for her we should be,' Eirlys said, 'that those two buggers, 'scuse my Anglo-Saxon, actually pulled their fingers out and found a decent place.'

Hannah laughed. 'It was so sweet when you gave her the cake.'

'Yes, it was, it was lovely.'

For when Eirlys had produced a lemon cake she'd baked for her, Megan's face had lit up in a glory of recognition. It was Proust's madeleine all over again.

'*Oh, Eirlys!*' Megan had said, naming her as she took the round cake-tin in careful hands and beamed. In naming Eirlys, she had seemed to bless her. *My favourite. You do so spoil me, darling.*

Eirlys hoped the cake would not go to the birds along with the biscuits Megan hoarded.

But if the feathered friends shared it with Megan, wasn't that a sort of communion? Her father would certainly have thought so: his gift was the delicious wine in your own personal communion beaker and the wafer. You let it dissolve on your tongue and an ephemeral goodness passed into you. A cake could carry the same quality but, heretically, more so. And how well the lemon cake had toned with the shocking yellow walls.

Hannah said, 'You are so generous with people, Eirlys, you always know just what to say.'

Who would not preen at such a judgement? Even as she disclaimed any such qualities, and knew that anything decent in her was a matter of upbringing, Eirlys warmed to Hannah. The car was stuttering down the coast road.

'I do think she's all right, Hannah,' she said. 'Don't worry. Pity about the walls, of course.'

'Yeah. Like having to live in a daffodil. Patriotic, though – eh, Eirlys?'

Hannah glanced sidelong, with a grin. Eirlys laughed.

'Or an egg-yolk.'

'She's very thin and threadlike,' said Hannah. 'It's touching the way she lays out the bits of biscuit for the birds.'

'And very practical, as I don't think she likes shop-biscuits herself. She wouldn't want them to go to waste. But look at the kiddies enjoying the water! Makes you want to jump in fully clothed.'

The entire population of Swansea's children seemed to be leaping and squealing in the Lido at Blackpill. The car crawled along in the jam of folk making for an evening at the beach or in a Mumbles pub. Over the road at Clyne the trees looked fresh and cool.

'Ice cream, Hannah? Then we could drift through Clyne woods a bit?' Eirlys suggested.

'Absolutely.'

They sauntered through the dappled coolness of the woods, along the straight path that had once been a railway line. The canopy of oak and beech above them caught the fizz of breezes in its foliage; birdsong wove labyrinths of sound. Eirlys's heart rose as her eyes luxuriated in a dozen shades of green, each of which seemed to quench a thirst. Late-afternoon sun fell slantwise through leaves, making them translucent.

They sat for a while by the pool, saying little, drinking in the cool, idly watching for fish in the green gloom. Then suddenly there it was, the kingfisher, a flash of cobalt blue that skimmed the still surface, flying into a shaft of sun and out again. So solitary and secretive, Eirlys thought, you never see them in pairs. In fact, you rarely see them at all. And they seemed to be more or less sociopathic: she had once watched one kingfisher mob another, waiting time and again while its victim dived, to savage it when it came up for air. Their kingfisher perched on a branch out above the water: Eirlys took in its orange breast, its legs red as the sealing wax Dad had used to secure parcels. A spider whisked over the grass around them. The kingfisher took off and vanished.

They wandered up through the trees to where an old winding engine from a disused mine lay rusting swathed in ivy. Because the woods had once been full of mines and works, something you never thought of when you came to take your ease. Eirlys led Hannah to the arsenic works deep in the wood. They examined the remains of a circular chimney stack, next to the dry bed of a canal. You could still see the flue leading up to the top of the hill to take the toxic fumes away.

'Old Tom Ching owned that,' she said. 'Or one like it.'

'What, the Ching that built The Eyrie?'

'Yes indeed. That's why he built his summer house so far around the coast.'

'Because of the stink?'

'Yes, the fumes. Smoke. Noise. Look, you can see crystals of arsenic still there on the walls.'

'The men will have died so young,' said Hannah. 'You can feel them all round you, can't you, the guys who worked here?'

They sat down in the shadow of the works and the girl's story began to spill out: the father who wasn't at Llangyfelach, a half-brother Hannah had never heard of, who'd also been ditched. What should she do? she asked Eirlys. Should she speak to the boy's parents, or not? How was she going to cause the least harm? To Jake. She had seen the family at Caswell, they went every Sunday. It would be the easiest thing in the world, Hannah said, to bump into them, accidentally on purpose.

But then it was the easiest thing in the world to upset someone's peace of mind. You sometimes had the power to change the world for a person, so that they could never go back. Just by saying a few words. But then, not saying could be a lie too. She wouldn't pursue the father, she was definite about that. The bastard had had his chance, hadn't he? Two chances. Anyway, he'd hardly welcome her with open arms. The prodigal father, still running: nice twist to the parable, eh? He doesn't deserve me or Jake, Hannah said, in a raspy small voice that seemed to beg Eirlys to contradict it.

'No,' said Eirlys. 'He doesn't. What about the mother? If you got in touch by letter, say? I wouldn't go bumping into them on the beach, Hannah.'

But there was more, Hannah told her. Ah, yes, now it all came out; a husband called Barry. Of course Eirlys had noticed, that first day when Hannah arrived, the indentation of a ring on her wedding finger.

11

There had been one more sighting of Rosa. Mother and daughter, both wearing slacks, had been trailed to Richmond Zoo by a spook. By the elephant houses, Dora had been greeted by two men and three women, who'd joined them and chatted their way around the zoo. The spook reported that the daughter seemed cross with the mother, refused to hold her hand and stamped off shouting, *I hate you anyway!*

But Rosa was a big girl by then, Dora objected. Of course she didn't want to hold her mother's hand. Why did I try to make her? Look at Angelica. No one could make Jelly do anything she didn't consent to. And Dora had always valued Jelly's unbroken spirit.

So was that it, then? she questioned, and her eyes swam with tears. Did I try to break Rosa's spirit?

The zoo episode stuck in her mind, partly because in the documents printed, Rosa was seen no more. It was the beginning of the end. The advent of the rows and rages, of twenty years of storming, unforgivable tirades on both sides. Oh, if only I could go back and try again with the bits of wisdom I've gathered, Dora thought. She had been so possessive. The lassie had been gripped by her mother's big bony hands – at the throat, it seemed. Dora sat back and looked down at her fingers on the keyboard. She hid them from herself like brutal evidence.

She should have let Rosa go. Then Rosa would have come back to her when she'd finished that painful spurt of growing that everyone had to get through.

But why be apocalyptic about the child being in a mood? And

of course there would be other documents, Dora realised. The sample ended in December 1950 but she could call the rest up from the National Archives. And don't forget the letters and documents you've buried, she told herself, looking round at the books that lined every wall. For there was a library-within-the-library. Dora's books constituted an archive of notes and letters. But what heavy work it would be to search through every book. Who could she ask to do it for her?

Hannah, of course, would accept the work.

Meanwhile, Dora must ready herself to visit Rosa's resting place.

But as she stood at the top of Tom Ching's elegant staircase, she suffered a qualm. Looking down, she was faced with an abyss. She couldn't move. Eirlys and Hannah had gone to visit Megan earlier in the week. On their return, she'd read more in their eyes than she'd heard from their tongues. Fright had set in like flu. But if you began to leak courage, the ninety-odd years you carried on your back threatened to sink you like a stone. She had seen it happen to others.

One could be shaken by changes. Changes (she edged towards the top step) not in themselves significant or dramatic. Small shifts, substitutions, tiny commotions in the little world you inhabited. so perhaps it was neither Megan's leaving that had unnerved her, nor the arrival of the young men the previous day, but Megan's replacement by those young men down there at the base of the stairwell. It was like being shown that, beneath one's own carpet, there was a trapdoor down to Hades and a queue of folk outside your door waiting to take over.

Irked by her timidity, Dora eased herself down the stairs, gripping the rail and letting herself descend one step at a time. She who had walked the Grampians had to grit her teeth. The step from risk-taking casualness to a timid sense that the stairs were a hazard had happened, not overnight, but in a moment.

At the bottom the post had been sorted and sat in neat piles on the hall table. Good. She took her letters and slipped them into her shoulder bag, pleased to spot a handwritten envelope among the bills.

It was natural to cast one's eyes over other people's post, and in no way reprehensible.

There was a postcard on the table. Good gracious. On a scarlet couch reclined a breasty nude, minus her head, for there was a cut-out oval where her head should have been. And through this hole poked a photo of a beaming face. The sender of the card that might be, or its intended recipient. Dora flipped it over.

A person named Josie proposed to visit Sandy and Alun on Friday.

Don't dirty them sheets, Dora read, *not till I come ha ha and stop dollying up large!!! don't do it boyz im telling yaz wel be PARTYING!!! so wait 4 it & give it me good.*

Dora replaced the card face down and made her way out, past the Testosterone Window, as she had named it, turning the text of the private message over in her mind. What a display! She opened the car door with the remote whilst reminding herself that it had not, strictly speaking, been a 'display', since she, Dora Urquhart, had violated the taboo that restrains civilised folk from reading other people's correspondence.

One could not blame the girl. No one had taught her grammar and by now, no doubt, it was too late. This Josie had fallen into the etymologyless chaos of the world of texting and e-mail and come out inchoate. Dora had never sacrificed the Scots tradition of rigorous parsing.

She drove scornfully out of the car park. She allowed herself to be amused, as she shopped, at the idea of cautioning the girl behind the Co-op counter, and dear Vicky the librarian, against 'dollying up large'. Once words wormed their way into your mental space, there was very little hope of squeezing them out. Probably this usage was already in the current Appendix to the Oxford English Dictionary.

And quite right too, she said to herself beside Joe's Ice Cream Parlour. For usage is everything in language, and what fogeys like me prefer is irrelevant.

Doubtless this Josie thought their sexual shenanigans very modern and shocking. Oh dear. Do you think, Josie, that you invented sex? Andrew Nisbet and herself and that wee man whose name escaped her had practised three-in-a-bed, and very exciting it was before it became predictable. Squabbling had broken out between the menfolk, allegedly on political matters, and the threesome had been dissolved.

Dora sat down peacefully in front of the Post Office with her choc-mint ice and watched the world go by. She silently postponed the visit to Rosa. Today did not feel right.

Howls of female laughter woke Eirlys. Sporadic ululations were followed by lulls, tempting her to hope for peace.

Josie! Josie! Don't!

Then the sound of timpani, as if someone were beating a saucepan with a spoon.

Come on, Al! Give-it-here!

A man with silver paper under Eirlys's window was holding a grave conversation with a drunken or stoned female other, whose lament was broadcast with echoes around the forecourt by his hands-free mobile, while he looked down at ... What was he doing with the silver paper? Rolling cigarettes? Why was he rolling cigarettes under her window? Should she ring the police? If so, what should she report? *There is a man rolling cigarettes under my window and I, boo-hoo, can't sleep.*

Eirlys stuck plugs in her ears and drifted off. When she awoke, there was no man beneath her window, but a line of people dancing the conga round the forecourt.

Aye aye conga! Aye aye conga!

Six o'clock: no more sleep possible. Bring in the milk, Eirlys ordered herself; start your day. I shall need to speak to them. We shall contact Hugh and Mary even if I have to go and stalk them in Mallorca. We shall summon a residents' meeting about this invasion. It will stop. All will be well.

The garden area immediately beneath Megan's window was covered with drifts of something white. The curtains in the men's flat were closed, the residents presumably sleeping off the night's exertions.

In the hush of morning air, Eirlys looked over to the hill. A grey cloud extended like a dove's wing over the castle ruins, while a plume of smoke rose from one of the houses in the valley. The quiet beauty of her world lay exactly as it had been last month, last year. Precious this was, to them all.

But now they were greeted with changes – for instance, this boogying in the middle of the night. And this – whatever was it? – white stuff on the lavender bush (and very dear that bush had been to Megan, always pinching a scent into her fingers, remembering to do that, right up to the very end, and smiling that inward smile, God love her). The white stuff had snowed onto the somewhat brutally pruned box bushes, and the classical urn with its profusion of dahlias had been caught in the same unseasonable blizzard. Whatever was it? Eirlys hunkered down and wondered if she should take a sample. Through her weary mind flickered the Prime Minister's advice to be vigilant against terrorist attacks. The white granules, with blue flecks, looked very chemical indeed and reminded Eirlys of the envelopes containing satirical talcum powder that Dora had sent to the Prime Minister, as her contribution to the antiwar campaign. Eirlys had been against this, privately considering it childish. Well, this was not talcum: crouching and sniffing, she decided it was washing powder. They had been throwing it at one another, Eirlys concluded.

From the curtained flat hung a couple of towels, what looked like a female item and one blue sock. Vulgar and touristy, she thought, and yanked hard at the sock and the towels. They were jammed between the window frame and would not budge.

Right! Eirlys knocked on the window; then, marching in, she banged on their door. Then she beat upon it until her fists hurt. Why should *they* be allowed to sleep off their excesses when they had denied sleep to everyone else?

No answer.

Incensed, Eirlys went back out, pressed their buzzer and kept her thumb there. It was the end of The Eyrie. The end of our gentle and courteous life together, she thought. The window opened and a man's head emerged. The towels and underwear fell down onto the dahlias.

'Fuck off!' he shouted. 'Just fuck the fuck off, you fucker!'

There was no time to open a dialogue with the head. It vanished and the window slammed shut.

Eirlys went upstairs for a pow-wow with Dora. But Dora did not want to come down to inspect the white powder. She flatly ridiculed the sock and the towels, and claimed not to have been disturbed by untoward sounds in the night.

Eirlys had noticed that the Dora-weather had been dour and overcast. She sat with her leg propped on her pouffe, for she had some kind of small boil or sore, she said. No, don't fuss, the discomfort was negligible and most certainly did not require the services of a quack or a nurse. A nurse, of course, was not a quack but a worker. You could trust a nurse, but still she did not want one. The nuisance was that the leg problem, trivial in itself, parted her to some extent from her computer, so that Rae would have to be laid off temporarily, just when they had reached a most interesting turn in their studies. If this went on, Dora would have to invest in a laptop. And she was concerned about Rae, in case that prodigy should take advantage of her free time to succumb to the bad, essentially hedonistic influences of her partying pals.

'Well,' said Eirlys, diverting her concern on Dora's behalf back to her own gnawing anxiety, 'but we've got partying pals *here*, Dora, and who knows what substances they're taking? I didn't sleep a wink; I heard Hannah stirring in the small hours, so she must have been disturbed. I mean, what are these people doing *barking*? Are they pretending to be dogs? It's the thin end of the wedge, really it is.'

'Are you sure it wasn't the foxes?'

'Quite sure.'

'*If* any genuine problem should arise, be sure, Eirlys, that I shall deal with it,' Dora reassured her loftily.

'Oh, well then.'

'I think we were all unduly panicked by dear Megan's departure. We must preserve our common sense. Would you mind passing that volume, the one on the desk, no, no, *there.* And the letter beside it. Someone wants me for an interview. I shan't give it.'

Dora jabbed with her forefinger towards a desk littered with books. Eirlys, gathering that she was being given her marching orders, discovered the required volume by a process of trial and error. But did this mean that Dora was unable to limp across to fetch it for herself? Was she able to get to and from the loo, the kitchen area? If not, the grandsons ought to be alerted. The possibility that Dora might be failing, going suddenly downhill, eclipsed all other concerns.

It flashed across Eirlys's mind's eye that Dora might soon follow Megan out of the door, into the ambulance.

'Can I do anything?' she havered, while Dora leafed through the pages to find whatever it was she wanted.

'In what respect, Eirlys?'

'Well, for you, *cariad.* Have you had your breakfast?'

No reply. Dora was reading, her jaw set. What a monster Dora could be though, Eirlys thought. Monumental, she sat there like a mountain of bare granite, no soft patches, just the massive bones articulating a forbidding presence with so little give in it.

'What is the matter, dear?' Dora asked, not looking up from the page.

'I want to look at your leg.'

'Very well, look at my leg then, if it makes you happy.'

Eirlys rushed to make use of the exasperated concession, while Dora continued, in a pointed manner, to read. She flapped the letter and cawed that she would not help these parasites out with their theses on the Spanish Civil War. Let them go to the Congo or Sudan and do some good. They were making a reputation on the backs of a previous generation's sacrifice.

'I think it's an ulcer,' Eirlys said. 'It does need seeing to, Dora.'

'Wants to know about the International Brigade and the

Comintern, but she cannot even spell it! You are sure about that, Eirlys, are you?'

'Almost.'

'It will clear up.'

'Not on its own it won't. Telling you I am, Dora dear. Our mam had those. Very nasty and incapacitating.'

'I am fine.' But her voice quavered. Dora flapped the letter again. 'Please put this down over there, Eirlys, before you go. I shall be writing her a strongly worded e-mail.'

'I'm going nowhere. I'm not sure you can even walk.'

'Of course I can walk. Stop fussing.'

'You've had no breakfast.'

'I am not hungry.'

'See, you've lost your appetite, *bach*. Not right, is it? And I'm going to sit here – yes, uninvited – and natter on about inconsequentials, as you call them, until you agree to eat and get that ulcer seen to.'

Quaking, Eirlys held her ground. She sat down on the recliner, hitched the lever back and floated up.

Dora sighed, rose and walked, scarcely grimacing with the pain, into the kitchen. She poured oats into a pan and measured out water and milk in equal quantities. She added a pinch of salt and no sugar.

'Now then, Eirlys, have *you* breakfasted? I can easily prepare a portion of porridge for you. You will have to wait the regulation twenty minutes for it to be ready – just say the word.'

She looked at Eirlys over her shoulder with a pouty sulk, so that Eirlys caught a glimpse of Dora at fourteen, moody and melodramatic. She recognised the family resemblance between Dora and her great-granddaughter, Angelica. Eirlys relaxed into a grin.

'Oh, honestly,' she said.

'If I've been rather, well, what can I say, grumpy, in the last few minutes, I trust you'll make allowances, Eirlys.'

Dora did not look at Eirlys whilst making this retraction, and somehow its effect was rather grim and off-putting. If she had been any other old woman, Eirlys thought, one would have been over there like a shot and had the wooden spoon out of her hand and given her a lovely hug. One would have softly rescued that stray wisp of hair between finger and thumb, and tucked it in at the nape of her neck. But Dora, even at her most benign, insisted on her electric fence.

Rapping at the door; then in bounced Angelica and gave her great-grandmother a warm cuddle from behind. Eirlys saw a spasm seize Dora's face, an untenable mingling of shock and bliss.

Bendy and supple, and taller even than Dora, Jelly hoisted herself on to the counter top and prattled. Her dad was such a lowlife sometimes. He was totally antagonistic to recycling and would not accept the special bins Jelly had bought out of her own money for the family: she had explained the difference between organic and non-organic refuse till she was blue in the face. She'd explained solar panels to her mum but all Mum could say was that she would think about it. *Thinking* was no good! The world might end while they so-called 'thought about it'. Infantile her parents were, and all her mates agreed.

Stirring the porridge, which hiccuped into bubbles, Dora listened to Jelly with adoration and neither rebuked her misplaced backside, nor her tirade against Keir.

'Well done, Jelly,' she said quietly, and glowed. 'Do you mind stirring the porridge? I've got a bad leg.'

Eirlys cut in. 'It would be a good idea if someone medical saw to that poor leg. It needs a dressing and your nan is always so busy.'

Jelly produced her mobile at once and had a run-in with the surgery.

'Of course she's a fucking emergency!' she bawled. 'OK, in that case you'll have to send someone round. Yeah. Right. I should think so, too. Ta-ra then. Honestly,' she said, coming off the phone, 'the NHS today! Bollocks it is. Don't worry, Nannan, the nurse will call this morning. Hey, did you see what those plonkers have thrown out of their window? Pants! And they've dumped a load of white shit on your garden.'

Jelly was just on her way to see Sam, she said, and then they had to go and see Laura, but she'd look in on her way back and make sure Nannan's leg was sorted.

How proud she was of Jelly, Dora said. So free of mindless compliance! She tried to get rid of Eirlys, but Eirlys, though feeling rather concussed, would not go. She suffered a lecture, as they waited for the nurse, on the sixtieth anniversary of the Civil War. *You can be a marcher. You're ambulatory, how marvellous! You can carry a Red Flag! Nothing heavy, just a small red flag*, the organisers had told Dora. *Just think, dear, what a statement!* They'd wanted to parade her with wheelchair cases, the remnant of the International Brigade, through the Madrid Sports Stadium. Dora had given them a short answer. What right did they have to make a show of her and her peers? Of course, no one else saw it like that, and perhaps they were right.

And now Dora might become a wheelchair case. She would not be seen dead in a wheelchair. Never.

'Of course not,' Eirlys said. 'No one wants you to be in a chair. I'm sure it won't come to that.'

The nurse knelt and peered. Not an ulcer after all, she reported. Dora must have banged her shin on something and the wound had become a touch infected. All at once, Eirlys saw Dora's balance tip and right itself. The pain subsided. Morale recovered. No question of ulcerated legs, support stockings and sticks.

The nurse giggled when Dora told her it was probably rock-climbing at Three Cliffs that had caused it, no doubt thinking the old lady was joking.

Sitting afterwards on the balcony with a mug of coffee, Eirlys and Dora looked down upon an unusual bustle in the car park. Hannah, coming round the block with an armful of towels from the washing line, looked up and caught sight of them.

'We seem to have left the towels out for two nights,' she called up. 'They've been baked and cooled and dewed and baked again. You can smell the buddleia in them.'

'Thank you, dear,' said Dora. 'You're as good as a wife. What's going on down there?'

'Not sure.'

The tenant from number ten, whose name Eirlys did not know, was loading her boot with black bin bags and cardboard boxes, chatting, or trying to, with a stooping, lanky man in combat gear. He was emptying his own car boot of cardboard boxes. Beyond them, one of the new tenants from Megan's flat was kissing a woman beside his sports car.

'Ah!' said Dora. 'The illiterate hussy who goes by the name of Josie.'

'Dora! I'm shocked!'

'Oh, well, I'm not shocked as such. I'm aesthetically displeased. Could he not canoodle with the hussy in the privacy of his own residence? Is it some kind of street theatre now, the forecourt?'

'No, not at that. I'm not shocked at *sex*, dear,' Eirlys said.

'What, then?'

'How do you know she's called Josie, Dora?'

'Oh, dear! The postcard.'

'Caught you out,' said Eirlys, making it clear that she too had been tempted to read it.

'It takes one to see one,' was all Dora could say in self-defence. But she had the grace to blush. 'Oh, dear, Eirlys,' she said. 'My blemishes are all on show today. I nearly bit your head off for your loving concern over my leg.'

'You are entitled, my very dear Dora, to bite my head off once in a while. Feel free. Though not too often, of course.'

Eirlys intuited the thought that had made Dora grouchy: how everything could curdle, just like that. She had felt it, too. A quiet community could be turned into bedlam: it took so little. A healthy aged person could fall in her own kitchen and initiate terminal decline.

This was why the old became conservative, she thought. Everything infinitesimally shifting and sliding away.

'*Another* new guy moving in,' mouthed Hannah.

Did the man in the flak jacket look quiet? Eirlys wondered.

Would he be the partying sort? His luggage was concise and neat, and he carried it in with swift strides, returning to lock his car and test the doors. Eirlys noticed the way he carried his head, craning so that it seemed to set his body at a forward tilt. She was relieved to see that he was not just quiet but mute, for he did not reply to the woman from number ten when she pointed to the water meter, and he said nothing to Hannah when she walked towards him, holding out her hand in greeting.

The kissing couple had decamped. Off to roister in some dune, Dora supposed, and roll home the colour of lobsters, or to drink themselves daft in the pub and return the colour of beetroot.

'Although,' she said, 'I do not want you to think that I am a prude, Eirlys. I took lovers well into my sixties. And why not? The salmon go on leaping.'

12

For a moment, when Hannah stumbled out of the sea, her muscles gone to jelly, the beach looked eerily different from the one she'd left behind. The tide had gone out, of course, sweeping her along with it. She made for that particular rock, the one like a clenched fist with the thumb and forefinger pointing out to sea, where, some weeks ago, she'd first spotted the boy. She and Eirlys had composed a letter to the mother. There had been no answer. Although it had been balm to pour out her heart to Eirlys, there in Clyne Woods the day they visited Megan, Hannah had not told her that she sometimes came to Caswell and watched the family. The grandfather – *her* grandfather, he might be – had a flat overlooking the bay. The family used it as a beach hut.

A light wind had sprung up and Hannah shivered as she reached for her towel. And there he was, a few steps away: the dark-haired child, equipped with a blue shrimping net, crouching over a rockpool.

'Hi,' he said.

'Hi. Do you remember me?'

'Yeah, I think so. No, not really. Want to see a crab?'

She crouched beside him to look. She could see both their reflections on the sliding surface of the water. 'It's Jake, isn't it? Oh, look, it's a baby crab.'

The tiny, almost transparent creature skittered across the base of the pool. There was no weed for it to hide in.

'I wouldn't hurt him,' said Jake.

'Of course you wouldn't. How's the bunny?'

'Fine.'

'Not run away?'

'No.'

'That's good then.' She knelt and dabbled her hand in the pool.

Jake looked into her face. 'Have you been in the sea? Your hair's all wet.'

'Yeah, it's great. Have you?'

'Nah, I've had earache, so I can't go in, I'm not allowed.'

'That's tough. Can't you use those earplug thingies?'

'Not allowed. My dad's here.'

'Oh, right.'

Hannah snatched for breath. She got to her feet and looked round. The guy who must be Jake's stepfather had been sunbathing and the whole front of his body was blushing. He was one of those pale-skinned people who couldn't look at the sun without burning. He was moaning about anti-social people who built barbecues on the beach. Not everyone wanted to smell burgers when they came down to the sea.

'I do,' said Jake.

'Well, I don't.'

'*And* I'd like to eat them.'

'Who's this? Oh, hi,' said the guy, tensely, recognising Hannah. He hardly tried to hide his hostility.

She tucked the towel in at her waist and twisted her hair to squeeze out the sea water. Behaving normally on the beach. She had every right to be here.

'Jake,' the guy said, 'how about you try that pool over there? Looks a whole lot more promising. I think I saw some shrimps there.'

'We got your letter, Hannah,' he said. 'I'm Paul.'

Hannah stood there, cold to the marrow. She felt horribly exposed and wished she were fully clothed. They had guessed who she was anyway, Paul said, as soon as she'd turned up. There were photos of her as a kid ... around. Or there had been.

'In any case,' he said, and it was not said pleasantly, 'you're the spit of Jack.'

'But your wife hasn't answered my letter,' she said. 'You haven't answered. You've said nothing.'

Wild whoops of joy interrupted them. The lad had found something in the depths of the pool. Something wicked, he said, something awesome.

They admired the shrimps together. Jake would put them back, he promised. It was their home. He's lovely, she thought. So gentle: wherever did he get that gentleness? But her father, she remembered piercingly, had had a very soft way with him. He was patient and calm. He would lie with you under a tree and just look up at the green. He'd had no hard edges. Under his long dark hair she had made a little world for herself. Of course, he'd been spaced out. She hadn't understood that then. And when he'd left, he just drifted off like a cloud. Hannah looked down on the back of Jake's head as he slowly lowered the net into the pool. So vulnerable, with dark little whorls of hair. A piece of cotton wool was poking out of one ear. His shoulders were thin and brown and his careful hands rather stubby, like hers.

'Can we go over here?' Paul asked. 'He's not all that well.' He led her away from the boy.

'I know,' Hannah said. 'His ear. Does he get bad earache?'

'Appalling. And then you have to fight the doctor to screw the antibiotic out of him.'

'Has he had grommets put in?'

'No.'

'Perhaps that would be a good idea.'

'Well, anyway.'

None of her business, he seemed to say. Paul put a halt to conversation about small, private things. She could see that he'd like to kick her off like a limpet. No way: Hannah was not budging. In the wind her skin was all gooseflesh, cold and naked: she didn't want him to see her shivering. In his eyes, she was a nasty little bit of Jack come back to spoil their cosy life. Fascinated with me, though, aren't you? she thought. She saw it in the way he darted glances at her, taking in her bare face with its cap of wet hair, making the obvious comparisons.

'Does Jake have any idea who I am?' she asked.

'No. Thing is,' he said, leading her further away, 'to be quite honest with you, Hannah, we don't want him to get hurt all over again. You can see that, can't you? I'm his dad now, see? And I'm here for keeps.'

'Good. I'm glad for him. I am his sister.'

'Half-sister, I think.'

She managed not to say that he wasn't even a half-dad. Because of course that was not true. She stood her ground.

'What does his mother think? I'd like to get to know Jake, if it's at all possible. And any other family I've got.'

'Speaking just for myself, like, I think it's best not to say anything. Don't get me wrong, nothing against you.'

'Well, how could you have anything against me? You don't even know me.'

'No need to get all upset now. Leave it with me, Hannah. I'll speak to Siân. But please?'

'What?'

'Leave us be until you hear.'

'Meaning?'

'Don't keep, you know, sloping round.'

'*What?*'

'You know what I mean. To be quite honest with you, we're worried that you're stalking us.'

'Excuse me. I live here. I exist.'

'Well, there you are then, Hannah. We'll sort this out. It just took Jake ages, see, to stop wetting the bed after his dad went, and then he had to get used to me. Which he has. Not easy for him. You can see that, can't you? I'll speak to Siân tonight. I promise.'

She kept up the pressure: 'How will I hear?'

He tapped Hannah's mobile number into his own phone. It would be soon, he promised. Best to get it over and done with.

And by the way, he didn't have an address for Jack Francis. And if she found out where he was, they didn't want to know. They wanted nothing to do with money from drugs. *Dim byd.* OK? Nothing. Full stop.

'He deals?'

'He is a lowlife.'

'OK, but just one thing. I might look like Jack, I can't help that, but I'm not Jack, any more than Jake is.'

'No, sure. Sorry, but you understand?'

'I'll leave you to it. Ta-ra,' she called brightly to Jake. 'Hope the earache clears up soon.'

Her heart howled as she dressed. She wasn't wanted. 'Well, fuck off then,' she said, 'I don't want you.' Need rose in her, intense and sharp. For arms to hold her. A mouth to want her mouth. Inside, you were still the same baby. You were an accident. Little Green. Go and find some young guy and fuck him. Go clubbing. You've been living like a nun in a bloody convent.

She began to walk towards a group of guys with cans who lay sprawled on the sand. Six or seven good-looking lads. Tanned and brawny.

But you've been there, done that. Hannah veered and strode straight past, towards the sea. No more offering herself around.

She stood at the water's edge and thought of Dora. Resting her mind on that one person who loved her, she seemed to gain perspective. A plume of smoke rose up from a boat in the bay. Was it coming or going? Perhaps in some way she could absorb Jake into her ordinary life and become an ordinary part of his. Oh, yeah, it's you. Hi, how you doing? Bye then.

Or she could stand back and do nothing and wait. Except that waiting was not doing nothing. It was the choosing of balance. The world wobbled and you repositioned at every moment, shifting your weight to hold your stillness. The tiny crab was still in the shallow pool, where the boy had pledged not to hurt it.

13

Dora lowered the newspaper and let it fall. She relaxed. What a place for lotus-eaters, this private area at the back of The Eyrie. Here they were in the August sunshine, basking in loungers, drugged with the scent of buddleia that had run wild over the lower slopes of the hillside. Tom Ching, who had lavished so much lucre on the veneer of his summer palace, had left its backside a messy muddle of drainpipes. The Elizabethan gardens at the front were complemented by a wilderness at the back, which Dora liked very well. Wild flowers had sown themselves amongst the rough grass, where bees, ladybirds and daddy-long-legs were busy.

The Italian Unabomber, she had just read, had used a child's chocolate egg to hide explosive. A yellow plastic packet containing a Kinder Surprise egg had been placed on a low wall at Treviso. When a boy gave the container a kick with his foot, the egg blew up. But the boy was unharmed.

Bombs from the same maker had exploded in a tube of soap bubbles and a felt-tip pen. In a tube of tomato puree. In a jar of Nutella. In a candle. The obscene ingenuities of the Unabomber were not as novel as he boasted. It had all been seen before. It would all be seen again.

The breeze made the tree canopy murmurous. She let herself be soothed in the swoon of warmth and perfume from buddleia and cut grass, and watched the lustre in the leaves of the birches at the top of the scarp as they bounced to and fro, revealing their silvery undersides.

'Penny for them, Hannah,' she heard Eirlys say.

Hannah did not reply. She was standing still and barefoot in her shorts, looking up into the woodland, listening to the birdsong perhaps. Or watching out for the foxes that had come out last night after Mrs Dark's heroic display. For one could call it no less.

There had been pandemonium. A fire alarm was going off. Dora had hobbled out from her bed to find people in their night clothes. One of the paramours who had taken over Megan's flat, dressed only in his underpants, had been telling the new neighbour, 'Your fucking smoke has set off the fire alarms and woken all these elderly ladies.'

The new resident had been standing aghast in his doorway wearing pyjama bottoms, smoke leaking out around him.

'We need our fucking kip,' the paramour had gone on. 'If you don't stop it, I'm going in to sort this.'

Then he'd barged past into the new man's flat. Eirlys had appeared and told Dora to take that bad leg back to bed. But Dora had held herself in reserve.

'Oh, now, no call to speak unkindly,' Eirlys had told the second paramour, who was swearing about his broken kip. 'Hallo, darling,' she'd said to the new resident. 'I'm Eirlys. And you are?'

The resident said something like 'Flood'. And at this moment Mrs Dark had appeared, stately in a long Victorian nightgown, her hair unloosed around her shoulders.

'Burnt chips!' the paramour had reported, marching out of the stranger's flat. 'Sorted. You can go back to bed, ladies.'

'Oh, no now, chip pans is very dangerous,' Mrs Dark had burst out at the stranger. 'You can get those modern ones, mind, self-regulating they are, so much safer. Please now, my boy, I am asking you *categorically* not to fry chips in the dead of night.'

So that was it, he spoke no English, Dora had suddenly realised. A torrent of words Dora could not catch (Eastern European?) had been accompanied by a flurry of penitent hand gestures. He'd gone in and shut his door. A refugee then, Dora had thought, from some horror in the east. What kind of echo had just been set off in his mind by the chip-furore?

Dora had been about to speak. But Mrs Dark had not finished. Standing there in her nightgown, buttoned and frilled at neck and wrists, this mild soul had begun to tongue-lash the paramours about the parties and the bedlam in the night. She would bring it to the attention of their landlords in Spain, she'd promised, oh yes, if it continued even one more night. And the police! The police would be called! 'It never used to be like this,' she'd said. 'The Eyrie is a quiet place for quiet people. If you don't like quiet, then take your noise elsewhere. Is that clear? Is it now?'

And off she had flounced. But the taller of the two had pursued her up the spiral staircase, begging her pardon and promising there would be no further housewarmings.

'Handsome is as handsome does. Good-night to you. To your beds now.'

Dora had retreated to her flat, amused. She'd taken aspirin for the pain in her leg and sat at her bedroom window, sipping tea, as she sometimes did when she found sleep hard to come by. The mother fox and her nearly grown cubs had been playing on the moonlit grass. Rolling over and over one another, play-snarling, learning to fight for their lives. Mrs Dark's light had also been on. Perhaps she too had been drinking tea at her window peering out, thinking her thoughts. How, Dora wondered, did Mrs Dark, sitting obscure as her name in her placid flat above Dora's head, construe the times she had lived through? She sat waiting in an antechamber to death, with nothing much to do. Husbands and friends had gone long ago. If you could know what Mrs Dark felt, Dora imagined, you would know pretty well everything. The human code would be cracked, like DNA.

Did the world look a different, more hospitable place, if you saw the marketplace as good and right? Did it make it easier to sit in your flat and age? Did Mrs Dark have a view concerning the marketplace? Or was it just there, like the floor and walls?

In bed, settling for sleep, Dora had thought she heard Hannah crying, so she'd tapped on the party wall to reassure her that she was there if wanted.

And Dora had suddenly wanted her mother. A kiss from Mother: *good-night, bonny bairn.* Parents had never kissed their children much in those days. But, had Mother known that kisses were permissible, she would certainly have kissed her, Dora thought. She herself had come late to cuddling and was a novice: she had Jelly to thank for her enlightenment. And Eirlys, of course, was a considerable cuddler.

Eirlys was now saying that it was her mission to remain in the shade and follow it across the lawn, since according to a dermatologist, her skin was fifteen years younger than her age and to preserve it she must eschew the sun.

'So eschew it I do,' said Eirlys. 'I pick up my bed and walk.'

'Quite right,' Dora said drowsily. 'You have beautiful skin, Eirlys. You do well to preserve it.'

Preserve was not, perhaps, quite the apposite word, conjuring up Pharaohs and pickles, but the feeling was right. Dora felt benign, sitting out here at the base of the steeply shelving cliff, the lower reaches turfed, the middle layer mauve with buddleia, the upper reaches a wilderness of unspoilt woodland. Eirlys, in a sun hat and a loosely flowing gown of brilliant blue that covered her curves and shielded her skin, smiled at the compliment. Dora's own arms reminded her of a toad's with all those speckles. She turned her eyes away, to where Hannah was sitting further up into the woods, on a fallen log, saying nothing, studying her mobile phone. Young people today were wedded to their mobiles. Jelly had three, 'just in case'. But she'd never seen Hannah with a friend.

Crying in the night, weren't you? thought Dora. Looking at Hannah, inscrutable behind her sunglasses, she thought: Bless her, I thought she was Rosa come back to me. Strictly speaking, of course, Dora had not been mad enough to believe this fantasy. She had allowed herself to entertain the terrible joy of it, rather as one enters into the emotion of a film, and this film had changed her. Opened her up. But now Dora was conscious of parting company with her illusion. Rosa was with Lachlan over there, where she was going. Hannah was over here in a dappled place of affection and happenstance. Of Hannah herself, she knew oddly little. I have always been selfish in my love, she thought.

'Come down, Hannah, and sit with us,' she said, holding out her hand. 'Are you all right?'

'I'm good. Just thinking. How is your leg today?'

'Fine. What were you thinking?'

'Wondering if the scarp puts us out of mobile range. I'm expecting a call. But I think it's all right.'

She plumped down in a deck chair next to Dora and opened her book. It was a book about Welsh mutations, with cartoon pictures of the thousand laws that made sounds change in a language that made Greek look like a picnic. She really wanted to learn, Hannah had explained to Dora. Eirlys's cousin Waldo had promised to teach her. Hannah's great-grandparents had been Welsh-speakers, as she'd seen on the censuses. And, as Dora and Eirlys knew, the English imperialists had imposed a law to prohibit their speaking it at school. So this was solidarity. It was a bit daunting. But the upside was that the book of mutations could put you to sleep just like that. It was infallible.

'But even so, *why* can't they use the washing lines?' Eirlys burst out, as if conducting a dispute within herself. 'Perfectly adequate they are. And what a colour scheme!'

Dora opened her eyes a touch and noted the rainbow display of swimming towels and trunks hanging from the back Testosterone Window.

Were people not taught the use of pegs nowadays? Eirlys went on. What would it have cost them to walk round to the clothes lines?

'Chill, Eirlys. Mrs Dark will trounce them for us,' said Hannah.

'Aye,' said Dora. 'She has unguessed leadership qualities.'

'She was magnificent! I hope it didn't take it out of her too much. And, you know, Hugh and Mary must have left Megan's pegs in the flat for them. Lovely pegs she had, and how proud she was of them. You remember Megan's pegs, don't you, Dora?'

'Not really.'

'Wooden, old-fashioned dollies, made in Yorkshire. Not the plastic sort.'

Dora was amazed at what a large subject clothes-pegs could be, when a person put her mind to it. It seemed there was a narrative of clothes-pegs which, as she dreamily listened in to Eirlys's discourse, bore on the social history of women in the industrial north of England, as well as Wales.

'Oh, God love her,' Eirlys said to Hannah in a loud whisper. 'I've bored her to sleep.'

'You have not and I am not,' said Dora, opening her eyes. 'You can tell me more about the pegs, Eirlys, it was most enlightening but perhaps elaborate over a pot of tea?'

Off Hannah and Eirlys went, the pair of them, into the cool of the flats. Dora yawned. She was weary. She wondered if she would continue with her computer studies. Her dream of attacking *him,* through mastery of a grand electronic project, was waning, though; in the course of their sessions, she had politicised Rae in a way she had managed with neither of her grandsons and certainly not with Angelica, who wasn't going to vote *ever*! It was her democratic right not to vote! And nor were any of her mates.

'Do you not know that your vote was purchased with the blood and torture of women?' Dora had responded, only the once, because at heart she sympathised with Jelly. Democracy had been mocked, scourged and betrayed by the Dear Leader.

A disagreeable pins-and-needles sensation crawled through her face; it seethed into Dora's lips and turned the thoughts in her brain to a dizzy blizzard of dots on the right side of her face. No doubt the effect of the heat. She found it best to give in to the pins and needles; drowse them away to the murmur of the radio or bees.

Well! She opened her eyes to mugs of tea and some kind of cake with nutmeg and walnut which Eirlys had baked in her workshop of delicate flavours. Always there was something tasty that Eirlys had somehow or other 'just whisked together and popped in the oven'. The whisking and popping had been no trouble at all. On the few occasions in her life when Dora had attempted such whisking and popping, incineration or heavy, stodgy droop had ensued.

She beamed at Eirlys, whilst flapping off a wasp that had taken a fancy to her portion. Two butterflies had taken Eirlys's blue gown for a flower.

'I wonder why it is, Eirlys,' she said, 'that whereas the butterflies come to you, the wasps visit me?'

'Can't imagine. Can you, Hannah?'

'I'll give it some thought.'

Eirlys prattled on in the background. Dora's mind drew off and in her imagination she was walking up, up into the woodlands, her body criss-crossed with shadow, past the vixen's lair. Hannah had taken her to Oystermouth Cemetery on the far side of the scarp last week, round by the road. So full of history, she'd said: all bourgeois Victorian Swansea was there, under marble bedsteads and flocks of winged spirits in white stone, the like of which Dora had not seen since she went to visit Marx in Highgate. She'd never before realised that there was a huge burial ground over the scarp. *I found it the first night I was here*, Hannah had said. Now Dora climbed in imagination through the rustling trees, until, as the scarp levelled out, she found herself in the city of the dead, where one-winged angels lay in long grass and an army of cherubs gestured confusedly to a better world, one pointing up, the next down.

'But when I was in Pucklechurch—'

'In *Pucklechurch*, Eirlys?' On the edge of sleep, Dora started and her heart skipped a beat. She could not have heard right. 'Whatever do you mean, Pucklechurch?'

'Well, it's a women's prison, Dora. Near Gloucester.'

'I know what and where it is, Eirlys, but when were *you* in prison?'

'Several times! Over the Welsh language.'

'Eirlys!'

'Shocked, are you, darling?'

'Surprised. You never said.'

'You never asked.'

Dora saw Eirlys's eyes kindle. *I love and admire you very much, but there is a region of me you do not know*, was the text of Eirlys's face.

'Were you at the prison near Sainsbury's?' Hannah asked.

'That is a men's prison, Hannah dear, so they could not put us there. Waldo was there. No, there's no women's prison in Wales, you see, so when we offend, they have to send us over the border. Do bear that in mind if you ever think of offending. Were you ever in Pucklechurch then, Dora?'

'No. My daughter was. In the autumn of nineteen sixty-eight.'

Ah. A silence. Dora looked away. What if they had coincided, Eirlys and Rosa? And could Eirlys bring a memory of her daughter out of hiding, add to the fragments that were coming from the internet and the letters in the books? Dora's heart hammered and she was conscious of that unpleasant fizzing sensation in her temple, as if Rosa might be about to appear from behind a tree and step lightly down to them in a cotton dress and sandals.

'No, I was there, I think in spring of that year. I don't remember any politicals by the name of Urquhart.'

'No, her name was Rosa Little. Her father's name.'

'Ah. Little ... Maybe she will come back to me.'

Dora had never, as far as she could remember, spoken Rosa's name at The Eyrie. Of course, they will have known that she'd had a child or children, seen Keir or Karl visiting. But perhaps they had taken the two men for her sons, or just not given the matter any thought. There was a pause. Dora could feel Eirlys and Hannah waiting to see if she would say more. They held their peace and did not ask the questions that must naturally have arisen in their minds. Dora saw them exchange a warning look.

'So tell us,' said Hannah. 'What was it like, Eirlys?'

'Vile. In prison you're nothing. They strip you bare when you get in and the doctors are not respectful; they examine, you know ... it's not pleasant. Dora knows.'

'It is a form of institutionalised rape,' said Dora.

Eirlys arranged her skirts over her knees and bunched the soft fabric of her top between her fingers.

'One pair of knickers a week. One bath a week. Shock to us nice, high-minded middle-class Welsh girls, I can tell you. We were not popular with the other girls. Tourists we were to them, and a hard time they gave us. Understandably. I went in a language protester, Dora, and came out a socialist and feminist. So there you are.'

'You are a dark horse, Eirlys. You did well.'

'Famous I was! Even mentioned in the English Parliament – think of that. When we got to Pucklechurch, you see, our visitors would come and we'd talk to them in Welsh. How could the screws know we were not fomenting revolution? So we were forbidden to talk Welsh, our own first language. And then it was raised in the House: "Women in an English jail not allowed to speak Welsh!" My poor mam thought Dad would have a heart attack. Not a bit of it. He came to visit and said – in Welsh, mind – that St Paul had been in prison for Truth, and he just wondered whether I was doing it for the excitement or for the cause? Which was a good question.'

'What was a good question, Auntie Eirlys?'

Oh no, here they came, Eirlys's nearest and dearest, to claim her, invading The Eyrie's private space. A round of kissing and exclamation began. And there was Waldo, late of Swansea jail, in a Patagonian hat, which did indeed raise him in her esteem, so Dora made an effort to welcome him by calling over, '*Bore da*, Waldo!' Perhaps he did not understand her Welsh, or even recognise it as Welsh, because he greeted her in English and stood looking up at the woodlands, as if trying to catch thrush-song or a haiku. Then he crouched to speak to Hannah, who came out of her shell for the first time that day.

Dora watched the family eating Eirlys alive. All of them wanted and needed Auntie Eirlys. They must have her. Would she be free to baby-sit her niece? Someone needed her to admire her daughter's bridesmaid's outfit, which was in claret satin with big puff sleeves that Aeronwy didn't like but they couldn't be altered because of the style and the expense. Well, will you tell her, Auntie Eirlys? Tell her she's got to like them? Could Eirlys lend someone that recipe for cheese straws or, better still, show her how to bake them? A lad in dungarees just wanted Auntie's lap to sit on and suck his dummy.

My God, thought Dora, she is a communal udder, and she raised her newspaper between herself and them like a barricade.

As she departed, Eirlys looked at Dora with an expression more moody than she normally allowed herself. *Don't forget, while I am being forcibly removed by my nearest and dearest,* her face said, *I am still the person who has been to prison for my beliefs.*

Feeble, Dora felt, lassitudinous. Sleep claimed her. The last thing that went through her mind before she nodded off was the fact that she still had her own teeth. Not every single one, of course, but the gaps were concealed at the back. She licked round her gums, allowing her tongue-tip to prowl the missing teeth.

A whirring of wings in the wood.

Then Rosa arrived.

She is here, Dora realised. She never went away. We made a mistake about that.

Mother and daughter seemed to be on a moorland, picnicking, the heather in bloom all around them beside a tarn. Dora turned her back on the black water. The wee lassie, no more than three years old, mustn't on any account tumble in. Great dark eyes and chestnut curls, plump cheeks and limbs. She's tendering her secret smile and holding her arms out, there she is, look at her with a lap full of bilberries, in her yellow dress, and Dora bends to scoop her up in her arms, to feel the darling armful of Rosa's heavy body. The bilberries will crush and bloody the frock. Never mind. We can pick new fruit. Dora's body knows, before she has fully caught Rosa up, how the lassie's arms will cling round her neck and her thighs will clasp her hips.

Such a characterful chatterbox, even at this age. What warm sunlight, perhaps too warm, for it becomes evident that Rosa is made of dark chocolate, the bitter chocolate Dora loves, and she is melting. She puts Rosa down. In the dream, Dora stands and can't help laughing through her tears to see the chocolate girl melt into a pool.

Awakening, Dora saw rust-edged buddleia blossoms bounce slightly in the heat; heard the surf of the woods, in the breeze. Rosa would have been in her sixties, the bittersweet chocolate girl. She would have had grey hair and a bus pass.

Dora's newspaper was lying on the grass, open at the article about the Italian Unabomber. Dora had seen children in Catalonia with their hands torn off. The Italian Fascists had dropped anti-personnel bombs marked 'Chocolate' and of course the little ones hadn't seen chocolate for years so they came scampering out and picked them up.

Dora had come rushing out into the sunlight, calling, *No, no! Don't touch!* She had scooped up a wee laddie spouting blood. She'd had to hold his foot on while she rushed him to the medics; it had hung by a cord.

It was something you tried to vomit out of your system. It tempted you to say with Sophocles: *Not to be born is best.*

'What is it, Dora?'

Dora must have cried out. She fended off Hannah's concern. And my goodness, in this touchy-feely age, how they pounced on your personal space without asking permission. Dora put out both hands to push Hannah away from the crevice in her armour that had opened to this disabling arrow of compassion. She had no wish to hear ignorant clichés about how terrible it was, against nature, for a parent to outlive her child. Instead of pushing Hannah away, she found that she had caught her by the shoulders and was staring into her eyes, tears pouring down her face.

Too late. Dora wished to be as she had been, sealed away behind walls within walls: at the heart of the silent, empty Russian doll of grief. Her safe place had been blown open.

'You're all right, Dora, everything's all right. I'm here. It's Hannah. I'd do anything for you, Dora.'

Dora calmed right down. 'I know. Take no notice. Sit you down now, Hannah,' she said, to put a distance between them.

But since Dora was holding both Hannah's hands, the lassie had no choice but to kneel beside her and pointed out that Dora would have to let go if she really wanted her to back off. They both laughed and Dora relaxed her grip, but Hannah stayed where she was on the grass and Dora was glad of it. She stroked the top of the girl's head, warm in the sun.

'Can you tell me what it was?' Hannah asked.

'I was dreaming about Rosa – that was my daughter's name; after Rosa Luxemburg.'

'Such a beautiful name.'

'Aye. Don't gush. Why are you crying? There's no need to cry.'

'Because you are.'

They both blew their noses.

'Rosa, you see, was a risk, she was a risk I took. All those poor angry Patiences of my generation – and lying Verities. She was an anarchist. To the left of me.'

'Wow!'

'You may say so. We did. And what did she do for a living? My dear, somewhat literalist Rosa did not believe in property of any sort, so she sponged off anyone she could.'

They had quarrelled, Dora said, and kept on quarrelling. Recriminations, grudges, scores to be settled, explosions.

'And I said things to her ...'

'But, Dora, that was normal.'

'What was normal?'

'Winding each other up. It's true, though, isn't it? Kids have to row with you to be free of you. Everyone does that. I wish I could have done that with my parents, but they weren't around to beat against.'

'Do you?'

Dora was oddly comforted by the banal perception that there was an element of normality in the relations between herself and her daughter, although Rosa had been nearly thirty when she died: hardly a teenager. She'd latched on to the Sixties youngsters and continued, or rather escalated, her madness.

Dora yawned. The right-hand side of her face seethed with

those pins and needles: all strong emotion must be paid for. She let Hannah bring her sandwiches and lemonade, and took the opportunity to ask her to sort out her archive. Hannah would love to, she said. She was taking a fortnight's holiday and it would be a great thing to do. When could she start? Whenever she liked, Dora said, but it would be a herculean task. Was Hannah sure she wanted to give up her precious holiday to start humping books around? But yes, she wanted to start this afternoon.

'In that case, please start with the atlas,' Dora instructed her. 'It is on the top saucepan shelf. I'm tired now.'

What a wonderful job, Hannah thought. She forgot to keep looking at her mobile phone, though she took care to check – surreptitiously – on Dora every half-hour or so, dozing in the shade under her Basque beret. How shocking it had been to see Dora lose control. Hannah had felt as if a landslide were beginning; the earth shifting beneath her feet. But Dora had steadied. It had just been a dream. She was all right now.

Hannah was to bring the books down, sort and catalogue them, dust and check for enclosures. Eirlys would be glad to hear that Hannah had been ordered to start with the books and papers that had strayed into Dora's kitchen. Coughing with the dust, Hannah took down the atlas and opened it. The volume contained a mass of newspaper cuttings.

She leafed through them. The obituaries for Rosa Little. Pictures of a striking young woman sitting on a man's shoulders, making a fist in a crowd of demonstrators. Long straight hair, almost black, jeans and a T-shirt. The paper was yellow with age but Rosa looked modern. You could meet her on the street and not think she looked out of place or time.

And there was a likeness. Hannah's mouth went dry. She poured herself a glass of water; sat down shakily with the cuttings in her lap.

Dora had wanted her to see and read these papers. And through them see and read something in herself.

The *Morning Star* and the *Daily Worker* glorified Rosa Little as a tireless fighter for the proletariat. An anti-fascist martyr. The broadsheets condemned her as, at best a *naïf*, at worst an assassin. They reported her foolhardy attempt to cross the Channel wearing a belt packed with explosives, with the intention of blowing up General Franco. She'd got no further than Harwich, where she had been taken into custody. Convicted as a terrorist, Rosa had died after contracting meningitis at Pucklechurch Prison.

Court case. Prison. Meningitis. Death. All within a year.

The face, with its dark, sad, scornful eyes, shook Hannah. The likeness was clear. For all the hostility between mother and daughter, Rosa had been trying to fight Dora's battle. She did it for you, Dora, Hannah thought. And you have had to live with that.

Dora dozed again. At one point Mrs Dark came out and advanced into the sunlight.

'Mrs Dark! Whatever are you doing out of doors?'

She was dressed in flowered navy-blue and thick woollen stockings that must be fiercely hot in this weather. Her forehead was beaded with perspiration. She looked into the heat haze with reproach and cautioned Dora against exposure to the destructive ultraviolet rays.

'It's your health, Miss Urquhart, your health you should be attending to. Sunbathing at our age, you know, it is not to be recommended. Not at any age. Not even in the shade.'

She complained about the noise the new people made and asked if Dora had seen and heard strange things.

'I do not believe I have, Mrs Dark,' said Dora. 'But what kind of strange things do you mean?'

'Well, up there, Miss Urquhart. Whatever is he doing?'

The fire alarm man was looking out through a pair of binoculars.

'Well, he may perhaps be an ornithologist,' said Dora.

'Or a peeping Tom.'

‘I hardly think so, Mrs Dark. I believe he is a refugee. I do not think he speaks English.’

‘Doesn’t speak *English*?’

Dora waved up in a friendly way to the man whose name had sounded like ‘Flood’, as far as she could remember. He withdrew at once.

‘Everything is changing,’ said Mrs Dark. ‘I for one do not understand what is happening. We shall be overrun.’

She retreated into the building, saying that someone should report this to someone.

Dora dropped off again.

Ruth and Max Norton appeared, carrying between them a red plastic basket full of wet washing, which they pegged out together, chirruping away, and walking back into the building hand in hand.

Adam and Eve in Paradise, Dora thought. She raised her hand in blessing.

The sun was behind the ridge when Dora woke again. The Testosterone Men had taken in their towels. Her mouth was furred from sleep but her burnt arms and legs were soothed by the late afternoon cool.

Then Mrs Menelaus appeared.

14

The luxury cruise liner anchored in Swansea Bay had been there, Eirlys's brother Tom said, for several days. Summer visitors drifting along the front pointed and gazed out, shielding their eyes with their hands. Tom said the liner would lie at anchor there for several days and nobody would come ashore. Eirlys imagined the cruise passengers frolicking and tippling out there on their floating island, occasionally coming on deck in the midst of their pleasures to glance to shore or peer through binoculars at all of us looking out at them. In the heat haze across the eggshell-blue sea, the liner resembled a phantom ship, built tall and solid; more like a building than a boat.

They have escaped, thought Eirlys, as they drove towards town. Then she asked herself: But for how long?

They too had to come home when their fortnight or month was up, didn't they? Think of the pounds they'd put on through all that stuffing of their faces with endless courses served by Filipino paupers. Think of their struggles with their cases at the docks, returning to their responsibilities with a fading tan. Also they might have caught the tummy bug that was one of the perils of the sea in these voyages.

So there was always something to be thankful for.

'Anyway, I never wanted to be a rotten bridesmaid,' Aeronwy continued. 'I only said I would to stop Mum nagging but now I've said, I won't be seen *dead* in that dress.'

Eirlys said she would look at the dress when they arrived home and perhaps some compromise could be reached. Personally, she didn't think so. She could imagine Aeronwy, who was at the age when one generally prefers horses to humans, stomping up the aisle in a prize sulk. Though when the time came, and the organ music and the bridal veil floated through the great chapel of Libanus, Aeronwy would probably be awed into playing her part appropriately. Probably.

At last Eirlys had told Dora about prison. And Dora's daughter had been there. She would ask around and see if anyone remembered her. Tom was saying something about a sturgeon that had been caught from Mumbles Pier, containing eight hundred pounds worth of caviar.

'A tidy bucketful was that,' he said.

Aeronwy said, 'Puff sleeves are *disgusting*. They make me want to puke.'

And she slapped the leg of little Dylan, who had been nodding off a treat in his baby-seat.

'Shushy shushy,' said Eirlys to both children, for Aeronwy was still a child herself, though she would not thank you for pointing it out. And her objection to puff sleeves was as understandable in its way as Dylan's bellowing rage at his sister's act of violence to his thigh. Eirlys reached over to rub the lad's hurt place, and blessed a kiss on to Aeronwy's forehead on the way.

'And purple!' shrieked Aeronwy. 'A purple fucking dress! I'll be a laughing stock!'

'It's not purple, it's magenta, the assistant said so in the shop, so you can shut up,' her mother snarled, and swerved around the West Cross roundabout.

Her father said that if Aeronwy *ever* struck Dylan again, she would be grounded for a week, and if he ever heard her fucking swear again, he would ... words failed him, they absolutely did.

'I think we're all feeling a bit hot,' Eirlys soothed. Aeronwy was squirming and twisting her entire body in her seat. 'Let Auntie Eirlys open the window and we'll get a good blow of air through our hair, shall we, darling?'

Aeronwy shrugged and then went quiet as Eirlys blasted her with the cool breeze.

Of course, thought Eirlys, I already have a cruise liner. What else was The Eyrie but a berthed liner, riding against the high green wave of the wooded cliff? And she was lucky, for there was nothing but ground rent and upkeep of the communal buildings to pay, and the cruise never ended, except when, like Megan, you were evicted by your nearest and dearest as an unfit sailor. How fortunate, she caught herself thinking, that she had no children of her own to winkle her out when the time came. Of course, she had decades yet before she had to deal with this, but perhaps it would be as well to ask, say, Hannah, to assume enduring power of attorney over her, rather than Tom or, imagine it, Aeronwy? Waldo's side of the family was, of course, more to be relied on. But she would not like to upset the Harries side.

Whatever she did, it must be kept secret from her nearest and dearest, that was clear. She had become close to Hannah and fond of her since their chat in the woods. She felt that the young woman would act with integrity. Of course, one could ask Dora: that was the natural choice, but Dora would hardly outlast her.

She could feel Aeronwy's soft head on her shoulder and, looking down, her eyes met the slate-greyness of her niece's. They signalled, *Sorry, auntie fach*, with a rueful smile that was purely in the eyes, not on the lips at all. Eirlys's heart twisted and she took Aeronwy's long, slender fingers in her own.

Aeronwy whispered confidentially, as if the news must come as a surprise to her aunt, 'I still don't like puff sleeves and I won't wear them. I want my dress to be strappy.'

'Stroppy perhaps!' said Tilda. 'Stroppy I can go with.'

'Hey, hey,' said Eirlys to Tilda, and allowed herself to wink at her niece. The television programmes on childcare insisted that adults must never betray one another's authority, and in general Eirlys approved of this doctrine. But in the case of Tilda she made exceptions. Aeronwy grinned and piped down.

Tom was saying something about the pier and how it was falling to pieces, it was a public disgrace, and the stink from the gulls that nested on the ledges was overpowering.

'Guava, that is,' volunteered Aeronwy.

'Guano, I think you mean.'

'I don't *think* so.'

Aeronwy waggled her head in a completely berserk manner, intimating that her parents were inane beyond all telling. She said she had done guava in biology, she ought to know, that bats defecated in caves, so there, and that her parents were mingers.

Eirlys mediated all the way to Glais, regretting that Aeronwy's parents had not seen fit to catch the olive branch the girl had proffered in the form of the guava remark, for she had created a moment where the tension might have been eased.

A relief to arrive at the modern, comfortable home which to Eirlys seemed spacious but to Tom and Tilda, whose friends apparently lived in splendour, was 'poky'. That was the price you paid, according to Tom, for wanting to live near your roots. It was beautiful, though, and tasteful, and always there was some new purchase to admire, an item of furniture or a vase. Was it Dora's influence, Eirlys wondered, that made her impatient with the family bosom where she had nestled gratefully and thought herself privileged? She was too often bathed in nostalgia for her days of protest. The Eyrie seemed a place where they dreamed of old certainties, dreaming inward to one another.

Eirlys found herself in the kitchen. She was showing her cousin Joan's tots how to mix a cake. Such fun it was. Three flaxen boys poked their forefingers into the bowl and sucked off the mixture, big-eyed, then cantered round and round the table when the cake-tins had been put in the oven, shouting, 'More! More!' and hanging on to Eirlys's blue dress in a rather alarming way.

'Gently! Gently!' In a hushed voice, she asked everyone to keep an eye on the glass of the oven door and let Auntie know the very moment they spotted the cake begin to rise. Two other nephews and several neighbourhood children made their way into the kitchen, lured by the scents of cinnamon, lemon and chocolate. The tribe all watched so devoutly, so silently, that Eirlys could overhear negotiations for her baby-sitting services going on in the lounge, where Tom had brought out a bottle of Australian plonk.

It was so nice to have Eirlys, everyone agreed. Eirlys was a darling. She was so obliging. Comfy she was, like Mam and Mam-gu.

The cake was rising, the solemn group of cake-watchers reported. Good, said Eirlys; it will go golden-brown, she told them, and the chocky one will swell all dark and yummy. So keep watching, everyone.

'Eirlys, you are so *good* with them!' someone called from the lounge. What would they do without her? they wondered, as they marvelled at her magic powers. For if they attempted to bake a cake with the kids (which, on the whole, they didn't have time to do because of the God-awful stress at work), all hell broke loose. One of the kids would be whacking his sister with a wooden spoon, and invariably an egg or something else would fall on the floor, and you would end up with a cremation on one hand and pandemonium on the other.

'Come on, Eirlys, you've done enough in here,' called Tilda, who had suffered postnatal depression three times and Eirlys had helped out, sometimes overnight. It had come as a shock to Tilda, on all three occasions, that when you got pregnant, a real live human being emerged, red and bald and puking, with a bunched face like a fist. But Tilda was cheerful and chummy now and led Eirlys by the hand out of the kitchen, settling her in Dad's old chair with the head-cloth embroidered by Mam still there. She rested her head back where his head, bless him, had rested. And whereas at first there had been great sadness at taking his place, now there was only comfort as she sank back into the dent his dear, good head had made. Somehow, with all his foibles and crotchets, his dry wit and warm beneficence, there was a calm he could still bring her, just through having been there.

'Tom, cut slices of Eirlys's cake, would you?' called Tilda. 'If it's cool. Well, even if it isn't. Stop fussing. If it's hot, it will cool down, won't it? You are so good to us, Eirlys.'

Oh, get on with it, thought Eirlys crossly.

'Give Eirlys that big slice,' Tilda pressed on. 'No, not that one, Tom – the one over there. God, you are hopeless sometimes.'

Tom, who was still the Tom who had gone tadpoling with

Eirlys, played ball games in the yard, who had dressed up in her frocks just to see what it was like being a girl, was ashamed and held back from the dirty work.

Eirlys was being treated to the best helping of what her own hands had made.

'Not for me,' she said. 'I'll pass on this one. I'm just cutting down on confectionery – cakes and ice creams and biscuits, everything sweet. Got to watch the pounds, isn't it?'

'Don't be silly, *you* don't have to watch your figure.'

'It's my heart, see. Cholesterol.'

Tilda, who was always dieting away the last pregnancy and was enviably slender, maintained it was different.

Oh, and why was it different?

Aeronwy said she would help out if Eirlys didn't want the grub, and stop nagging at Auntie to eat, she knows if she doesn't want to eat, she's not a baby. Don't keep on, boring, boring. She bit into her slice vigorously. Eirlys laughed.

'You will not speak to your father like that!' said Tom. 'Go to your room.'

'No.'

'I said—'

Tilda interrupted them. 'Leave it, Tom. It's her hormones. Eirlys, I'll cut you that nice slice.'

I'm going to be as slim as you are, thought Eirlys. Nobody's ever going to bounce me like a ball again. Force-feeding it was, like the suffragettes or what they do to geese. Cramming it down their gizzards.

'Aeronwy,' she said.

'Yes, Auntie?'

'Come and sit down by here with me. And no cheekiness, right?'

'Right.'

Aeronwy quietly folded herself down into the chair next to Eirlys, licked her thumb and began to leaf backwards through a magazine. Nice as ninepence. The other children were turned out into the garden. They carried their huge ball of noise away to someone else's house.

Played right into their hands had Eirlys. Digging her own grave.

'See how good she is with the kids,' Tilda cooed. 'What we were wondering, Eirlys, is, if Tom and I could somehow or other get away from all the stress for a week or ten days?' She had not been feeling herself lately, and Tom was completely knackered, he was annihilated by the pressures on him at work, life in a solicitors' office could be mean, they would both end up on Prozac, she had seen the doctor and he had said, *You must de-stress, Matilda, or you will self-destruct.* Those were his words. It was an order. The doctor had said, hadn't he, Tom?, that she and Tom must take a proper break; a weekend was neither here nor there.

Tom said nothing, but was blushing to the roots of his hair. Eirlys had known him from before his birth, when he was a bundle of knees and elbows squirming round in Mam's belly, the first of the longed-for boys. He'd left all the work to his wife: the thumbscrew and the arm-lock.

'I didn't know you were ill, Tom,' said Eirlys. 'Should you be in bed?'

'Well, not ill exactly. As such.'

'Yes, you are, Tom. He won't admit it, Eirlys, he is in denial.'

'What are your symptoms, dear?' pursued Eirlys relentlessly.

'His blood pressure,' Tilda came in.

'Is?'

'Giving cause for concern.'

'Yeah, cool,' said Aeronwy without looking up from the magazine. 'Let those two buzz off to Spain. They've already booked, I can give you the dates. They want you to come and look after us. It's a fortnight they've booked.'

A small red fishing boat was becalmed in the great oval pearl of the sea.

'Cruise liner there was, this morning,' said the taxi driver.

'Yes, I saw it. Do they never dock at all?' Eirlys asked him.

'Don't know, my darling. Doubt it. They might do in Venice or Athens, for the history and the ruins. No ruins, see, in Swansea.'

'Oh, I don't know.'

'No exotic ones anyhow. 'Cept me, of course.'

They passed a small band of Highland pipes and drums, proceeding with melancholy skirling around the bay towards the pier. Eirlys thought it must be hot wearing those white spats and heavy plaids in this weather.

'You would think so,' said her driver. 'But heritage it is, see.'

As they drew up at the flats, Eirlys felt such a wave of relief that she stumbled getting out of the cab and had to grip the door for support. She would draw down the blinds on both windows and sit in the friendly and unexploitative dark.

But even as she secured the chain on her front door, the rot of guilt set in, and the knowledge came that it would eat away at her and prey upon her peace of mind until, her stomach in knots, she would wish she had yielded to their claims rather than, uncharacteristically, rebelled.

Almost. But not quite. The moment when it had been suggested that Eirlys was so like Mam it was uncanny had been the point at which she turned.

Their idea of Mam was evidently less bracing and more conventional than her memory. She supposed it was partly that, being a boy, Tom had been more indulged. Mam had perhaps confirmed his sense that a cut knee was a tragedy; but the girls, their knees all grey and scabbed from frequent tree-climbing and tumbling, were taught stoicism. They did not boo-hoo at every small calamity, for boo-hooing was not countenanced in girls. The boys had a softer mam.

Was that normal? She did not know.

'I'm not available,' she had told them. 'I have a life of my own to lead. Me! Good old Eirlys! A life!'

She could not now remember what else had come tumbling out of her mouth. She, the peace-loving Eirlys. The kangaroo pouch. She'd stayed all day, doing everything expected of her, meek and mild, before exploding. They had gawped gormlessly at one another as she allowed the dam on her reservoir of resentment to burst. A great big hand-knitted jumper, the size of Wales, was unravelling.

No, she would not like a lift home. No, she would not accept one. Thank you, it was nice to be independent and do things under your own steam.

Aeronwy had squealed with excitement and trampolined on Dad's chair when Eirlys vacated it. *Good on yer, Auntie Eirlys! Give them hell, man!* she'd squawked, letting out a great yodelling rugby call. And this had to be taken as disinterested solidarity, for Aeronwy had stood to gain a fortnight's liberation under Eirlys's more mellow regime. She could have brought her mates home and fed them with the products of Auntie's slaving, handed them roll-ups over cans of cider at nightly sleepovers. Stayed out late and been tattooed from head to foot.

Nevertheless, the twanging of the aged springs of Dad's chair and the shouts of an excitable fourteen-year-old could hardly count as the most credible back-up. Plus there had been mayhem in Aeronwy's voice and the suspicion of panicky tears building behind her eyes. One does not take a niece's needs lightly. Nieces are given by God. Almost as soon as she had spoken, Eirlys had begun to flutter with panic. Most people had partners with whom to form a *folie à deux*. The partner would stick up for you whether you were right or wrong. Tom and Tilda were now glued together at every pore. Tom was no longer the brother he had been, united by tadpoles and ball games.

Eirlys felt, as she dropped her handbag on her settee and filled the kettle, woefully alone.

The doorbell rang. Deep breath. Now for it.

But it was only Hannah.

'Oh, dear ... How are you, Eirlys? You look down. Am I in the way?'

No, Hannah must come in. Eirlys, her head bursting, sat Hannah down by the busy lizzie and looked round for something to give her. One must always give something. But she had come over all trembly and apologetic, and she was not sorry to have her neighbour fuss over her for a change.

'Talk to me,' she begged, and the room was magnified and blurred through a tear that wobbled on her eye. 'About anything. About what you have been doing.'

And it seemed that Hannah had had a phone call from her half-brother's family – she'd tell Eirlys about it another time – but anyway the call had given her such a turn that she'd put down the work she'd been doing for Dora and gone out on her bike for a while to calm down, and had forgotten to check on Dora. But she'd glanced into the back garden when she'd come home and found Dora sitting exactly where they'd left her. Hours and hours ago. Hannah had felt awful about it because she'd meant to keep checking up on her.

'What, all day in the sun? Oh, no. Was she all right?'

'She was a bit burnt. Not too bad because she'd been in the shade for a while. But she was a little odd.'

'Heatstroke?'

'I don't know, Eirlys. She'd been dreaming. Said she'd seen Mrs Menelaus.'

'No. Oh, dear.'

'Yes, but she was all right about it. They'd had a nice conversation.'

'But still, chatting with the dead? That does not seem like Dora.'

'And she said Mrs Dark came out—'

'Into the sun?'

'Yes. Imagine.'

'Well.'

'She didn't stay long apparently. Anyway, Dora was desperate for a pee but otherwise she was fine, I thought. And we stayed out till Dora said she could hear bagpipes, which, for some reason, she particularly abhors. You don't expect them here, do you? But Dora has a keen ear for that kind of kitsch, so she says, so we ... are you feeling better?'

'I saw the pipes and drums promenading along the front. By

Blackpill they were, with the chappie whirling the baton in front. It's funny Dora is hostile to them. Being a Scot.'

'Ah, but Dora is a sort of pacifist Internationalist, isn't she?' Hannah pointed out, and Eirlys could see how it followed that she would detest the march of kilts. It was the militarism behind the sporran that Dora objected to, they agreed.

'Listen. She's coming,' said Hannah. The slow clumping on the stairs signalled Dora in her heavy sandals. 'Chance for you to see whether she's all right after all that.'

When Dora put her head around the door, she said that she had come all the way to South Wales to escape the pipes and drums and then, when she believed herself to be quite safe, what happened? They followed her all the way down here. For now they were apparently on the march from the pier and headed back to town.

'Ah, but I do love a good lament,' said Eirlys. 'A pibroch, say. There's nothing like a good lament to lift the spirits.'

'I was thinking about Mrs Menelaus out there,' said Dora. 'Such a memorable lady. And dear Hannah has begun the cataloguing of my archive.'

That was all right then. Eirlys felt Hannah relax.

Later Eirlys wandered down to the front. A blessed coolness had followed the intense heat of the day and the sunburnt people had taken their children home or disappeared into the pubs and clubs and eateries that had mushroomed round the bay. Alone by the inky sea she sat on a step and listened in to the plash of the waters.

Around the bay's not quite closed circle was suspended a beaded necklace of amber lights. *Lovelier than Naples*, their dad used to say in that last year before he died. He'd only been able to walk slowly. All his children and their families had walked with and around him in a gentle, protective swarm. Dad's human shield against death.

Human shields have no effect. The water at her feet was darkly troubled.

There was no need for Eirlys to be alone. There was no

possibility of that, no. None. The black waves now made a chuckling, plopping sound as they broke along the steps, coursing down to her, passing her by. Gentle and monotonous. Eirlys was not like Hannah and Dora, wild and renegade. She did not condemn their footloose condition; in fact, she envied them. But she would never be vagrant. They could go anywhere and be equally at home, or not at home. Eirlys could only be fixed here. Planted.

It was not only the craven guilt that held Eirlys in place and told her she would surrender to the designs of Tilda and Thomas (despite knowing that Tilda had been grossly at fault and that Tom was hiding behind his wife), but Eirlys was also part of a root-system to which her being clung with every blind filament.

Still, she could and would still slim. She'd shed the blubber she carried around as if she were bearing the weight of half of someone else's body. She need not be quite as comfy, Eirlys thought, walking up the dark hill through pools of lamplight; Hannah would lend her her bike, or perhaps she'd get one of her own. She let herself into the flat to find the phone ringing.

Waldo had been composing inside a stone circle, he told her on the phone. Having expected Tom or Tilda, ringing either to activate or to forgive her, Eirlys was doubly pleased to hear her cousin's voice.

'Lovely that is,' she said. 'I can't wait to hear them.'

Not many poets, he said, had attempted the haiku in Welsh, and he expected to be laughed to scorn. If you were a genius, you could go your own way. Of course, he was not a genius, no really, thank you for disagreeing, but he wasn't. There was nothing he respected so much as an englyn, he said, she knew that. But when a series of haikus had struck him like frisbees, what could a poor hack do but put up his hand to receive them?

'*Ah, cariad*,' she said. '*O'r gorau*.'

'You always understand.'

'You've spoken to Tom and Tilda, I suppose?'

'Aye, I've been Tilda-ed. Plenty.'

'So you heard about my outburst? My not being "comfy"?'

Waldo denied indignantly that Eirlys had ever been comfy. If anyone said so in his hearing, they would have him to reckon with. He would knock the buggers down. He would not have Eirlys spoken of as if she were some kind of sofa.

'By the way,' he went on, 'I agreed with Tom that Ianto and I would move in to give them a break. No probs. I'm afraid they're a bit insensitive sometimes. Tom feels bad about it, Eirlys. You know he thinks the world of you. Please don't imagine otherwise.'

Eirlys immediately went into a nose-dive: he mustn't put himself out, she'd been a bit temperamental what with the heat, and said things she shouldn't. She would sit in, of course she would, it was only a fortnight after all, what is Family for?

Waldo took it all obliquely but resolutely, and would not be diverted.

'You can visit, of course, if you feel like it, Eirlys. We always like to see you for a bit of intelligent conversation. And, well, comradeship. Oh, and how's Hannah, by the way? Doing very well with the Welsh she is: it must be your good influence. And I nearly forgot, *bach.* Aeronwy sends her love and says, "Tell Auntie, hey, she's a star, she's a shooting fucking star."'

15

Hannah had passed through the door into her father's world. The house where he had been born and his father and grandfather before him.

High on Trewyddfa Hill, she let her eyes wander over the panorama of Llangyfelach beneath her. She looked down over the complex of slate roofs that led over her people's Chingtown, across Tyrpenry and Pentrepoeth, Tan-y-Lan and Clasemont; her gaze paused at the spire of Libanus and moved west over the flat plain where the enterprise park had taken the place of the tall chimneys of the Dyffryn tinplate works, and, a little nearer, the Morganite. The labyrinths of streets, unchanged for centuries, her stalking-ground. She knew them like the back of her hand.

Panic had shaken her as she'd knocked on Siân Taylor's door, wiped her feet on the mat, stepped over the threshold. At once she'd known in her bones that her brother was not there: all the toys had been tidied away. Paul had taken Jake out for the afternoon, Siân said. There'd only been Siân – well, and the people in the photographs.

They'd sat in the kitchen by the open window, and Hannah had thought, I'm in now, I'm into his space at last.

The interior was plain and uncluttered, the walls painted cream to lighten the cramped space. Outside, Hannah could see the hutch for Jake's rabbit. Siân looked impossibly young, a small, sturdy, no-nonsense woman with short curly hair, dressed in white T-shirt and jeans. She was tense and abrupt, understandably. Hannah had seen her in a bad temper before, throwing shoes around, as mothers did.

What had been said? Something about Jake's earache. Then Hannah had asked about a blurred photograph, which turned out to be of her great-great-grandfather Francis with his work-mates at the Dyffryn, wearing leather aprons, cloth caps and white cloths round their necks. Another picture showed him in the uniform of a private of the Welsh fusiliers before going off to France in the Great War. And Siân had let fall that she'd known him. Not only known him (he'd been two years short of a century when he died) but for a couple of years he'd lived with them here in Quarry Street. Lovely man he'd been, according to Siân. Never discussed the war. A quiet soul. He'd liked to put his feet up on the fender and smoke his pipe of St Bruno's tobacco and listen to his budgie cheeking him.

Siân had been born round the corner in Pwll Glo Street. And her grandparents had had seventeen children. All in a house as small as this, she'd said, two up, two down, think of that – though they'd farmed some of them out, mind, to relatives, and some of course had died in childhood. Think of the mathematics of that, she'd said. You'll see that everyone is related to everyone else round here – and people tend not to leave, or, if they leave, they circle back, like your father.

The conversation had only really begun when Siân asked, 'What do you want with us, Hannah?'

'What I want, what I would like, is for you to think about whether it's in Jake's interest to know that he and I are related.'

'There must be a hell of a lot of hurt in you,' the woman had said, coldly, as if you had to be careful of people bringing their hurt into your house.

'I've got a lot more sense and apparently more good feeling than he ever had,' Hannah had said quite sharply. 'I've no idea why he left us for you, or why he never tried to keep in touch.'

'Oh, he didn't,' Siân said.

'What?'

'He came back for a while, but of course he quarrelled with

his parents, and then he took off for London. I was only a kid at the time. He came back again when his parents died and that was when we got together. And you know he can be so charming. Dreamy and gentle. I can't see that it would have lasted long, but then I got pregnant with Jake. He's nearly eight.'

'And then he just cleared off again?'

'I threw him out.'

'Good for you,' said Hannah.

'Yeah, best thing I ever did. And then he was inside for a while.'

'Dealing?'

'That's right.'

Hannah had done some sums on her fingers. Over ten years of her father's life were unaccounted for.

'So there might be a whole string of children between me and Jake waiting to turn up on your doorstep.'

'Oh, my *God*! I hope not!'

Laughter had melted the ice between them. Siân had fetched a couple of cans from the fridge and they'd drunk together. Hannah had explained that she'd like to get to know Jake, on an ordinary, day-to-day basis.

'Let's give it a go,' Siân had said. 'Why not?'

The sense of home-coming was strangely divided between relief and a new apprehension of loss. Loss of heightened feeling perhaps.

This is the territory of *hiraeth*, Hannah thought, burnishing the everyday world with nostalgia. But now that she'd gone through the door, the excitement that made the past a novelty would fade. She'd enter into the ordinariness of family and perhaps, like Eirlys, occasionally cringe from the awfulness of it.

I've got through to you, she said to her father, *but you aren't here.* Yet it was odd: the early dad was the same, untarnished. He read her a story about a green bear. He blew her smoky bracelets. Jack carried Hannah on his back up a steep hill, her arms around his neck, her cheek in his long, tangled hair.

He lay beside her in her rhododendron den, looking up at the patterns of leaves against the light, for hours and hours, perhaps for ever.

16

The Eyrie, with all its petty concerns, closed in on Dora. Pipes gurgled, other people's spin cycles erupted on their washing machines, and radios murmured through the partition membranes.

The heatwave had taken it out of her. She was out of sorts, dragging her weariness about with her. Most depressingly, Max Norton had been singing 'Always look on the bright side of life', round and round, in his rumbling bass, while he hoovered. Well, but the weather had broken now and the castle was shrouded in a veil of wet mist. She thought of coffee and, maybe, cinnamon toast. But what a fag to get up and make it. Mrs Dark was shifting about upstairs in her methodical fashion, performing the small round of her activities at her regular times, treading in her own footsteps, her heels in their serviceable leather slippers drumming softly on Dora's ceiling, like a child's ball bouncing.

Cars swooshed along the wet road. Dora crossed to the window and down there on the forecourt, in his shorts, was Sandy Sanderson hefting out two bags of shopping from his car, saturated in the mesh of fine Swansea rain. And here came Eirlys, bobbing up to him under an umbrella, which she raised jauntily aloft to serve the two of them.

Back, then, are you? And what gratification Eirlys could derive from looking after her brother's children, who had all come down with gastroenteritis, taking over from her precious Waldo, likewise stricken, Dora could not imagine.

She could hear Eirlys now, giving her gamp a good shake on

the doorstep and exchanging a few words with their neighbour. She sounded perky.

Suddenly, enchantment: a silver thrill of birdsong. Through the rainy windowpane, the steep woodland trembled with that call. Dora had the impression that Mrs Dark had paused by her fridge, stooping for the milk (it was precisely her coffee time), arrested by the same outburst. Hannah, perhaps, had laid down a book on her table, catching the arabesque of notes.

Again, amaze me again, thought Dora, and the bird obliged.

Goodness, had the paramour invited Eirlys into his flat? Had she gone in? How strange to enter Megan's world without Megan in it. To view the beige settee where her slight frame had perched and where, in her pretty gentleness, she had smiled. At what, Dora could not conceive. From where she stood, Megan had possessed no earthly reason to smile. But perhaps she too used to hear the bird sing, Dora thought.

Odd how one at first missed Megan's presence; then let it blanch and fade; until, at the very point of disappearance, one was seized by remorse. A vein of querulous superstition warned Dora that a penalty would surely be exacted for turning her back on her neighbour. These things were a system. Very well then: invite Megan here for the day, for surely they were not confined to quarters at Myrrh Lodge? Surely the more able-bodied were permitted – criminals thought unlikely to reoffend – home-visits? But might it unsettle Megan, to spy her own door sealed against her? And if the paramours came strutting out with a surfboard under one arm and a trollop under the other while Megan was passing, how would she feel?

Eirlys and Hannah had reported that Megan, recalling Dora's name, had suddenly stood up and expected her to come through the door. I am remembered, thought Dora, when everyone else is forgotten, and her ego vibrated with the old vanity.

Tell it not in Gath, but she shrank from visiting Megan in that place. Dora knew in advance what its smell would be. The smell, not of dirt, but of need and humiliation, of being at the mercy of others' ministrations. Moral squalour. In her filing cabinet lay the metal box with the escape kit she'd been assembling.

She went there now, just to check: unlocked the file; unlocked the box within the file. She took out the two bottles of sleeping pills she had wheedled out of the doctor. Gently Dora shook them into her palm. She opened and smoothed out in her lap a carefully folded plastic bag with a tie, holding it up to the light to check that it was airtight. Fine. Tried it on at the mirror like a weird item of millinery. The woman with a roomy plastic bag on her head, coming down over her shoulders, looked at her reflection in the glass. Through the plastic, Dora thought her eyes looked sly, crafty, like a child's, playing some solitary game and telling herself that this game is for real. But the child knows fine that she will put her fantasies away and run home to tea. Dora could not, if she were honest with herself, credit that she would actually come to use the kit for real. It was hard even in age to believe that one's darling self could come to an end.

All men are mortal. Socrates is a man. Therefore Socrates is mortal. And history rather reinforced the syllogism.

A-ha! she thought, catching herself out in her vanity, but you, Dora, half-believe a god will come down to save you. How could the world do without your intellect, your brilliance, your sheer goodness?

Yet this strong, craggy body must decay. And when my time comes, I must recognise it, thought Dora, and use my nous, keep my nerve. The loneliness of that final choice made her shudder. All this while she was wearing the bag on her head, breathing in her own carbon dioxide.

Oh, take it off, woman. She did so, shamefacedly. The flat-haired old person in the mirror looked baffled, fearful.

Dora turned away and folded the bag. Teased up her hair. She picked up the bundle of farewell letters she had deposited with the tackle, and sorted them, breathing more easily now. The panic that had towered above her had subsided, for when the time came, she could ask for aid. She could count on Hannah. Coerce her, if need be, though she felt suddenly nervous in case

Hannah should get away. As softly as she had entered Dora's life, she might slip out of it.

It was only transparent plastic that divided Dora from Rosa now. Hannah's excavation of the archive was not so much delivering Rosa to Dora as delivering Dora to Rosa. It was like the hole in the school hedge Dora and her pals had tunnelled out bit by bit as very young lassies, six years old perhaps. And in the event only Dora had had the courage to escape through the privet tunnel. She had found herself on the other side, anathematised and alone.

The rain had lifted and water steamed from trees, grass and roofs as the sun pushed through. Dora poured almonds on muesli and brewed a pot of coffee. Mr Powell was hawking in his flat. How could one cough that loudly, through so many intervening walls? Atrocious, the reek of smoke that hung about his door. Likewise the new man with his burnt chips and binoculars. He smoked, too. They should at least open their windows and give themselves a chance.

But what chance had these men ever had? Weren't they just victims of the cynical cigarette companies, she thought, seeking to work herself up into a customary passion. Of course, I have never really smoked, except when we were young, and then we were all perfect chimneys. It was politically modish to hang a fag from the corner of your mouth, especially for a woman. But not for half a century have I touched the gaspers. Mr Powell has wilfully corrupted his lungs. He has very little healthy lung tissue left. I have all mine. Mr Powell is sixty going on ninety. I am ninety-plus going on sixty.

Dora washed up her bowl and spoon, plugged in the computer and logged on. Rae would be here soon and Dora wanted to push on with the work, for all her doubts. They had found that US military sites were laughably easy to penetrate, even if you had no password. All they needed was some software they had bought legally online and a port scanner. They could see other unauthorised users getting into the same networks from China, Turkey and Holland. Dora would return when Rae had gone home, against her mentor's advice, *for you'll make yourself visible, Miss Urquhart.* Dora would leave little notes on the system administrator's machine. There was a thrill in this forbidden work, for it might well bring the police to The Eyrie one fine day with an arrest warrant.

Such a grey and lifeless day, though. Am I ill? she asked herself. Nothing seemed to enliven her, not even the customary chatter in her brain. Leaving the computer to its own devices, Dora settled herself in an armchair and dropped off into the gloaming of a dream in which she was breastfeeding Rosa in the old lumpy bed in Peckham. Bombs and snow were falling.

Dora gave a start and a quiver. Someone was calling for her! Someone was at the door. She felt for the milk leaking on to her bodice but of course her breasts were dry.

The door was now being quietly tapped and of course here was the prosaic Eirlys, hotfoot from Glais and with tales to tell, Dora supposed, of her numerous kinfolk suffering the throes of a twenty-four-hour bug. On the third day they had all arisen from the dead and ascended to the Chinese takeaway under the care of guardian angel Eirlys. She had been told this on the phone.

'Are you all right?' asked Eirlys. She looked fit and glowing.

'I am always all right. I saw you with our neighbour.'

'I think we misjudged him, you know, Dora.'

And it seemed that the paramour had charmed Eirlys's socks off. He and she had come in under the same brolly; he had invited her in for a cuppa and sat her down, making a flattering fuss of her. The umbrella, Eirlys felt, had created a bond between them, or over them, and allowed him to see that she was not just a boring old spinster past her sell-by date, and her to see that he was an interesting person with lovely manners.

'How old do you think he is, Dora?'

'Hard to say. Which one is he? The tall one? In his forties, perhaps.'

'Yes, I think so, too.'

'But what about Josie? Is she not his partner?'

'No, Dora, Josie is *Alun's* girlfriend. Well, apparently she clings on to him and Alun is too nice a bloke to hurt her . . .'

'Bad psychology.'

Dora was not going to indulge Eirlys's credulous and puerile infatuation with a man, just because he was a man. Nevertheless it was good to see her glow. She felt a chill in her fingers and feet, although it was not a cold day. Dora raised her hands and turned them round meditatively, as though her friend were a coalfire one could bask in. An urge arose to declare her symptoms and have them soothed away. But what were her symptoms? A vague fizz of pins and needles in the arches of her feet and the palms of her hands. Uneasy thoughts dotting her mind like the perishing images that appear on the verge of sleep. Tongue-tinglings and slight nausea. A moment of fear that one was about to pee oneself. She must snap out of this.

'And how are Tom and Matilda, Eirlys? Did they have an enjoyable fortnight?'

'Wonderful, apparently. In Spain they were. And they mentioned that they crossed the River Ebro.'

Instantly Dora felt sour again. She could not bear it that this footling pair were coming back prattling about the Ebro. What did they know? Had they ever been to the real Spain? Hardly. Every inch of soil had been fought for in a land that was now little more than a theme park.

'The place is a holiday camp! It is a burger bar! Well. Go on, do go on with what you were saying. About,' and Dora gave a hollow laugh, 'this place you call "Spain" and I call McDonald's. And your brother's seaside holiday. Just think, they might have had the pleasure of bumping into Hugh and Mary.'

Eirlys wavered. Dora was sorry so she smiled and nodded more cordially, and Eirlys went on.

'Well. Tom is not calling Tilda "woman" any more. They are both very tanned, I will say that. But Tom called Aeronwy a little slut almost as soon as he was in the door, and she flounced off to get "wasted". And the youngest one is acting up and calling his mam "baddy lady" for leaving him – and I said to her, now, don't be hurt, Tilda dear, he's just saying he needs his mam, which made her quite angry with me, which I suppose is understandable.'

'Pardon me, Eirlys, but it is not understandable: it is shameful, if we are seeking an apt epithet. Ingratitude of the most deplorable kind.'

'Certainly,' said Eirlys, and Dora was pleased to see that her Christ-like neighbour was indulging a short flight of vindictiveness, 'they were not what you would call grateful. I expect they had jet lag. I heard them in their room going at it hammer and tongs – I don't mean sex, of course – the word "divorce" as plain as anything and the kiddies howling, and of course the poor little things had not been well. Eventually I just said I'd have to go and called out ta-ra and went. I shouldn't really be telling you all this, but I know it will stop with you.'

Such a relief, Eirlys confided, to be back under her own roof. And Sandy had invited her out for a drink. Should she go? Dora hoped Eirlys would be careful whilst squeezing a little juice from life. Generally it was a case of other people squeezing Eirlys like an orange. She hoped her friend would not be hurt, and was visited by an inappropriate urge to rush downstairs and catechise this potential suitor on his intentions. She supposed that he was just being neighbourly or placating her. She reminded herself that, so far, all the paramour had given to Eirlys was a cup of tea.

'I thought you did not like their music,' she said. 'And their nocturnal performances.'

'Quietened down markedly, though, they have, don't you think? And don't worry, Dora dear, I've got my wits about me.' Eirlys scrabbled in her handbag, saying, 'I've got something for you: ah, here.'

Dora received the tiny shells on her outstretched palm with pleasure. Together they turned them over in the silver-grey light. Each shell stood open on its tiny hinge, yellow, grey or white. They lay on the palm of Dora's large hand and, as Eirlys told her about how the children had gathered them combing the shore for 'exactly the right ones', Dora drifted. The last thing she said was to remind Eirlys that they must go to see Megan. Tomorrow.

'But both our cars are in the garage. Let's wait awhile.'

'Can't wait. We must go by train.'

Now Eirlys was removing the shells one by one and laying them on the glass-topped table. She was placing Dora's loosening hand down upon her knee. She was brushing the hair back from an old woman's brow. Dora, slipping into a doze, heard the tiny ping with which each shell met the glass. She was the old woman. How rude to nod off with company in the room, but then it was not a stranger, it was Eirlys.

Shaking herself awake, Dora insisted. No time to lose. She would brook no delay. But when Eirlys rang Myrrh Lodge, she learned that Megan had been moved to a place near Carmarthen. *Yr Hen Ysgol.*

As the train slid to a standstill overlooking the Tywi estuary, the women looked out over the expanse of grey, lapping water. Through St Ishmael they had passed, and St David's, like the landscape of Scripture.

The home was a converted Victorian schoolhouse of red brick, half-covered in ivy and creeper. The playground was still marked up as a miniature football pitch and the Thomases' car was parked in one of the goals.

The beast with two heads was there in the hall. Dora was on it in a flash.

'Why have you moved Megan?'

'Oh,' said Hugh. 'What are you doing here?'

'Visiting Megan.'

'How did you know she was here?'

'We asked. But what we did not discover was *why* she had been deported?'

'Oh,' Hugh replied. 'I don't know why you're using that word, *deported*, Dora – seems a bit OTT. We only want what is best for Mother.'

'In what sense? What was wrong with the first place?'

'In a word, pounds and pence. Extras they were asking for – podiatry, hair-dressing, incontinence pads. Could never have been sustained for long. It is Mother's security we have at heart. Go out of town, see, and you can find a bargain.'

Hugh seated himself on the chair lift, which was labelled 'Out of Use', and delivered himself of a beery belch. Dora took advantage of the opportunity to tower over Hugh. He was wearing a turquoise shirt with an orange floral pattern, to which she felt an all-but moral antipathy. She hankered to poke him with her stick between his splayed legs, where it would really hurt. The chair lift appeared to be patched with parcel tape, and there was a dingy look and a cabbagy smell in the stairwell, which had been carpeted and wallpapered with crimson roses decades ago; they had been darkening ever since.

'The true, the blushful Hippocrene!' exclaimed a wraith-like gentleman positioned in front of the door. He made a cheery motion of raising a glass to his lips.

A blue-aproned carer attempted to lure him away from his vantage point with the promise of a nice cup of tea and a Welsh cake. 'He's ninety-three,' she explained to the visitors.

'I am ninety-two, lassie,' Dora riposted. 'How is that relevant?'

The carer seemed confused. 'Are you a resident, dear? What is your name? I'm new. What room is she in? Can she remember? Are you her daughter? Ronald, where are you going now?'

'No, I am not a resident! Certainly not.'

Ronald mentioned that he was just off down the pub for a quick lunchtime half, and made a feint at the door, but was frustrated by the carer.

A tall mirror stood over a semi-circular table, on which the visitors' book lay. As Hannah bent over to sign them in, Dora met her own dismayed eyes in the mirror. Megan's daughter said she must just go off to the ladies' room to powder her nose. Hugh, suddenly finding his voice, forbade this retreat. He said she would stay just where she was. Dora hardly knew where to target her contempt: there seemed so many candidates for it. But being mistaken for one of the residents had unsettled her nerves.

No doubt Ronald had the right idea, in attempting to make a dash for it. Dora wished she had never come. Why had she insisted upon it? Not her kind of place at all.

Hugh said, 'Mother won't know you.'

'Well, maybe not, Hugh, but she'll know we come as friends,' Eirlys managed. 'Anyway, we want to see Megan for our own sakes.'

'Come again?'

'We are *fond* of Megan. We miss her at The Eyrie.' She explained this as if stooping to the understanding of a child.

'Oh,' said Hugh, and shook his head. 'Of course.'

He gave a small, bored groan. His complexion was that of a prune, thought Dora, from lolling in the Spanish sun. And just look at his belly. As for Mary, in a white cotton blouse and culottes, she looked fit and well. The idea of dumbbells at dawn came to Dora's mind.

'What is the matter with you, Hugh?' Dora asked. 'Why are you sitting on that chair lift? How can we get past you?'

'Had a heavy lunch he has,' Mary said. 'Down at the Church Arms. And I don't know that it agreed with him.'

'Don't talk about me as "he", please. I'm not the one who's lost his marbles. I don't think I'm well, Mary. You'll need to drive. Sorry I can't offer you ladies a lift.'

The carer opened the door with one hand, holding back her prisoner with the other.

'How do the residents get up and down the stairs?' Hannah asked her. 'When the lift's out of order?'

'I don't know, I'm afraid. I'm new.'

'Well, who does know?'

'The owner will fix it as soon as he's back, don't worry.'

'Back from?'

'Florida. On holiday, see. Lovely it is there. Apart from the tornadoes.'

Dora could have shaken the woman. But of course she was just a skivvy. Cheap labour, doubtless transient. Who'd do the work, anyway? Not me, thought Dora. I'd run a mile.

'So, who's in charge?' Hannah went on. She offered to look at the lift and see if there was anything obvious. She was an engineer by profession, she told the carer.

'Sandra, I think. But Sandra's off today. I couldn't let anyone loose on the chair without her say-so, I'm afraid.'

'And I suppose,' said Dora, 'you're going to tell me this Sandra is also at Disneyland?'

'Gracious, no. In Bangor she is, with her uncle. You go into the day room, Ronald. That's right. Toddle in, there's a darling.'

They got a glimpse of the day room. Ladies were silently suffering in a row of chairs, like clients at a hairdresser minus the curlers. In the centre, a cheerful but robotic woman was kneeling, coaxing them to throw a plastic quoit at a target to win a box of Smarties.

'I'd rather be shot through the head like a horse,' said Dora and, to her own shock, she staggered backwards and uttered a high-pitched sound like a whinny.

'Don't say that, Dora. Never-say-die.'

It was Megan. She was standing behind her like some small creature in a cage that had abandoned its treadmill. Taking Dora's hands, she led her into her own room, Hannah and Eirlys following. She explained to Dora that she should not be worried about the chair lift, since she herself lived on the ground floor, so it was no problem getting up and down. She personally did not think those marooned upstairs particularly wanted to come downstairs anyway. Communal meals were a terrible bore, she said, because of having to speak to people. And you had to sit up straight and exercise your table manners. Gravy was the devil for dribbling down your chin, and as for custard – oh, terrible. But if you were allowed to eat in peace in your room with nobody coming in and saying, *Finished, dear?* you could tuck a tissue into your collar like a serviette and there you were, happy as Larry! Breakfast they could all have, she explained, in their own rooms. So the people up there on the first floor were leading the life of Riley because they got all their meals sent up on trays and did not have to eat sardine salad with a lot of old ladies.

She sat Dora down in her best chair and assured her, as if comforting a child, that everything would be all right, not to be alarmed, all would turn out for the best. And there was corned beef for supper, her favourite. Hannah and Eirlys wedged themselves into a miniature sofa.

'Who are these two?' Megan queried. 'Are they the sort of ladies who live together?'

Gently, Dora reminded Megan that these were her old neighbours at The Eyrie.

'I've transferred,' said Megan. 'To a cheaper place.'

Yes, thought Dora, and we know which two scrooges are responsible for that. Yet Megan seemed more tranquil than she remembered her and it was moving, too moving really, that she knew Dora perfectly. Megan sat with a fluffy pink rabbit in her lap, a toy which she petted, tying and retying its ribbon and occasionally nuzzling it with her nose. Yes, I would rather be shot, thought Dora. She forced herself to remember the dignity of her exit kit and itemise its contents to calm her beating brain.

So long as I don't lose my faculties behind my own back. How shall I know when my brain has gone and I am no longer in control? She flashed Hannah a yearning look. Hannah smiled back: she looked blooming and healthy, her complexion glowing beside those of her elders. Hannah will not deny me, Dora thought.

Megan was saying that she had no objection to gay marriages, and that that awful duffer Hugh was living in the nineteenth century.

'He would not tolerate you,' she told Eirlys and Hannah. 'But luckily he's not here today.'

Hannah asked, leaning forward and taking one of Megan's hands, 'Megan, dear, are you all right? Tell us in confidence.'

'Yes, and I don't mind you patting my knee, dear. It wasn't nice, you know, in that lemon room. Although I miss the birdie-boys.'

'That's right. You used to feed the birds, didn't you?' Eirlys asked.

'Swallows and sparrows came to my window. And once upon a time a magpie.'

'Are there no birds here?'

'None so far.'

'I can hear gulls,' said Hannah.

'Pigeons of the sea,' Megan corrected her. 'You wouldn't want one of those scavengers beaking you.'

'There must be other birds.' Eirlys went to the window to check. Not a great view, the back of her head acknowledged. The lichened roofs of outhouses, wheelie bins and part of the car park.

'Aye,' said Megan, 'but how do you attract the nice birds and keep the nasty ones away? I am always on the look-out for an eagle or a kestrel. One of those I'd love to see.'

She remembers me, thought Dora, when all the rest of them are aliens, and what does that say? She looked round keenly to assess the conditions in which Megan was to finish her days. A dark, mahogany world, heavy with pastness, but clean enough. To Dora, Megan looked impressively well-ironed. And she appeared no thinner than she had been before.

'May I look in your wardrobe, Megan?' Eirlys asked.

'Since it's you. What are you looking for? You want to find out if I'm all right, don't you?' she asked with more clarity than Dora remembered seeing in a long time. Would it be better or worse, she wondered, to be incarcerated here in a lucid state?

'It's nice to be fussed over a bit,' said Megan. 'Thank you. But you see that? You see who has come? Dora is here! My ducky Dora! It's quite funny, you know,' Megan told Eirlys, 'because I have see-through doors.'

'That's nice,' said Eirlys cheerfully. Then she thought for a moment and asked, 'Is it?'

'Well, what do you think?'

'I don't know. I suppose it is.'

'Do we get a cup of tea?' asked Hannah. She looked round with a grimace Dora realised they must all be wearing: *when can I get away?*

No, I shall not come again, Dora thought, but at least I have been the once. Her heart throbbed in her throat, a disagreeable sensation, even a dangerous one, and it did not seem to be keeping time with itself, pausing and then galloping to make up the lost beats.

They sat subdued through the journey back to Swansea.

'Do you think she's all right in there?' asked Eirlys.

'Aye. She's fine. As these things go,' Dora answered. Imagine Megan now sitting motionless and distracted, fondling the pink bunny like a simpleton. I could be like that. And I have an intellect to lose. Would I not know when it was compromised? For after all, Megan was a simpler organism than herself. She was content, always had been, with very little. Megan had only ever had a sparrow's appetite for intellectual nourishment. No daily newspaper even. She had loved the rubbish on TV, so that Dora had felt bound to point out that the characters in the soaps were not real.

But then again, she thought, looking out at the desolate marshlands of Pembrey, compared with herself, Megan has always been placid. What had she ever known of the fighting spirit? Only in relation to her duties at the Inland Revenue could dear Megan have shown this spirit, and then of course she was acting in strict deference to the codes laid down in her handbook. So it must be easier for Megan to reconcile herself to what must be. The same quietist spirit could never be expected or exacted from Red Dora.

I still seem to think I'm God, she thought, and, for no reason, fixed a fierce, covetous stare upon Hannah.

'Is there anything wrong?' asked Hannah. 'Something I said?'

'Of course not. Was I making faces? I was far away. As a matter of fact, Megan seemed to me very sharp, very much in control of her faculties.'

'That's because you were there. It gave her such a lift.'

'Don't flatter, Eirlys.'

Megan had suffered a loss and come to terms with it, she

thought. I am too prone to belittle. Megan feels this loss of bearings as any human soul would feel it, but she has the resolve and the coherence to make some adaptation.

She looked again into Hannah's pensive eyes as she listened to her walkman. Yes, Hannah was devoted to her, and would do for Dora anything she asked.

'I suppose they'll move her to Pembroke next,' she said scathingly, 'away from our bad influence. Next stop, the sea!'

17

A serial bell-ringer was treating every flat to a carillon. Mrs Dark's ladylike bell could be heard tinkling out its peal. Now Mr Flood was buzzed hard. The men in Megan's flat got a blast. The unknown thumb pressed the Urquhart bell. Waldo and Eirlys were teaching Hannah early-morning Welsh prepositions, one shooting from either side, with plenty of laughter and coffee to wash them down. Eirlys picked up Hannah's receiver. 'Yes? Who do you want? ... Hannah, there's a man demanding to see you.'

When she got downstairs, Alun had opened the door to Hannah's nemesis.

'Hannah? Oh, right. You mean Miss Francis from number four? Cross-purposes, mate. Here she is.'

He stayed on to listen, pretending to sort through the post on the table.

'At last,' said Barry. 'Miss *Francis*.'

'I use my own name,' she said. 'You know that. I don't think there's a lot of point in speaking, Barry. Best to leave it with the lawyers.'

'She doesn't want to talk to you,' Waldo said. 'So you'd best be going, hadn't you?'

Dressed in well-pressed chinos and a navy, short-sleeved shirt, Barry shifted nervous car-keys from palm to palm. How handsome he was, tall and willowy; and how dull. The thought that he may have come with the idea of bringing Hannah back to that haven of dullness in Bristol aroused a half-forgotten feeling of suffocation. But at the same time, seeing him like this out of the blue brought back their early days together, when Barry had taken her under his wing and cared for her. He'd shown her so much tenderness when she needed it that Hannah had felt she'd be in debt to him for the rest of her life. Only she had outgrown him and wanted her independence. What had started as comfort had turned into smothering. How was that his fault?

'I think you had better go,' said Dora.

Mortified, Hannah realised that Alun was choking with laughter. She'd never be able to hold her head up again, and whatever was Waldo going to think, Waldo whom she liked so much, and perhaps it was more than mere liking? Barry was standing his ground, his hands in his pockets jingling his small change. With an angry timidity Hannah recognised, he scowled at the faces confronting him. She was stricken with pity. She'd been vile to him, hadn't she?

'What's going on?' quavered Mrs Dark from her upstairs window.

Eirlys stepped out into the sun, squinted up and called out, 'Nothing, Mrs Dark. A small misunderstanding. Don't worry, the gentleman's going now.'

'I'm going nowhere until I've spoken to my wife,' said Barry. 'Because she's still my wife. Oh, and by the way, Hannah, I've got Lara in the car. Perhaps you'd like to explain to your daughter why you abandoned her.'

It was more a public accusation than a private one. Hannah's face burned.

'You're thinking of her real mother, Barry. Lara's not my daughter and I didn't abandon her. We've been in touch. She's OK with it.'

'She's heartbroken.'

'Who's heartbroken?' called down Mrs Dark. 'I can't hear properly.'

'Nobody, Mrs Dark. Don't catch cold with that window open,' Eirlys said.

Lara appeared behind her father.

She arrived silently, dressed in dark clothes and wearing

around her neck a crucifix on a silver chain. The daughter stood at her father's shoulder, looking younger than her years, although she was taller than Hannah remembered. Her hair had been cut in a new, more feathery style, which softened features Hannah had sometimes seen as harsh and judging. She looked beautiful.

'Oh, Lara!' Hannah said, burst into tears and threw her arms round her.

'*Don't*,' said Lara in a whisper. She squirmed and winced away, blushing to the roots of her hair. 'Who are all these people, Hannah?'

'Come inside. We'd better talk,' said Hannah to her husband and his daughter.

Waldo would be in with Eirlys, he said, if he was wanted.

Hannah led Lara and Barry up the stairs.

Lara stood with her back to her father and stepmother, looking out of the window at a patch of empty air above the castle. Barry sat down and accepted a mug of tea. He commented that she seemed to have done very nicely for herself – a pad in a stately home! He had no idea how she could afford it. He took a swig of tea, his eyes roving round the flat with a quite scared look, Hannah saw, as if he were trying to ascertain who this person was through the objects she had selected without consulting his taste. He lay back in Mrs Menelaus's elderly settee, his long legs stretched out. Into her mind flashed their visit to Tintagel that first summer, the four of them, standing at the edge of the cliff, completely safe, and the girls for once tranquil. Hannah had felt Lara's small fingers twining with her own. She'd stood there with her husband's arm round her waist, not looking down, in case Lara snatched her fingers away, but she'd given the hand a little squeeze. Lara had fallen asleep on Hannah's lap in the car. She remembered the warm weight of her trust.

'Where did you get all this stuff?' Barry was asking. 'Car boot sale? It's a bit of a junk heap, if you don't mind my saying so.'

'Fine, if it makes you feel better.'

'Well, it doesn't.'

'What did you want to talk about?'

Barry looked into her eyes for the first time. His eyes were still beautiful, grey, long-lashed. He'd meant the world to her once. Hannah had felt she could never do enough for him, ironing his clothes, cutting his hair. At what point had her excessive devotion turned into a laundry service? No wonder he was perplexed.

'An apology would be a start,' he said.

'I am sorry that you were hurt.'

'That's not good enough.'

'Then I can't help you.'

'Who said we thought you could help us?' Lara said. She was flushed and her voice was high and small. 'Who said that? We don't need helping.'

Hannah remembered that resentment from her four anxious years of trying to mother Lara. Whyever be surprised that she's hostile when it comes down to it? Hannah asked herself. Of course they had texted one another affectionately over the months and Lara had promised to come and stay, and made it clear that she wanted to be friends. But what was Lara but a child caught up in adult chaos and her own ambivalence? How could Lara not take Barry's part and see his pain as her own? Texting was one thing, the reality of Hannah's world and Lara's need another. Twice the child's home had been broken up. Two women had cleared off and left her. It must be such a shock for Lara to see Hannah at home amongst strangers in her own world. She watched Lara place herself on the settee beside her father, sitting on her hands – an unconscious gesture Hannah recalled from early days. What it meant she had never quite worked out, but it went with a faint smile on one side of her face. Lara had some new boots made of a soft fabric that looked like suede. Every so often she would comfort herself by raising one of her legs to admire them.

'Are those new?' Hannah asked her.

'Quite new.'

'Lara, I never wanted to hurt you. I am truly sorry. I tried very hard for you but it wasn't enough. Some of the stuff that hurt you wasn't to do with me. I mean, your real mum going away.

Some of it was. Now you just have to cope with life as it is.'

'Don't speak about my real mum!'

'OK.'

'If you hadn't come, we would at least have had my dad.'

'But, Lara, you do have your dad.'

Lara's body twitched, as people do in their sleep.

'So tell us about lover boy,' said Barry, getting up to wash his mug, which he placed neatly on the draining board. She had once been so comforted by the rituals that had given stability to each day. She had tucked in under Barry's arm. She had sat with him watching football on the box on Saturdays and enjoyed the fact that he was enjoying it. Until she didn't any more. It was unfair on him that the life he'd lived in good faith had come to torment her.

'What do you mean, lover boy?' Hannah asked.

'The bearded carrot-head with the fake Welsh accent?'

'How's your girlfriend?'

'Well, that's different,' he said, and a guilty look came into his eyes. 'Emma and I, we started when you'd gone. Anyway, how did you know?'

'I didn't, I guessed. Anyway, I don't have a boyfriend. I didn't leave you for a man, Barry, though I don't suppose you'll believe that. I left, well, for me.'

'You've been watching too many soaps. You were happy.'

'Was I?'

'Course you were. Well, when I say happy, you were OK, you were content. As good as it gets in the real world, Hannah.'

'So why did I leave?'

'Kids probably. You could just have waited till they were grown up. You won't get a penny out of me, Hannah,' he said. 'You know that, don't you? I hope my solicitor has made it crystal clear. I've bagged your stuff and left it in the shed.'

'I don't want anything,' she said. 'You are well aware of that. I haven't asked for anything, have I?'

When he got up to leave, she said she hoped Barry would find true happiness with Emma. She had much to thank Emma for.

Barry walked off towards his car, shoulders down, hands in his pockets. Hannah's silent stepchild walked at her side, wearing the suede boots that were evidently the anxious darlings of Lara's heart, for she kept reaching down to finger their soft tops. They must be hot to wear in summer but Lara had clearly meant to make a statement.

'Who is this Emma?' Hannah murmured.

'You know. Next door but two.'

'Oh, right. I don't remember her at all.'

'Young. Chubby. Fucking cow-eyed. She started coming in when you left, bringing him meals and stuff.'

'He has to have someone, Lara. He can't manage on his own.'

'No.'

'And it shouldn't be you.'

'No.'

'You've a life to live.'

'Right. News to me.'

'Lara, I'm so sorry.'

'Yeah.'

'Come on, Lara. I thought we were going to try to be friends.'

Then Lara burst out, 'We gave you hell, we gave you shit when you were our stepmother. We tried to get rid of you, I know that, but that didn't mean we didn't, well, you know, care about you, Hannah. After all, you cleared up our sick.'

'Come on if you're coming,' Barry called across the forecourt. 'One hour from now we'll be in Eng-a-land!' Preposterously, he punched his arm in the air yelling, 'Eng-land! Eng-land!' before swinging into his driving seat and slamming the door. A St George's Cross was hanging from the window.

'He'll be OK,' said Hannah. 'I like your hair in this style.'

'You look a hell of a lot younger, Hannah. Wish I had a flat like that.'

'Would your dad let you come and stay? Of course, you might not want to, I'd totally understand, but there are things I'd like to explain to you.'

Lara said, 'Someone's kicked the bollard over. Yeah, he'd let me come. He'd be glad to have a break from me. Soph won't come, though. She hates your guts.'

Barry inched the car forwards. 'Lara, are you coming or not?'

Hannah walked out to wave Lara off. It was hard to let her go. Lara was dearer to her than any long-lost brother could be. Let Barry think she was weeping for him, or out of guilt, if it made him feel better. And off her back. It was the last time in her life she would be Barried.

The car, blaring its hooter, veered around the bollards at the base of the roundabout, and shot off towards Cardiff. Turning, Hannah was confronted by pairs of eyes on stalks, viewing the drama from open windows or, like Mr Powell, from his balcony. Hannah felt that she ought to gratify her audience by taking a bow. Instead she rushed indoors, head down.

Eirlys gave Hannah plenty of time to reach her flat. So that was the husband. She could not help but be surprised at his good looks. Not that Hannah wasn't a good-looking girl, but somehow the way Hannah had spoken of him had left her with an image of a baldy with a paunch wearing a football strip. Should Eirlys knock on Hannah's door or leave her in peace? Did she ever miss her handsome husband, waking alone in Mrs Menelaus's dark bed? Waldo, who liked Hannah and was liked in return, was no beauty: at least, Eirlys could not see that he was. But then Waldo was family. And more than she could admit, Eirlys had become preoccupied with Sandy. And he apparently with her. When Sandy saw her bringing the shopping in, he was out of his flat in a flash to carry it for her. Always a kind word and a charming smile when they passed in the hall. Perhaps they might pass one another now?

She went out, just in case. The quiet newcomer, Mr Flood, was lingering in the hall, evidently seeking someone to confide in. He dug a phrase book out of his pocket and pointed to *I do not understand English. Please speak more slowly*, hesitantly reading it aloud. He revealed, *I am a refugee/asylum-seeker. My country of birth is Bosnia.*

Eirlys invited him in, pointing to *I am pleased to meet you* – and he smiled and replied that he was a keen student of the respected English language, adding, without bothering with the phrase book, 'Cup of tea! Very nice home!'

Between them they managed to fix him up with a GP, though not a dentist, for there were no National Health dentists in South Wales, as Eirlys knew, whatever your nationality. Only last week a desperate man from Clydach had resorted to pulling out his own tooth with pliers. It had been in all the local papers.

And this interesting Bosnian, who had found sanctuary in The Eyrie, had, it turned out, been a meteorologist in his native land, until he was forced to flee. *Later in the week/month we shall see rain and gales.*

Eirlys went shopping and, as she was putting her groceries away, there was a knock on the door.

'Delivery for Miss Eirlys Harries!' said Sandy. 'Stand aside, please!'

He would help her in with it, he said. And might he assemble it for her? No problem. Eirlys beamed and blushed. Her new exercise machine took up much of the lounge, which had been converted into a mini-gym. Sandy, tall and rather ruined in looks, stood smiling upon his handiwork.

She explained, with a series of her big, self-deprecatory laughs, how she was going to pump iron and swim to bring herself up to peak fitness. Don't laugh, she added. He wouldn't laugh, he said, whyever should he? All for fitness, he was. He'd had a bit of a health scare a few years back when he lost his ... well, someone dear to him, a loved-one, he said. Eirlys wondered why he seemed unable to be more precise, but perhaps the person had been a Grand Passion? Or married to someone else? Eirlys did not condemn the adulterer: Christ had not, so how could Eirlys Harries? If an opportunity presented itself, she could not absolutely rule out grabbing passion with both hands. He'd gone to pot a bit, Sandy admitted, he'd a beer gut on him like nobody's business, but he'd taken up exercise and now he walked the cliff path to Caswell and back every Sunday.

'Oh, my goodness, Eirlys,' he said, 'why am I telling you this?'

'I'd no idea you had suffered a loss. I'm so sorry.'

'You're the kind of lady it's easy to talk to. I suppose everyone tells you that? I often think of you, you know, when I'm in my quiet room.'

What quiet room is that? the sage part of Eirlys wondered. Sandy and Alun seemed to live in a perpetual stew of pop music. But the susceptible part of Eirlys was touched. An image of a pensive Sandy at his window came to mind. Sad spaniel eyes were raised to hers. What was it that beat up in her, she thought, at hearing other people's woes? Did she want them to be afflicted so that she could nurse them? Was she a bloodsucker? Did they know she was a leech?

'Oh, dear,' she said.

'Tell you the truth, Eirlys, I got to be a bit of a soak at one point. Never touch the stuff now, though.'

Liar, she thought. I've seen you there in the forecourt legless. Middle of the night. But he spoke with such feeling that she felt in touch with the inner Sandy, the one he would like to be.

'Anyway,' he said, resignedly. 'That's all behind me. What's the phrase? I've moved on! And speaking of moving on: what a beauty!'

He meant the exercise machine. It was splendid, he said. What a good buy. How he envied her. Might he have a go? They adjusted the mechanism to Sandy's larger frame and off he went, powering his way across the floor. Eirlys hummed and put the kettle on, retrieving the chocolate digestives from where she had hidden them from herself.

One day quite soon, she thought, perching on the kitchen stool while Sandy rowed on, she would step out of this plump body. One day she would look in her mirror and see an appealing and pretty reflection. She would like to sashay round in tight jeans like Hannah's. Older people could these days. And if Dora can wear jeans, why shouldn't I? she demanded. She'd never managed a successful diet. Only in prison had fear and inedible food created the right conditions. She'd gone in a bread pudding and came out a raspberry sorbet.

'Fantastic machine,' said the man sweating on her living-room floor.

'You should get one.'

'Don't think the landlord would appreciate it somehow.'

He eased off his sculling as if he had reached the tranquil waters of an inlet or lagoon. 'Funny guy. Bit of an old woman.'

'Hugh.'

'Yeah.'

'But it's not his flat, you know.'

'No, so he says. Says it behoves him to keep an eye on his mum's pennies. Blimey, that was good. Gets the toxins out of you!'

Oh, no, he's not starting again. He seemed to have forgotten the tender passage between them. But before Sandy could make his way out into open water, Eirlys reminded him of the cup of tea he'd thought wouldn't come amiss.

'Landlord's a bit of a damper, to tell the honest truth,' Sandy observed, sitting down in a lather of sweat. 'He and Mrs Landlord came and did an inspection. Eviction awaits us apparently unless we pull out socks up. Lovely cup of tea you make, Eirlys. Choice, is that.'

'In what way, pull up your socks?'

Perhaps Hugh had spoken sternly about the illegitimate hanging of washing from the window.

'He's trying to raise the rent, we reckon. Had a bit of a reversal in his Spanish property investment. Operation White Whale, heard of that?'

Ah, so that was it. Hugh's villa was on an estate which, it turned out, had been built by a company with laundered money, illegally siphoned from a Russian oil giant. Although he and Mary had bought it in all innocence, they were facing the sale of their dream to repay creditors. Which was why poor Megan had been moved to a cheaper place.

'What I think is the guy wants us out and then he'll tart the place up a bit and charge double. It's a scam. He's saying we're dirty tenants.'

Eirlys had an intimation of what was coming.

'Well, you know, a couple of bachelors living together,' he went on. 'You can't expect them to keep things as nice as two ladies would.'

'Really?' Eirlys tendered no help and no chocolate biscuit.

'So we were – well, really I was – wondering if you knew of any lady who might care to earn a few pennies doing a bit of cleaning, and maybe washing and ironing, to help out a couple of lonely guys. We can't pay much.'

A woman who had lately stormed out on her own flesh and blood could easily face down a stranger. She held Sandy's eyes until he looked down and said he really ought to make tracks.

'Just before you go,' she said. 'A word about the noise levels. And what was that white stuff we found all over the lawn?'

18

Autumn in the air. One must draw up one's accounts. Dora made her plan and agreed it with Eirlys. Good that she had paid the visit to Megan. She had meant to cheer her but it had been rather as if Megan had blessed Dora for her journey.

She'd opened the tiny hinge in her heart, like the hinge of one of those delicate pink shells you glean as the tide goes out, and now her heart was ajar. Down on the shore at Rotherslade, she found herself writing Rosa's name and dates, together with her own name and dates, crouched at the edge of the incoming tide. Then she paused, offering both names to the sea. The foam tongued its way forward and lapped the twin names into itself. Bending again, Dora rewrote the names and a message to Rosa: 'I am still your mother.'

The wide grey eye of the sky read this truth over her shoulder. When she turned around, there was a kite being flown on the beach, racing up the wind current, scribbling all over the parchmenty cloud, and trailing a blood-red tail. It could not be over soon enough. Tired, hectic children were out of school, and all the dogs of the area had come out to tear up and down and bark.

She wrote to Rosa: 'Your mother is near you.'

Although the membranes of her heart tensed around their – at last – acknowledged burden, Dora was glad that she had been able to turn to Rosa. *Pock-pock*, went her heart, then a pause and a scramble to catch up. She laboured back, digging her hands in her pockets, bent against the wind. Looking back down over the bay, Dora gazed at the broad, sombre sea, where several jolly yachts with yellow and red sails were rigging and tacking.

Dora was coming closer to Rosa with every breath. True. But she must eke out her strength. A relationship can go on unfolding, she thought, beyond the death of one partner: this recognition seemed a gift greater than any wisdom she had been granted for decades. Dora stood considering her position in relation to the horizon, like an athlete preparing her run-up to a high bar. It was a matter of balance, she thought, a stillness you could find within yourself which quietened and slowed the mind.

She drove home to The Eyrie. The here-and-now was populated by midgets, clowns, parodies. And here was Hannah, who had clearly sustained some crisis in her own life, and was occupied with emptying her flat of Mrs Menelaus's massive furniture. Dora drew up to the sight of a wardrobe being swung out of Hannah's window by a baby crane. This eviction of Mrs Menelaus's effects was accompanied by the shouting of instructions and counter-instructions between Hannah and two men. A huddle of scowling Victoriana already stood exposed on the forecourt. A pow-wow of dinosaurs. Hannah breathlessly confided that she was going minimalist. No clutter, no junk, she said. A new start! What did Dora think?

Dora said she was sure it was a good idea. Space had to be cleared. Hannah would give a flat-warming party, she said, a very quiet and unorthodox one with only two honoured guests. She hadn't forgotten her archive work, she assured Dora: should she come in later on?

'Not today,' said Dora. 'I have plans for today.'

'Oh, of course, Dora. Whenever you like. Just say the word.'

I have made her love me, Dora thought. In a way it had been on false pretences. The glow on the young woman's face echoed the devotion Dora was used to from decades of disciples. The veneration that takes you for something you can never be, a source of gifts that are not in you to give. Now that she'd turned for home, the will to mime this charisma for the benefit of others was weakening.

That afternoon Eirlys drove Dora up to All Saints. The day Dora had dreamed of, lived for, procrastinated about, had arrived. Nervous as a child at the school gates, Dora peered through black railings into a green and homely churchyard. The garden of rest centred in a rectangle of turf, surrounded by a well-tended border of bushes and bright flowers. A paved path parted the turf into two equal areas and led to a Celtic cross of dark-grey granite.

Eirlys wandered away, to allow Dora space. A girl and boy were playing marbles on a gravestone. Why were they playing up here in a churchyard? She wondered where the parents were, and why the two little ones did not speak. Perhaps they were the Rector's children, or came from the fishermen's cottages surrounding the graveyard on three sides and regarded sacred ground as their legitimate territory. This would be quite Wordsworthian. The marbles, she saw, listed into the grooves where the lettering of the names of the departed had been engraved two centuries back. It was an interesting surface. She heard the chinks of glass against glass.

The little girl erupted, 'Ha! You got "Morgan"; I got "Departed"! Yee-ha!'

'Did not so.'

'Did. You can't read, you. Can he, miss?'

Eirlys squatted and saw that a blue marble had lodged in the O of Llwyd Morgan, a nineteenth-century curate, while a red marble had lodged in the D of his departure for a better world.

'Well,' she adjudicated, 'if the red one by here's yours, dear, that's right. Does that mean you've won?'

'Ya-ha!' sneered the child in the lemon cotton dress, her fair hair clipped back in a slide.

'Cheated you did, you louse.'

The girl skipped off though the iron gates, singing, 'Yee-ha!'

'Delyth's a monster; her mam says,' said the morose boy. He

paused in his collection of the marbles in a pouch. 'Do you want a game?'

'Just one game, then, on another stone. This one's spitty.'

As the boy was the only one who knew the rules, he was guaranteed to win. Eirlys joined in, but glanced over to see how Dora was getting on.

She was standing in the garden of remembrance where Eirlys had left her. And she looked peaceful, meditative.

'Right, that's *it* – you've won,' the boy told Eirlys, shovelling marbles into the pouch. He left, honourable and disconsolate.

Eirlys had no idea how she had won. Her marbles had been flicked randomly. Most of them had wobbled into the pious admonitions at the foot of the gravestone.

Boo! You can't catch me! That had been Rosa. A rush of green skirts, full tilt into the bracken or, once, in the Louvre when the bored lassie had dashed from room to room. Each room had proved as empty of Dora's daughter as the last. A sequence of near misses. Only the echo of Rosa's giggles had greeted the mother.

Gone! A muffled explosion of laughter might be heard from some nook like the one Rosa had found at a Manse where they had stayed that time – a dark, cool larder with pickles and cheese and a dish of pilchards, where they'd found her and the son of the Manse, hamster-cheeks stuffed with forbidden food. Rosa had not been in the least afraid. *Because it's fun, isn't it, Mam, to eat secret food and hide away*?

Standing here in the garden, she could not see Rosa's death at all, only the girlish face of the mortuary attendant who'd prepared Rosa's body for viewing. Even her name came to mind: Isobel. This Isobel had partially closed Rosa's eyes and stood obtrusively in a doorway in her white uniform. A box of tissues was placed handily on a small table. She had to be there, she explained, by law. Dora had glanced at her scrubbed hands. Isobel had said (and Dora had been grateful that the girl had stood between her and the body, the very cold body from the fridge) . . . Isobel had said . . . yes, that was it, *this is very hard.*

To her, death was a livelihood, Dora had thought, not looking around the body of the living girl to that of her and Lachlan's silent daughter. You are like the fish-gutters or the chicken-packers on the conveyor belts. As such, you are worthy of my socialist respect as a valued worker.

Isobel's hand on Dora's forearm, steadying her. But then she had moved away and Dora had seen Rosa's face.

Yesterday those eyes in all their dark, lustrous boldness had been open, but today they were partially closed; nevertheless, Dora could see that under the lids their gleam had dimmed. Rosa seemed absorbed in deep, eternal thought. A hospital blanket, pale green, had been pulled up to her neck, and the single stalk of a carnation lay on her chest.

Dora had knelt and spoken to Rosa in Basque.

Euskara, the isolate language.

But what had she said? It came back to her now as she stood on the turf where Rosa's ashes were buried: she had poured out her thanks. Yes, that was it, she realised: I thanked her for existing. For being Rosa. And all in the Basque tongue, as if this might reach her world more readily than English or Spanish or Latin or Greek. And she had spoken also, as she now realised, on behalf of Lachlan, who stood – yes, *over there* – in the other world, ready to receive their daughter.

When this torrent of thanks had dried up, she had turned away and shaken Isobel's hand, praising her work. Such work was doubtless ill-rewarded, she had observed to the youngster, who was dressed like a butcher but with no blood on her bib.

They do help you, these people, they are midwives who see you and the child across the threshold.

She turned briefly. Over there crouched with the children was Eirlys, a shepherd in leaf-green and white. She was gravely playing marbles with the wee lad over on the path.

A marmalade cat stalked along the bushes and exploded into the sunlight. Plump and well-fed, it reached up its head and, Dora was amused to notice, held its tail standing up on end, with a curious kink in the tip. Now, what did that signify? What are you insinuating or expecting, fellow creature? As she stood upright, it padded away, back into the bushes. They know when the cupboard is bare. Don't come near me with your begging eyes. I don't lactate. I don't melt for parasites such as you. The grass blades cast complexities of shadow across the path of a beetle that was labouring over a leaf. So much toil and where did it think it was going? Two of Dora's tears stood on grass blades like dew.

The marmalade cat pounced on some creature beneath the shrubs. Some frog perhaps, with its vulnerable skin dried out and now raked with the claws of the playful creature that neither needed nor wanted to eat it. That was how it was. There was no moral stance to be taken on this. Yet she could not help but weep.

She remembered – it was clear as day – the morning before Rosa had left for Spain, telling Dora nothing of her real intentions. She was going to visit the Cave of Santa Lúcia at La Bisbal de Falset, she'd said, and hoped to see where her father had been buried. Dora had been touched.

Ultimately, both had spoken out of character. For Rosa had been a sponger and Dora a skinflint.

Rosa, take my wallet, I wish you would. Take all you need for you and the boys. Do.

I don't need anything.

I wish you would.

Thanks, Comrade Mother.

You are most welcome, Fiery Particle.

And before she'd left for Spain, Rosa had kissed her mother's hand four times. Dora had looked at the hand her daughter had kissed. She'd curled it in a mitten and stepped out into the snow.

Eirlys was beside her now.

'How are you, Dora? Oh, come here, *cariad*.'

'Don't take any notice.'

Looking at her hand, Dora curled it softly in against her heart.

'But I do take notice, lovely girl, of course I do. And to lose a child – well, that I cannot conceive.'

Dora looked at the maternal woman who had missed her chance to conceive, and stretched out a hand to her. They stood together, arms loosely round one another's waists. Dora was conscious of the soft, private give of Eirlys's flesh. Light on leaves. The ordinary sky, the simple grass. The plain slate of gravestones. Nothing said. No face looks back at us. This counterpane is all we see.

19

'It was a bloody century,' Eirlys said. 'And no mistake.'

She and Dora sat in their old places at either side of Dora's magnificent window, looking out into a plum-coloured sunset, fading to violet. Beneath the lamp Dora sat composedly, telling Eirlys about Rosa. Dredging around in her memory, Eirlys found the name Stuart Christie, the anarchist boy, Dora's countryman, who'd been imprisoned in Spain in the Sixties for plotting to assassinate Franco. She mentioned the Angry Brigade. But Rosa Little had not made the headlines apparently?

No, Dora told her, Rosa had failed even to generate publicity, as she had always been destined to fail. She had been too nervous, naive and highly strung. And what a good thing that our secret police had detained her at Harwich before Franco's could. For had she been caught in Spain, Rosa would have faced the garotte. She would have been strapped into the garotte-vil; received the *ultima pene* – Dora's nervous Rosa, who'd made a hysterical fuss at the dentist or when the school nurse came to give her a jab. But perhaps, Dora speculated, Rosa might have risen to it. After all, the dentist's chair is both something and nothing. There is always an element of play-acting. But they would have tortured her first. For Spain had been a terror state, Franco a jackbooted tyrant, comrade to Hitler and Mussolini.

'You will have been too young to have taken Franco seriously. But what you have to understand, Eirlys,' Dora explained, 'is that so far as Rosa was concerned, Franco had murdered her father.'

'Murdered her father?'

Rosa's father had died before she'd been born. Eight months before. At the battle of the Ebro.

Were they sitting here discussing real things? Eirlys asked herself. She felt as though they were reminiscing over a film Dora had seen. In black and white. Yet this was no film. Having visited her daughter and wept her tears, Dora was calm as she passed Eirlys the information. Rosa had believed that, in the end, politicians and states would be superfluous. Sovereign individuals would respect one another and live in natural, self-regulating communities, the means of production and distribution being held in common. But rage and violence and acts of murder, Eirlys thought, had apparently been necessary to achieve this peaceful, godless state. How do we live with our paradoxes and contradictions, she asked herself and, as she thought of this, she imagined rashes of contradiction all over her own skin.

'Your Rosa was a dreamer,' she said.

'I have been a dreamer, too; so have you, Eirlys.'

'True. It was a bloody century,' Eirlys repeated.

She remembered the blood on her bed. She'd been thrust into a cell by the worst kind of Pucklechurch screws. They'd called her *it*, they'd said, *We'll put it in with one of the psychiatrics.* They leered through the hole in the door, to where she stood shrinking and wondering if it was menstrual, this dark patch of blood on her bed. Or had the 'psychiatric' been self-harming? Or had she attacked someone else? Eirlys had spent the night in a moment-by-moment terror, waiting for the 'psychiatric's' return, afraid to sleep on the stained bed.

This had been the closest Eirlys ever came to the bloody violence of the century. The stain and smell of her fellow woman's despair.

'Are you tired, darling?' she asked Dora.

'Oddly not. I feel wide awake. And thank you for today. With all my heart. But before you go, just let me show you something. You know of course that Hannah has been sorting my archive?'

'Yes, but she doesn't tell me much about it.'

'She is loyal,' said Dora, and she extracted a picture from a folder on her desk. 'Who do you see here?'

The girl in the black-and-white photo had a pale face with a strong jaw and vivid, lustrous eyes. Her long hair was almost black. Eirlys recognised the likeness at once.

'Ah, I see,' she said. 'Yes, Dora, I see the similarities.'

'It is Rosa at eighteen.'

Dora did not seem to want Eirlys to comment. She began to hum tunelessly, turned away and took down a random book from the shelves that Hannah had cleared and catalogued. Then, with what Eirlys recognised as Dora's habit of willed absent-mindedness, she slipped the photo between the leaves and returned it to its original place. Hannah would have to start again at the beginning, Eirlys thought. Round and round we go, hiding things from ourselves. It is an ingrained habit. She smiled at Dora.

'What is it?' Dora asked.

'Oh, I was just remembering, *cariad*. Our reading sessions.'

'Och, they were lovely. We must carry on with them,' Dora said, and treated Eirlys to one of those smiles which placed you at the centre of Dora's world. 'Wherever did we get to, can you remember?'

'We were halfway through Dickens, weren't we?'

'Well, then, what could be nicer than to give our autumn to finishing him?'

Returning to her own flat, Eirlys mentally travelled back to Hannah's arrival, which had marked a break, as it turned out, in their reading. There had come a time when Eirlys had thought, flinching with embarrassment for the dignity of her friend: *oh please no, she has fallen in love.* But it had not been so. Dora had – how could she put it? – reinstated her memory through Hannah.

Acts of God these summer storms were, Eirlys thought, shutting the bay windows. She quite liked a tempest, as long as the pot plants were safely indoors: the free firework party of a moody God. That's it, Jehovah, get it out of your system! We don't take it personally any more. The exercise machine was a damn nuisance, tripping her up as she brought hot chocolate and buttered crumpets over to her chair. Who needs you? she asked it. If she wanted exercise, there were gentle mountains to climb at Ystalyfera, cliff paths to run round, the coast path to cycle down. She'd ask Hannah to dismantle the machine.

What a treat to settle down in front of her best soap, *Pobol y Cwm*, and fill herself up with comforting food.

She had thought Dora would be worn out with the emotion of the day, but apparently she had gained a second wind. She heard Angelica and Rae arriving. There was a roaring outside like a standing ovation. Various rending noises, as branches were perhaps torn away from tree trunks on the scarp behind The Eyrie. The birds would be huddled in the trees, the foxes crouching in their lair.

On the whole, Dora was well pleased with Rae and Angelica. They would carry on the struggle for her, she thought, despite their different – what one might call *fluid* – perspective. She was slightly concerned at Rae's spaced-out, dopy smile; it made her want to click her fingers in her face. Since they had scaled down their computer sessions, she was afraid that Rae had gone downhill. Her smile reminded Dora of that smiling hypocrite, the warmongering Prime Minister.

'Why are you smiling like that, Rae?'

'Hey, chill, Nannan,' said Jelly. 'Rae and me've—'

'Rae and *I* have . . .'

'We've been standing with candles and stuff with the Quakers on St Helena's Road against the war. In the wind and rain. Bit of a problem keeping the candles going 'cos we forgot to take jars. Rae needed a bit of a smoke after that. It's only drore. Weed, you know.'

'Right,' said Rae.

'Surely the Quakers would have provided the jam jars? They are so well-organised.'

'They were doing Silent Witness. We didn't like to interrupt them.'

'It's a well trippy night,' Rae observed.

The wind gusted through the firs beside the flats and blew panpipes down the drains. Dora's spirits were high, too high somehow. She ought to be tired by now, after the day she had had.

'People don't bother much with beetles and stuff,' Jelly was saying, 'but I try to step carefully over them. No, I do really. That's if I see them in time. There's a lot of, you know, invisible killing goes on.'

'In Baghdad ...' Dora began, and forgot what she was going to say.

'Well, everywhere in the world, isn't it, Nannan? There's creatures as small as dots. I've made a list of ones with nervous systems. That's a start.'

Rae said she was not stressed about the plight of insects. But she was concerned about lambs and their transportation, and she wondered why mutton was called lamb when people were going to eat sheep.

'The more apposite historical question is why sheep are called mutton,' Dora said. She tried to explain about the Normans oppressing the Anglo-Saxons and making the serfs rear *sheep* so that the ruling class could eat *mouton.* Her argument seemed to get rather twisted up but then she went to the window and pushed it open, and let cold air rush around her scalp and neck and ears and down her sleeves. That was better.

'Are you tired, Nannan?' Jelly asked. She came up and took her great-grandmother in a tender hug. She held her body lightly, not wanting to squeeze her too tight. When she kissed her, Dora felt the warmed gold of Angelica's earring, delicate against her cheek.

'We'll give you a break from our fascinating company,' Jelly said, picking up her various possessions that lay festooned around the room. Dora was not conscious of weariness as she shooed the two away. She reminded Rae to keep a very cool head.

She would just see if any new documents had appeared on the government website. But the text coming up on the screen seemed cryptic. As Dora looked away, the wall of the kitchen bent backwards like a dancer.

A crash somehow inside the flats. Within the body of the building.

Should she phone Mrs Menelaus? But what was her number? She had surely opted to go ex-directory.

Dora looked round and checked her possessions. Nothing had fallen down or been thrown across the room as used to happen after Rosa's death. One had had a poltergeist. One had been fond of the poltergeist and missed it when it absconded.

Was the computer doing the right thing? The screen was blue and flashing its eye.

No: it sternly told her she had performed an illegal operation and that she must abort the present task.

Dora had done everything in her customary punctilious fashion, by the book, but she sighed and turned off the computer at the wall. Logged on again. The light from the screen was now all pins; multitudes of pins shooting into the pupil of her eye.

Oh! She had lost a millisecond.

Everything was changed but in what way, Dora could not assess. The harsh light of the lamp seemed too much for her.

You heard of this happening, to weary drivers on motorways. A fraction of a second's sleep and you had caused a multiple pileup. And this, when your ambition was nothing less than the salvation of the planet, was ironic in the extreme.

How could a person's heart be said to be beating in her throat? Yet Dora's was. It skipped and then it waited. Oh, dear. She held on to her throat. Then it laboured. Her bursting heart was toiling now, up some impossible hill. Striving. To pull her body up.

Come along now.

Volts of electricity hit her mind with a swoosh. The currents rushed up through her hair, which burned, and her brain burned, too. She had been struck by lightning, surely? The only explanation. She shot to her feet and peed herself, on and on.

In a flash she saw. It was a system. Behind a wall was Megan; beyond Megan was Emma Menelaus; beyond Emma was Mother. They ranged to infinity in a superfluity of diminishing mirrors.

But Rosa was not with them.

Dora sagged in the chair and her jaw hung open. She was drooling a little, how deplorable, and now she was sliding.

Another lost moment and she found herself wrecked on the floor. A terrible crash. Ear-splitting shriek by some poor blighter.

Yet Dora knew, to her profound shock, that the poor blighter was not Megan, as she would have liked to think. Nor was it Mrs Dark. It was the ill-wisher called Dora who had dominated this body but now lay at its mercy.

How long had gone by? An aeon, an instant?

Waking into the clarity of reason after who-knew-how-long in the narrow bed, Dora considered her position. Her exit plan had not been put into execution; no time had been vouchsafed, no warning given. Instead she had been struck, removed to hospital and delivered into the hands of the State. The State had stuck her full of needles and a tangle of cables, clamping a plastic muzzle on her nose, and attaching a plastic bag for urine, along with many other abject humiliations. This had gone on for an indeterminate period of time, until, by and by, she had been freed from these horrors, only to awaken into the knowledge that she had lost the use of half her body and the whole of her voice.

Dora Urquhart cannot speak, she told herself.

Her left arm had, for some time, dangled heavy and useless, growing flabbier than her good right one, though now she could open and close her fingers. They pressed her excitedly to practise this opening and closing. It was a 'good sign'. Through the window Dora watched the changing sky and the branches of a tree turning colour from green to red and yellow.

Dora was unrepentantly aware that she had shown no courage: a euphemism for deference. Those in the beds on either side had seemed bent on riling her by showing Christ-like patience and fortitude, and also the inclination to chat. Her silence had discouraged them not a jot.

In her silence, Dora had smacked off hands laid on her arm to coax or comfort her. She had not co-operated. Indeed, she had swiped at the consultant with her good hand when she had overheard him asking someone to check in the notes whether Miss Urquhart had suffered from dementia before her stroke.

The lurking presence of Keir and Karl at Dora's bedside had proved not the least of her ordeals. Clearly they had been plotting with the doctor and social worker to arrange her eventual discharge into the company of Megan. She had made it known to Hannah, in writing, that she did not want them here.

Eirlys had been holding Dora's hand, it seemed, for weeks, or months, and Dora had not on any occasion resisted. She had allowed her talon to rest in that plump cocoon, permitting Eirlys to think she was comforting her. She wasn't.

Latterly Dora had been unearthed from the bed and cajoled into taking her first steps. Now she was subject to daily ordeal by physiotherapist. She had eaten very little. They were concerned about her weight and frailty. But nothing tasted of anything. She responded to all calls upon her attention with the same stony face.

'Soon you will be fit enough to make a home-visit, Miss Urquhart,' said a bright woman in blue uniform. 'That will be nice, won't it? Just as a preliminary assessment visit, mind. Not going home for good yet, but we shall still have a nice time, won't we?'

Dora uttered her first word: 'No.'

It seemed that a team would be accompanying Dora to The Eyrie; a team consisting of a social worker, an occupational therapist and a nurse, to assess the appropriateness of her accommodation and what changes would need to be made. And Dora herself was to undergo a test: they would ascertain whether Dora was capable of making herself and the team a nice cuppa.

Dora repeated her first word. And a few more to go with it.

Then a further angry and raucous flood broke out, filling her hearers with, so it seemed, awe.

Seated on a leather recliner in a place referred to as 'home', Dora was wearing a (what *was* this?) pink shawl-thing. She tried to shoulder it off. The flat for which she had longed had changed. She gripped with her good right hand on to the arm of the recliner, her left hand and leg seeming to float away, so that she felt she must keep an eye on them. How high Tom Ching's ceilings were. Far too high: whenever she looked up, the copper light-fitting at the centre gave her vertigo. Books upon books towered up the walls, and the planes and curves of her private space seemed unfamiliar. Everything was wrong.

A man with red hair was in the kitchen area lining up mugs and spoons for Dora's tea-brewing test. Eirlys's Waldo, of course. But why Waldo should be making free with her things in her kitchen, Dora could not imagine. He had never been invited to do so before. Her person was now public property apparently. The so-called team could be heard in the bathroom, fussing about the construction of new rails to help Dora cope with getting in and out of the bath and pulling herself up from the loo.

Glancing out of the window, she met a scene of such tranquillity that, letting out a long sigh, she could finally allow her shoulders to relax. The castle ruins lay under a haze of silver-grey cloud. With her eagle vision, Dora could see the grass and weed clinging to its ruined walls and a flock of gulls perched at the summit. Mild rain had been falling but now had cleared, and the roofs and road in the valley were shiny with evaporating moisture. The trees upon which the castle ruins floated were luminous with copper, scarlet and ochre. Smoke twisted up from a peaceful bonfire at the base of the hill. And she could see the allotment-holders in their little world going about their business. This was in order. It was all as it should be.

She would never recover entirely; never be the person she had been. But recognising this brought Dora closer to the person she had been.

Dora understood that she had suffered a stroke. I shall be struck again, she thought. Another almighty blow from behind. Without any warning, or with ten seconds' warning at the most. The killer would always be lurking, to smite but not yet give the *coup de grâce.*

The Being that made us hates his handiwork, she thought.

But there was no such Being. It would have been a bitter pleasure to fight the monster. Instead, there was no one to fight.

Where was Hannah?

'Oh, Dora,' said Eirlys, rushing in. 'Ever so sorry, my love, I've taken so long. They are being very thorough about their measuring. Has Waldo been looking after you, *cariad*?'

Dora snorted.

'What was that? Are you comfy? You'll need some help for a while, till you get your full independence back.'

'Piffle.'

One must be kind to dumb beasts. Dora laughed.

'Nice to hear you laugh, my lovely,' said Eirlys.

'Magnificent intellect,' she told the two of them. Tears brimmed.

Waldo's hand on hers felt leathery and hard. 'Your language will come back,' he said. 'Completely. The consultant said so to Eirlys. I was there.'

'Don't take me to Megan again,' Dora pleaded with Eirlys. 'Promise me.'

No question of that, Eirlys assured her. But, just to please the hospital people, would Dora mind taking the tea-making test? Just humour them, she said. Waldo had arranged the mugs and so forth to make it less of a chore. Although, of course, it was supposed to be a chore.

The occupational therapist and the social worker could now be heard in the bedroom measuring the height of the bed.

'Pink article,' said Dora. 'Who put it on me?' She plucked at her shoulder in disgust.

'Oh, dear, I knitted it. Do you hate it?'

Dora shook her head and gave up. She cast her eyes up as if to indicate to an invisible ally that it was a hopeless struggle against mass moral blackmail. They had all knitted you something ghastly and unsuitable in pink, or brewed you a mug of tepid tea with too much milk, and you were expected to ingratiate yourself with these do-gooders.

All actions were exercises of power. This was known. And Dora had better knuckle down and try to please them, because she was dependent on their goodwill. She had better take the tea-making test.

Don't put their hackles up. She feigned a submissive, little-girl look and said, 'Lovely tea. Nice pink shawl. Sweet doilies.'

Perhaps she should not have included the doilies. She giggled, and Waldo, sitting hands on knees, threw back his head and laughed.

'Where is Hannah?' Dora asked with an intense qualm.

Hannah was registering for another engineering degree at the college apparently. She'd be here as soon as she was through the system. She had wanted to put it off but everyone had told her, Dora would want you to do it, Dora would be proud of you. Dora concealed the fact that she couldn't care less about the degree. Why should she care? She needed Hannah to come and be putty in her hands.

In came the team. They grouped around her wearing uniform smiles.

Dora had intended to co-operate with the tea-making and all other demands. Yet when officious women came in with tape measures and shouted questions to you as if you were deaf, flesh and blood rebelled.

'Detested kite!' she said to the occupational therapist.

'Pardon?'

'Dora is quoting Shakespeare,' Waldo explained. 'A kite is a bird.'

'Got me there.'

The social worker bent down to ask Dora how she felt about being home.

'It must feel so weird at first,' the young woman said in a natural, conversational voice. 'Especially with us lot hassling you. A bit of a shock to your system. You'll soon settle down, Dora. You will.'

Dora would have liked to explain to the young woman that she had had enough now. That she wished everything to be brought to a swift and painless conclusion. No more struggling. It came over her to explain that she had resisted in the Spanish Civil War in '38, on the Paris barricades in '68, at the miners' strike in '84, even though already a pensioner, the first Gulf War in '91 and now this one – and wasn't that enough? Could she not hope for a quiet end? She wished to raise the question of Megan and how that poor lady stood as a reminder to us all of how not to manage things. To add a few words anathematising the filial impiety of Hugh and Mary, roasting themselves in the cancerous sun of Mallorca; also to note that Hugh was a vulgar prole who'd never read a book in his life. That Mary had the brain of a feather duster. To denounce Keir and Karl and capitalists in general. Mankind, she wanted to explain to the social worker, could not progress. And that, while all you nice chapel people insisted on singing 'Abide With Me' and '*Iesu Mawr*' every Sunday, it was a waste of breath. Nobody was listening. Her work therefore was done on this planet. But Dora's tongue would not conform.

I have spoken, she thought bleakly, on hustings. On soap boxes. On platforms. I have taught girls world history. Never needed a microphone.

'Well now, we've done our bit,' said the occupational therapist. 'We can all sit down and put our feet up. It's Dora's turn to do the work.'

'Aye,' the nurse agreed. 'A nice cuppa will go down a treat. Milk and two sugars for me, please, Dora. I shouldn't, I know – but it's my only vice.'

They all sat down on Dora's chairs and looked expectantly at Dora, who didn't move.

'I'm sure you can do it, darling,' prompted the occupational therapist. 'I have every confidence in you, Dora. After all, we've had plenty of practice, haven't we, in Rehab? But hang on a minute, who has set out the cups and milk ready for her? She has to do that herself. Honestly! Put them back where they belong. We have to see if Dora can bring the whole thing together, see.'

Waldo asked if they really needed this charade.

They did apparently, it was standard procedure. They needed to assess whether Dora could live independently, as they knew she wished to do.

'And what if Miss Urquhart does not independently choose to make you a cup of tea?' asked Waldo.

'Shush, Waldo,' said Eirlys.

'Well,' said Dora. 'What if I refuse? You going to put me away?'

In rushed Hannah. 'Oh, Dora!' she cried. 'You're here! You're back!'

She burst into tears and Dora's resistance broke down. But, recovering herself, and holding Hannah's hand, she asked, 'How was registration, dear?'

'Bloody awful. Standing in queues with forms like zombies. All I could think was that you were coming home.'

'Glad you're going to study, Hannah,' said Dora. 'And glad you're here. Let me make you a cup of tea.'

Eventually they were on the move. She was exhausted, asleep on her feet. Waldo half-carried Dora to the car. Tickly beard. Likes Guinness. Must get Hannah to buy him some. Hannah – where had she gone?

Dora had chosen to make the tea. Passed that test. She had spoken. In vain. Lachlan had been shot. In vain. They tucked a blanket round her legs. Oystermouth flew past in a ragged riot of autumn colour and when they got down to the coast road, she took in with a sigh of relief the calm surface of the pearly grey sea. Holding Eirlys's hand, and squeezing tight, Dora thought, that's right. She might have been mean to Eirlys. She leant over to kiss her friend and tasted the salt of the earth.

20

Hannah listened to Dora questioning Waldo about whether he was still swimming. Oh, aye, he and Ianto went surfing at Llangennith, he said. They carried on all year round, wearing wetsuits, of course. Dora, who had been out of hospital for over a month, seemed very interested. She went on to ask when high tide was and how high the waves were. She intended to take to the water again, she said. Not the sea, until next summer, of course. Penlan Pool had been recommended to her, as a civilised place where there were not too many of those muscle-men in goggles hurtling up and down without regard to lesser fry.

'Lovely swims we had this year, didn't we, Hannah?' she asked fondly.

Apparently Waldo's extra-mural duties teaching the art of strict metre to the tiniest possible bunch of veteran devotees at the college did not take up too much time. Hannah was drawn to the companionable way he sat and chatted to Dora during her recuperation, and how much he knew about the history of socialism in industrial Wales. From seeing him as a bit of a joke, Dora had come to feel an unfeigned affection and respect for Eirlys's cousin.

Eirlys's cousin and my lover-to-be, Hannah hoped. He spoke to her of T.E. Nicholas, the Communist Christian, who wrote his poems on scraps of toilet paper in Swansea jail; of his namesake, the Quaker poet, Waldo Williams. This was a rare man who would understand that you would love to be read to sleep, she found herself thinking. But what chance would a woman raised in England have with a man like Waldo? What interest could he take in a Saesneg engineering student who could not pronounce *sglodion*, though it was the national dish of both countries; a woman who knew nothing of druidical lore?

He and Hannah went for chips. They stood in the queue at Joe Davies the Chip, and Waldo tested her on the Welsh for 'chips'.

'Well, I know that, Waldo. *Sglodion*, of course.'

'*Sglodion!* That's it! Well done. Or you can just say "chips". That will be understood.'

'*Sglodion, os gwelwch yn dda!*'

There were unique things, it had turned out, that she could do for Waldo. He had a passionate interest in the contents of Hannah's toolbox. He went through it with her, with a kind of reverence, weighing the hammer and screwdrivers in his hand, asking the names of the jobs she did and how exactly they were performed. He took out a small book and jotted her answers down. Occupations, he said, have fascinating argots.

What if he only likes me for my argot?

'Can you blow smoke rings, Waldo?'

He looked shifty. 'How do you know I smoke?'

'Don't you?'

'I take a very occasional gasp. In good company. But don't say a word to Ianto. He doesn't know I smoke.'

'Bet he does.'

Kids knew pretty well everything you didn't want them to know. Either that or they were bent on finding it out. She had brought Jake to The Eyrie for what he called a sleepover. She'd put him on the sofa bed in the living room and found in the morning that he'd scoffed the tastier contents of the fridge and had explored the drawers of her desk. Although, on the face of it, Jake seemed to take Hannah for granted, obviously he was quietly curious about her. They'd gone on to their grandfather in Caswell the following day. He had given Hannah a cautious welcome. She could see Dad in him, of course. But father and son had quarrelled a decade ago. Jack Francis's name had not been mentioned.

Hannah asked Davies the Chip for *sglodion*, and he said, sorry, no seafood. Except cod and hake.

'She means *sglods* – chips. Three portions, please,' said Waldo. 'Not a Welsh-speaker, are you, Joe?'

'No fear. Ruddy nutters you lot are, no offence, Waldo my boy.'

'None taken, Joe my boy.'

'See me dead at one of your Eisteddfods, gasbagging, all done up in sheets.'

'You do surprise me.'

'Never done a day's work in their lives, those ruddy harpists and drag queens.'

'As it happens, Hannah, I can blow a passable smoke ring,' Waldo boasted, propping up the counter as if it were a bar. Mr Davies was spading golden chips into triangular paper bags.

'Will you blow me some?'

'Course I will. Pleasure. When Dora's gone down for the night, I'll drop by. Eirlys is not too keen on me smoking, bless her. And Carly, Ianto's mum, hates it. By the way, you do know we aren't together, don't you, Hannah?'

Joe asked, 'Salt and vinegar?'

'Oh, aye. Lashings.'

Dora shouldn't have salt, Hannah knew. Salt would kill her more quickly. She and Waldo both knew. They were complicit in this encouragement of Joe Davies to give Dora what she was asking for, rather than what was good for her. She watched Joe's wrist wielding the shaker and heard the secret sound of killer salt-grains fall.

A great success. Dora ate nine or ten good-sized chips and some flakes of cod. Hannah counted and tried not to show that she was doing so. That was quite a bulky meal for Dora these days, and she evidently enjoyed it. Only three months ago Hannah had experienced Dora as rather a massive woman. Now her face was thinner and she looked drawn and grey. One eyelid did not fully open and the left side of her mouth had somewhat lapsed. A new feebleness expressed itself in the static hands that lay on the arms of the recliner like tree roots weathered out, and seemed too heavy for the twiggy arms.

She would recover most of her functions, the nurses and doctors and carers all agreed. If she would just try. They exhorted Dora to cooperate.

What was it about Dora's look, when it fell on Hannah, that seemed to want to reel her in?

Waldo's smoke rings were of variable quality, as he modestly admitted, but the best he acknowledged to be works of genius. Guinness seemed to help production, but it also inspired the chanting of an ancient lament by Aneirin in which the bard recalls the expedition of a warrior tribe from Edinburgh, at that time a part of Wales, all of whom (except the bard) are slaughtered at Catterick. A shocking waste, as Waldo commented, one arm loosely round the back of Hannah's chair. 'Nothing changes, does it, Hannah?'

'How are you, Dora?'

'How do I appear?'

'You look much more yourself, but how do you feel?'

'Well, I feel nearer to myself.'

'Oh, *good.* Dora, I know it's hard, but you've made huge strides.'

Hannah was relieved to see life creeping back into Dora's frame, the mottled hands warming, balance reinstated. And there were times when her friend's eyes beamed at her over cheeks that seemed rounder somehow, bonny as a baby's straight from the bath. What was it, though, that frightened her about Dora, as if she held something cruel and unrelenting up her sleeve? She heard a lickspittle whine in her own voice from time to time, as if she were pleading with Dora: spare me.

'All I ask is . . . all I ask . . .'

'What?'

'Is that you do not treat me like dear Megan.'

'How do you mean?'

'As if my brain had turned into a cauliflower. I have my *mental* faculties.'

Hannah rushed in with words of reassurance. No one could think of Dora in that way, ever. Yet she saw that they could and had. And Dora had registered that, knowing herself demeaned.

'I am weakened,' Dora said, and her powerful eye snared Hannah's and commandeered attention, obedience.

'Yes, but—'

'Significantly weakened.'

'I know, Dora, but you're so much better.'

'If you would listen. Stop running away. I am not running away, am I?'

'No.'

'So if I can bear to face it, so can you. You know, Hannah, how much I have come to love you. For yourself.'

Hannah tried to respond with her own words of love and attachment, but Dora wouldn't listen. It was as if this were just a preamble that had to be gone through before Dora could reach the core of what she wanted to say.

'And remember, dear,' she said, 'you have Eirlys and Waldo – and dear Lara too, of course. But you have, more importantly, your own self to fall back on.'

Hannah sat forward in her chair. Whatever Dora wanted to ask, she must be prepared to listen. She could always refuse. Because, of course, she knew, had known all along, and Dora had read this prevarication in her eyes. She thought, I have grown to love Dora Urquhart more than she can ever love me. I am just a person she happened to meet and be fond of in her closing scenes. The main body of Dora's drama had all been played out years before. But then, Hannah thought, isn't that quite an honour for me? That she offers me affection, when warmth does not come naturally to her? She switched off the Mozart CD and came to sit close by Dora on the settee. Took her hand. Was ready.

‘I can be churlish,’ Dora began and smiled. ‘So forgive me if I sometimes am. I forbid you to disagree!’

‘Yes, miss.’

‘For instance, this bed jacket affair. It was woven with love, was it not, by Eirlys. And what did I do with it? I maligned it as a pink horror.’

‘Well, Dora, it *is* a pink horror.’

‘But the love that created and offered it is not a pink horror. And here, you see, I was churlish. From the Anglo-Saxon *churl*, meaning slave or thrall. This is how I behave if my dignity is threatened. I always have done so and I always shall.’

Dora’s breathing was rather shallow and irregular; there seemed to be mucus on her lungs, which she had to pause to cough away. Hannah had the sense of someone surviving at altitude, way above the line where it is practical for humans to climb.

‘If I am struck again, I want you to help me go. No, don’t speak.’

‘Dora—’

‘I said, don’t; don’t speak now.’

She had Hannah by the wrist. The grasp of her good hand was monstrously strong and it really hurt.

‘Not a word. I’ve got my exit kit, it’s all prepared. You may not have to take any active steps. You may not. But you may.’

The grip on Hannah’s wrist was tight and Hannah looked down in wonderment that a creature so frail could exert such force.

‘There is no one I can ask but you, my Hannah. To deliver me from evil.’

Hannah thought, I can say no.

‘Come in and just inspect the kit. There’s nothing frightening about it.’

In the bedroom Dora opened the drawer of her filing cabinet. As Dora took her through the procedure – *here are the pills, this is the plastic bag with a tie which must be secured carefully, and a spare* – Hannah was conscious of the party wall between her flat and Dora's. Dora had been creating her exit kit a metre from where Hannah slept, for months before her stroke. Through the party wall they heard one another pacing; caught and interpreted one another's small movements, and sipped the small fare of hints and clues. Imagine, thought Hannah, if you put a glass to the wall and caught it all. It would be unbearable. You would be destroyed.

'You are my father and mother,' she told Dora.

The lassie had said yes.

Hannah's mercy and devotion, and perhaps her weakness, too, had been such that she had felt unable to resist. She would keep her vow. She was a vow-keeper. Look at how she'd remained with that oaf of a husband just because of a vow. Dora had left red marks on her wrist: did I manage to do that? she wondered. She had always been brutal in her affection. With Rosa the same, and how we fought. Hannah does not fight back. She yields.

Dora would hear Hannah with Waldo in the evenings when they all thought she had gone to bed. The reverberations of his rather booming voice carried through the flimsy wall. Waldo would be there for her, when Dora was not, to keep her off the straight and narrow. So, good for him.

Dora lay in her cell and heard the small, shuffling sounds made by Mrs Dark above, like a bird under eaves or a mouse in a wainscot. She listened to the goings-on in Hannah's flat that included the playing of a harmonica and rather a lot of laughing. And the squeaky shoe-leather of the refugee, Mr Flood, and his considerate but doomed attempt to close the fire-doors quietly outside Dora's flat. She heard the men and maidens in the Testosterone Flat, seizing the hour. She smelt good cooking smells from, presumably, Eirlys's kitchen, and heard Eirlys burst out of the front door at sunrise and gallop off down the hill for her jog.

These days Dora only got to sleep in the morning – sleep like a shallow grave – and Eirlys's rushing out, the paper boy having a fight with the bulky newspapers, the nymphs abandoning their playmates, irked her by arousing her into a world in which she enjoyed no active role. Then came the ceaseless round of nurses and carers. And neighbours 'popping', as they put it, in and out. She had told herself that she would get rid of the computer, which she blamed, probably unfairly, for triggering her collapse. But there were marine sites which she began to frequent.

Hannah had said, *I will.*

And here was her central comfort. This forced complicity.

There had been another comfort, greater by far. Dora had lived through months of – how could she describe it to herself? – romance with the past. Rosa had come to her, day and night, breaking through the crust of buried memory. Dora's love flowing out towards her daughter had brought her to visit the garden of rest, a place where grief met bliss. Dora's quest had been completed.

And then the light had gone out. After the stroke, it had all gone to ashes in her mouth. But just as she had given up on them, here they came, into her dream world, Lachlan and Rosa with linked hands. In some odd way they had grown to be considerably older than Dora. She was a little child who stood at the door and knocked. In her left hand was a small valise.

Behind the smoky glass door were her husband and daughter, the family likeness speaking on their faces. They had been waiting there, Dora felt, with some impatience. Was she knocking too quietly? Were they unable to hear her? Did she really want to go to them? Certainly they paid Dora no attention, so perhaps the glass partition was one-way.

She was a sort of refugee, of this she felt convinced, for she had no home and there was no way back. The world at whose threshold Dora stood, an evacuee, was some kind of vast Kindertransport, in documentary black and white, to show that the film was over.

When she awoke, the television was on. Fuddled, Dora looked into the blindfold face of a hostage in Iraq. They were going to cut his throat for the camera, said the men in black hoods.

Hannah said, 'Oh, look, the television must have been on all night.'

'Where did you spring from?'

Happy to see Hannah, Dora held out a hand.

'Shall I switch it off? It's so terrible. What is the answer, Dora?'

What was the answer? The answer was that there was no answer; our generation's solutions, Dora thought, are all down the pan. The future lay with mad lasses like Jelly and Aeronwy, Rae and her new girlfriend. Perhaps they would be able to pose the right questions and come upon answers. She doubted it. Perhaps, like Hannah, they would do the work near to hand without intellectualising it. She nodded to Hannah to switch off the record of this man's sufferings, playing round the clock behind the screen.

As Dora perched on the edge of the bed after her bath, Hannah massaged her shoulders for her. It was quite a chilly morning, she said. Eirlys had pretty much had to skate along the front rather than jog.

'I can dress myself, Hannah,' said Dora. 'If you will just be there to help with the socks.'

The dream had brought resolve. Dora would get strong again. Dora would be Dora once more.

She told Hannah that she would soon be seen leaping over the hills like a young roe. Look out for me, she said, as she nudged the unwilling arm into the sleeve of a tracksuit. That arm had lost muscle tone, according to the physio, and it had swollen up rather strangely, like a broken wing, in its disuse. It didn't seem to go with the other one. She was asymmetrical. We need symmetry for balance, she thought, but I, typically, have allowed myself to remain lop-sided. For of course Dora had spurned the training schedule. This morning, however, she and Hannah performed the exercises together at the window, chanting, '*One* – two – three!' Then Dora insisted on preparing porridge for both of them, pinching the salt in her good hand but stirring it with her bad hand.

'You promised me,' she said to Hannah.

'I know.'

The lassie flushed red. She stopped eating, holding her breath, wondering if this was the moment. Everything in her posture said: *No, don't ask me, Dora. Not now.* She could not meet Dora's eyes.

'I absolve you from your promise,' she told Hannah briskly as they ate. 'How could I ask such a thing of you? I might have landed you in prison.'

'It's a difficult one, Dora. I should have thought it through first.'

'That is quite correct, Hannah. You mustn't be such a limp dishrag.'

Hannah dabbled with her spoon so that the brown sugar melted on top of her porridge. 'In principle,' she went on, 'I am with you. And I want what is right for you, Dora. What *you* feel is right for you. On the other hand, I'm not all that keen on being sent to prison. And how would I live with it afterwards? But, Dora, you don't want to go now, do you? You're getting better, you said so yourself. Don't you feel that?'

'Aye, I am getting stronger every day.'

'Oh, good. Perhaps we could just ... play things by ear ... try to hope for the best? But, Dora, if you need me to, you *know* I will do it.'

Dora brushed the matter aside. She suggested they gird up their loins later in the week and go for a dip at the National Pool, since the season for skinny-dipping in the sea was over. Or the smaller pool at Penlan, perhaps, to start with.

'What's that, Nannan?' Angelica had entered without knocking. 'Going swimming? Can I come?'

She flashed Hannah a filthy look and did not bother to greet her. Dora saw and understood the hostility Jelly felt. Hannah was not family.

'I sent a message, Jelly, I didn't want you to come.'

Dora's face said yearningly otherwise. Angelica kissed her and held her by both hands.

'Don't you want to see me?' she pouted.

‘I don’t want you to see *me* like this. Remember me as strong. As me.’

‘I don’t want to remember you as anything. I want to be with you. Are we going swimming?’

‘Aye. I’m training for the Big One.’

‘I can’t swim, though,’ said Jelly. ‘You’ll have to teach me, Nannan. But I’m up for it.’

Dora could hardly credit that her great-granddaughter, living in this watery place, had not managed to learn to swim. She promised that in due course she would teach Jelly to stay afloat. For the time being, she would confine herself, she said, to the small pool for crones and tots.

Spain must not revive ancient conflicts, the so-called People’s Party had stated. The vast majority of Spaniards did not want to rake up the Republic and Franco. There must be no digging up of mass graves, the Party insisted; and the idea of granting members of the International Brigades the right to take Spanish nationality without having to renounce their own was outrageous.

Dora read this aloud to Eirlys as they sat in the pool-side café after their swim.

‘Would you like Spanish nationality, Dora?’ asked Eirlys.

‘I cannot imagine that it would make the slightest difference to my life.’

Through the glass partitions they could see elderly members of a fitness club having the time of their lives, performing exercises of an amphibious nature, to the accompaniment of music. Wearing pink and blue arm-floats, they all stretched this way, waving their hands, and then the other way. A hearty lady in a red tracksuit directed operations from the poolside.

Dora watched Eirlys take a sip of coffee and return to her book. They had finished *Bleak House* and progressed to *Great Expectations.* Because she read almost all night, sleep being hard to come by, Dora had now overtaken Eirlys. The two of them read together and visited Penlan Pool several times a week, Dora’s strength having been significantly restored through her resolute and sustained efforts. Hannah, now engrossed in her studies, joined them at weekends.

Dora had put her all into freeing herself for this one last action. It would soon be the New Year, and look how far she had progressed. But, she thought, it must not be left too long. One must guard against getting too cosy. The pretence of normality might easily slip into the real thing: there lay the insidious temptation. But even in her regained strength, Dora's world felt brittle and precarious; her field of vision was dark at the margin. There was a tedium to topics that had previously engrossed her. And Dora's appetite had failed: the salt had lost its savour.

Eirlys looked up and smilingly reassured herself that all was well with her friend. That she had all she needed. Not cold? Not bored? Not tired? More coffee? A cake or biscuit? Having reassured herself, Eirlys immersed herself again in her book, with a small chuckle of appreciation. Through the partition, the water-babies were leaping in their turquoise world.

Dora looked down at her newspaper: the disappeared were being brought to light one by one, the report said, so it was just a matter of time. There was a picture of young people mobbing a rally of old Fascists at Franco's grave in the Valley of the Fallen.

Rosa! Rosa! There it was again.

Dora raised her head and closed her eyes.

In the moist hubbub of the pool's acoustic, a strange effect recurred with each visit. The girl's name echoed across the water and Dora listened, inwardly assenting, in an ecstasy of impatience.

21

There had been trouble with the intercom. Strange voices would confide to Eirlys, *It's me, is that you, Hannah?* or, *Hallo, parcel for you, Mrs Dark.* The pharmacist attempted to effect a delivery of suppositories to Hannah. Now someone was ringing every doorbell in the block, so that a serenade of chimes, buzzes and the opening bars of *Eine Kleine Nachtmusik* were let loose.

'Really, it's too bad,' said Hannah. 'He's pressing three at a time. Honestly.'

Eirlys said she was on her way downstairs anyway; she had her weights to lift. She dropped a kiss on Hannah's head in passing and said she'd see her later for their walk with Aeronwy and the youngsters.

A removals lorry. Two melancholy men with cartons said they had half a load to drop off here and then they had to get to Pembroke with the other half by teatime.

'No need to go mad with the doorbells, though, boys,' Eirlys admonished. 'Wait for an answer I would, before you ring the whole lot. Some of us might have been enjoying a nap.'

A legitimate nap, she thought. Sometimes the very thought of all the swimming and the power walking was so exhausting that she needed a rest before she'd even begun. Nevertheless, anyone could see that the doughy mass of Eirlys's hips was being shed; she now had ankles, and only the flaps at the top of her arms were still causing her concern.

'I could do with a nap, I can tell you,' said the driver. 'Know how long we've been on the road?'

'No. Now, what do you want?'

'Number three, but there's no answer. She said she'd be here but she's not, and we can't hang about waiting.'

Oh, no, thought Eirlys. Oh, no.

'If *she's* not here, I can't let you in,' she said. 'Wouldn't be right and anyway, I don't have a key.'

Well, she did have a key, of course, but not legally. Somehow, she had been reluctant to surrender it.

'We have to get to Pembroke, see.'

'Yes, you said.'

'Well, not Pembroke, but this small village we can't even pronounce. Here, look. How would you say that then?'

Eirlys spoke the word slowly, in three distinct syllables, which appeared to confound them even more.

'Clan – Oik – Zet,' said the younger of the two.

'Not really.'

'It's beyond me why they can't talk English,' said the first. 'Like every other bugger.'

'Really.'

'Aye, we're in Europe now. Listen, Jason, got the mobile? Ring the estate agent bloke, tell him we're dumping it on the doorstep if we can't get in.'

'Oh, no, you're not,' said Eirlys.

'Eirlys, what's going on?' came Hannah's voice through the intercom.

'We want access to number three,' said the driver. 'Can you help us, miss?'

Eirlys listened to Hannah's silence, which rang in her ear. Internally she argued with that silence, insisting that this moment had had to come sooner or later. And, Hannah, she went on inside her head, this must be better for us than to pass by that door each day and know it's just a hollow box, with no life in it. Much better, her silent voice went on, although her heart was bursting.

'At last!' said the removals man, as an elegant Mercedes came sweeping into the grounds, executed a flamboyant circle, and reversed into the space reserved for Mrs Dark. Mrs Dark would not like that, despite the fact that she did not own a car.

'Hey, Mrs Walters, we have to get to Pembroke by teatime, right, so we need to unload sharpish.'

Eirlys went upstairs two at a time. She and Hannah looked palely at each other and then moved to Hannah's front window, their arms around one another's waists. Down there a large, immaculate lady in a dark skirt and very high heels, perhaps in her thirties, was haranguing the removals men in an authoritative transatlantic accent. She seemed to be taking them to task for their bitter attitude to their labours. If they were contracted to deliver two halfloads, she said, her view was that they should set aside the time to do so and perform their undertakings without grouching. And, no, in point of fact, she was not late: they had arrived early.

Eirlys and Hannah watched as she directed her team, seeming to be here, there and everywhere, despite the towering heels. They blenched as the heels clattered upstairs, through the fire door and into Dora's flat.

'She's in,' said Hannah.

Eirlys nodded. They both looked at the party wall, and tracked the stranger's movements around the flat. Now she had pulled up the blinds and thrown open the sitting-room window, letting the chilly, sunlit air into the stale space. She would have stepped out on to the balcony to survey the view.

'It's good really,' Eirlys said. She fell back on the elder sister role that she had resorted to after Mam and Dad went, but this time it was without the suppressed desolation that accompanied their passing.

'Yes, I know it is,' Hannah said, more resolutely. 'Do you think we ought to offer her a cup of tea or something?'

Eirlys, about to charge into missionary mode, scattering benevolence and cake crumbs, changed her mind. She shrugged. 'Not really,' she said. 'She can ask if she wants something, can't she? I mean, pair of lungs she's got on her, tidy pair of lungs!'

'Gracious! Put it down! That is an heirloom!' they heard.

'Bring it up with appropriate care, please, and mind the door – it seems unconscionably narrow.'

'She doesn't like the door,' said Hannah.

'Apparently not.'

They rested their arms on the windowsill to watch the removal drama unfold. Mrs Walters gave her men hell. She had made them unpack everything on the forecourt, after the heirloom fiasco. That, the driver had explained several times, was not how it was done in England. He wanted to know, no disrespect, whether she was a removal expert.

As a matter of fact she was, said Mrs Walters.

'It's all right, love,' said Jason, the peacemaker. 'We'll do it how you want it, don't worry.'

'Well, that might be how it's done in the US of A, lady,' said the driver with folded arms. 'But not here. You've got more room over there to spread your clobber.'

'I beg your pardon? I do not come from the States. I am a Canadian.'

'Whoops,' said Hannah.

'Have you heard of Canada?'

'Look, come on, George lad,' said Jason. 'We can get all this stuff sorted and be on our way in twenty minutes. Just do what the lady says.' He rolled his eyes for his partner's benefit.

'Canada is that land mass directly north of America. I come from Ontario. I am a professor at the university there. I am a professor of midwifery . . .'

Hannah said midwifery was a kind of removal, if you looked at it like that. Eirlys saw her transforming her grief, moment by moment, into jest. They had become so close when they were sorting Dora's clothes and belongings: had even squabbled a bit over what should go to which charity shop. Looking up from the bin bag she was filling, Eirlys had seen that they were behaving like sisters. Keir and Karl, having probated the will and taken possession of the bank account and valuables, had been glad to leave them the clearing of their gran's bits and bobs. Angelica had arrived, carrying a teddy bear, which she kept alternately punching and cuddling.

'Your Nannan wouldn't want you to be upset, Angelica,' Eirlys had said. 'Just to remember her and get on with your life, isn't it?'

But Jelly had tossed her head, saying nothing, and, seating the teddy beside her, had opened up the computer and entered into Nannan's private world.

'Oh, wow, Nannan!' she'd exclaimed. 'Thank *you*!'

She'd turned to the two intruders, saying, 'I'm to take all her files and stuff for myself, meaning everything on her computer and also her papers. I have to sort them out and decide what to do with them.'

Laughing and crying, she'd saved that private world to a memory stick and carried it away in her jacket pocket. She would be back with boxes for Nannan's private papers and books, she'd told them at the door, and please would nobody touch them while she wasn't here? They heard her sobbing into her mobile phone on the way downstairs.

Eirlys and Hannah had washed and ironed Dora's T-shirts and trousers, and shined her shoes. Dora had never cared about such things. Eirlys had started to sort a drawer in the bedside cabinet containing personal things. The first thing she'd come upon was the nail-clippers. Dora had such lovely nails, Eirlys remembered, with perfect moons. She had always wanted nails like that herself. When she had confided her envy to Dora, Dora had looked at her as if she were, frankly, deranged.

'Oh, Eirlys,' Hannah had said, 'let me do that drawer. Please.'

'No, it's all right. What is it, Hannah?'

Hannah had not explained but agitatedly took over. Whatever she had been looking for she did not seem to have found.

Professor Walters now announced to that amphitheatre, the world, her intention to return to Oxford for the weekend before returning for the new semester in Swansea. The removal men, unimpressed, set off for Pembroke at speed, with a long hoot of derision. Professor Walters clattered about a bit and also left.

The building settled back into drowsy brooding. A vacuum cleaner hummed; the spectral presences in Eirlys's fridge-freezer murmured in lamentation. They knew they would never escape their icy tomb. Eirlys wished she had bought a quieter model. She caught the post as it tumbled through the flap and grinned at the post girl through the glass. A bulging letter from Waldo for Hannah, she saw, airmail from South America, and a card from him to herself. And a brown envelope franked by the Inland Revenue for Sandy Sanderson, the dirty tenant (for so she uncharitably called him to herself) from the Testosterone Flat.

She examined the postcard from Waldo: he was in Patagonia, far more Welsh than Wales, he said, and although he missed them all like mad, he was in his element. She felt Hannah's letter. It was satisfyingly chubby, with folded pages and perhaps photographs. Last time he had sent several pictures, to give them an idea of the poetry of the place, its peculiar Cymric flavour. He was getting thin as a broomstick, he'd written. People here didn't eat as much, because they didn't have as much to eat. And after a while, you didn't want it.

Odd how fond he was of Hannah. She could never have imagined his falling for a monoglot. But Hannah, perhaps sharing her doubt, had purchased tapes and videos, although as yet she had scarcely floundered beyond greetings, thank yous and a perpetual announcement that it was coffee time.

'Mind,' Eirlys had said kindly, 'your vocabulary may be limited but it is to the point. And your pronunciation of the double "L" is lovely. And don't tell him I said so but Waldo's consonantal mutations can be woeful.'

'*Amser coffi?*' asked Hannah.

'*Da iawn!*'

'I'm not poking and prying,' said Lara.

She was into Hannah's wardrobe, clocking the coat-hangers along the rail and sizing up Hannah's anarchic outfits. 'You never used to wear this kind of stuff. I mean, purple! Hey,' she said, pulling out a dove-grey parka and holding it up to assess the effect in the mirror, 'this isn't bad at all.'

'Don't sound so amazed. Try it on. Go on.'

'No way. It's a good coat, this, Hannah,' she pointed out, as if trying to confer a little tactful education. She tried it on anyway, and under the eskimo hood, flirted with herself in the mirror. 'That's really quite fashionable, you know,' Lara said kindly.

'Oh, I'm high fashion now,' Hannah said.

'Course you are. You ought to do more girlie things, Hannah. I suppose there's no one in these old people's flats to be girlie with, though. Why don't you move to a hall of residence? There can't be many girlie people on an engineering course.'

'Not really. A few nice girlie guys.'

Lara, standing half a head taller in her spike-heeled Jimmy Choos, took off the coat and draped it over Hannah's shoulders.

'Anyway, I'm not a girlie person, Lara, am I?'

'Not yet. Getting there, though. You haven't been brought up properly.'

'No, you never took the trouble with me,' Hannah said, as Lara arranged her hair over the furry collar.

'You were a crap pupil, is what. Dad used to say you needed a makeover.'

'Great.'

'I wish you were back, Hannah.'

Lara followed Hannah into the kitchen, walking her forward, hands on her shoulders. She accepted a cup of coffee and could she have some cereal to tide her over with banana chopped into it, as she was quite hungry. She'd only had a chicken curry roll and crisps on the train.

'I thought things were OK with Dad now?' Hannah said.

'Yeah, but I don't like to see him making a plonker of himself with that Emma one. It's gross. Embarrassing.'

'Does she like football?'

'Yeah.'

'Does she support Bristol City?'

'Of course. Off every Saturday to the match or the pub if it's an away.'

'Then he'll be all right.'

Lara stared. She pushed the bowl away and half-averted her head. 'You do look down on him, don't you? I mean, he's dirt in your eyes. I used to watch you, you know, looking at him behind his back. I wondered the back of his head didn't go on fire. Dad'd be prattling on about this and that, and you'd be, like, drilling him with your eyes.'

'What kind of face was I making?'

'Blank. Dead.'

'Not thinking anything in particular, probably. Just tired or thinking about lunch.'

I'm sure I *was* giving him the evil eye though, Hannah thought. Lara and Sophie did not miss a thing.

'You used to hold us,' Lara said.

'Yes. If you were ill and let me. But I understood, it would have felt like a betrayal to you to love me back.'

'You were shit-scared of us. And you were pissed off because we spoilt your nice dream by acting up and puking and not co-operating. But you were there with the sick-bucket.'

'I was.'

'So,' said Lara, with an air of drawing the meeting to a conclusion. She put out her hand and Hannah squeezed it.

'If you need someone to hold the sick-bucket, Lara, I will always come and hold it.'

'Yeah. Right. And vice versa.'

Hannah chopped tomatoes and red peppers for salad while Lara went off for a walk up and down Newton Road on the stilts of her Jimmy Choos. She'd talked about exploring the beach or the castle, but she'd never get down to the beach done up like that. Hannah crossed to the window holding the chopping knife in one hand, a pepper in the other. Lara had her own key, so there was no need to look out for her and let her in. But it was sweet to imagine and then admire her sashaying up the path. No, there was only twilight coming on too early, and Mrs Dark being helped out of a white taxi, and Dora, whose name she had managed not to think of for half an hour, was nowhere to be seen.

Hannah strolled round the cliff path from Bracelet to Rotherslade, her eyes stung by the thrillingly cold air rushing in from the sea. Lara had been gone a week and, for all her enjoyment of the visit, Hannah had been relieved to reclaim her own space again. She was free to think of Dora, to walk in her footsteps, going over and over her unanswered questions. The sea boiled and thrashed against the rocks and bellowed as it powered into the caves. Last year's bracken was smashed into strange shapes, and lay in tongues of ochre round the cliff. Out to sea, ribbons of silver light tussled with the cloud and were confounded.

How had it felt for Dora, going the way she did?

Hannah stood still on the cliff path, pondering, and made her way down to the beach at Rotherslade. The green and white beach huts were padlocked, the café was closed and the sands deserted except for a handful of dog walkers, down towards the edge of the water. With the tide half out, the two beaches of Rotherslade and Langland had joined into one. Clambering down over the banked pebbles, Hannah began to walk towards the edge. A happy place, it had been for them. She remembered sitting on a tartan rug with Dora, drinking a flask of coffee, feeling safe and secure. How monumental her friend had seemed, everlasting.

Such a small parcel of bone you were, she thought, smashed against the rocks when the lifeguard pulled you out.

The rocks. There. Those rocks. Hannah made for the exact spot. She paused to take off her shoes and padded across the cold sand, hood up.

The wind slammed in and Hannah's cheeks felt scalded. How did you make it all that way down the beach in the icy wind? I think you flew. Your shoulder blades grew wings and lifted you to the edge. No one saw you, so perhaps you crawled. Or rolled, over and over, down the sand. I'd believe anything of you, Dora, anything at all, Hannah scolded her against the wind's tirade. It came screaming round the headland, the nearer she approached the sea.

You were determined and devious, she accused Dora. You plotted to leave us. She'd been gripped by surges of anger towards Dora for leaving without a word.

It had been a grey windy weekday like any other. Hannah had been preoccupied with an assessment she had not quite finished for college. Getting up before first light, she had brought her bike on to the forecourt and loaded the pannier with her books and papers. When she'd glanced up at Dora's bedroom window, the light had been on and the curtains open.

Going to Rosa, she was, Eirlys had counselled Hannah, going home to Rosa: she needed that and we must let her go, let go of her. They had advised Keir and Karl to do what Dora wanted, burying her ashes alongside Rosa's. So, yes, Eirlys had said, we have done right by her, *cariad*. Come away now.

Hannah had resented losing Dora to Rosa. The way Dora had been recovering suggested that she might have had years left of a not-too-unhappy life. But Dora had never had much time for common sense. She wasn't content with crumbs and morsels. And of course they ought to have sussed her out, but had taken her at her word that she'd been exercising for sensible reasons: to live and make the most of it. Hannah remembered the endless trips to the pool both with her and Eirlys. The crash course of swimming lessons Dora had given Angelica, which Dora had seemed thoroughly to enjoy. Hannah had admired the astonishing progress Dora had made, so that she'd been able to swim fifteen slow lengths side-stroke. She'd thought it was scientific curiosity that made Dora so eager to know about tides.

The waves were high and pounding. Hardly had one thrown itself down on the shore than the next one reared up behind it. The roaring echoed from cliff to cliff. And Hannah couldn't help but feel exhilarated by it, though she huddled into herself, turning away from the wind, arms folded.

After the first shock, Hannah had known and accepted that Dora had needed to go. But, Dora, I would have helped you, she said to her. If you'd got into those straits, I'd have been there to help you go softly, in your sleep, holding your hand. I *promised.* You ought to have realised that, whatever my reservations, I meant it. Did you need to take the way of violence? It filled Hannah with horror to think that Dora might have chosen this violent way out to save her from fulfilling her promise.

Hannah's heels had sunk into the wet sand. They came up with a sucking noise. The tide was driving in. And actually there was a violence in Dora, that was true. Perhaps Hannah ought to cheer her on her way. Such a fighter she was. And as far as Dora was concerned, all the battles she cared about had been lost. There was nothing left for Red Dora to do. Just being an old person with failing health was not enough.

The new woman from Canada had finally moved into Dora's place. Which was inevitable, of course – the market was, after all, a seller's market, as Keir had said, so it was bound to be sooner rather than later. But Hannah had got used to letting herself in at night and secretly lingering in Dora's space. Not really thinking or remembering: just being in the place where her friend had spent her last years, and finding it peaceful.

She'd heard Eirlys do the same once or twice. Hannah had stood with her head against the party wall in shared vigil.

It came to Hannah that there was only one way to understand Dora's escape. *Just wade in. Go on, do it, I dare you. Follow her.* Hannah took off her backpack, coat and trousers, securing them with rocks. She stood for a moment. Then she ran. Plunged bang into the breathtaking shock of the surf. The first wave reared over her; Hannah crouched before it and leapt as high as she could as it crested.

The drag before the second wave hit had her off her feet and carried her under. She was pulled up into the cresting wave which then, now, smashed down on her skull.

Up again. Hannah burst up above the turmoil, spitting; had caught the drift of Dora's violent last pleasure. A terrible, exciting game of dares. Dora would not have lasted moments. And for Hannah the violence and the cold and the danger were what? Elating? She dived clean under the next breaker, deep into its body beneath the roaring surf, but the next struck her hard and carried her head over heels.

Yes, that was it. Hannah dragged her shaking, exultant body out of the water. A few aghast walkers had paused to watch a madwoman take a dip in the middle of winter.

With that, the child who'd been strolling with, presumably, her nan on the beach, slipped her mittened hand free, gave a little skip and pelted down towards the sea.

Note and Acknowledgement

Chingtown is a fictional area of industrial Swansea, 'Copperopolis', situated in the area of the old parish of Llangyfelach and built by the equally fictional copper master, the Cornishman Thomas Ching. I have modelled his enlightened philanthropy on that of the Morris and Vivian dynasties: Sir John Morris began to build Morriston (Treforys) in about 1779. The Vivian dynasty, originally from Cornwall, extended their copper concerns into South Wales during the early nineteenth century. Thomas Ching's summer house, *Nyth Eryr*, is conceived as a less palatial version of Sir John Henry Vivian's neo-Gothic house at Singleton, redesigned in the mid-1820s. I have taken the liberty of situating Tom Ching's arsenic works at Clyne.

Although Dora Urquhart and Lachlan and Rosa Little were absolutely real to me as I composed this book, they are imaginary people. I found clues to their characterisation in many wonderful books about the International Brigades, including Paul Preston's moving *Doves of War: Four Women of Spain* (HarperCollins, 2002); Angela Jackson's *Beyond the Battlefield: Testimony, Memory and Remembrance of a Cave Hospital in the Spanish Civil War* (Warren & Pell, 2005); James K. Hopkins's *Into the Heart of the Fire: The British in the Spanish Civil War* (Stanford University Press, 1998); Stuart Christie's *Granny Made Me An Anarchist: General Franco, the Angry Brigade and Me* (Simon & Schuster, 2004); Alvah Bessie's *Spanish Civil War Notebooks*, ed. Dan Bessie (University Press of Kentucky, 2002); Hywel Francis's *Miners Against Fascism: Wales and the Spanish Civil War* (Lawrence and Wishart, 1984); Alun Menai Williams's *From the Rhondda to the*

Ebro (Warren & Pell, 2004); Antony Beevor's *The Battle for Spain: The Spanish Civil War, 1936–1939* (Weidenfeld & Nicolson, 2006).

I would like to thank my friend, the poet Menna Elfyn, for her overwhelming generosity in giving me insights into the experience of the Welsh language movement. Nigel Jenkins, poet and comrade, has been of constant help in understanding the history of Swansea; and Professor M. Wynn Thomas has answered questions concerning language and the history of the Welsh and the Spanish Civil War, with immense patience. Any errors that have crept in are wholly my own.

Stevie Davies